Redesigning Happiness

Redesigning Happiness

NITA BROOKS

Dafina
Books

KENSINGTON PUBLISHING CORP.
www.kensingtonbooks.com

DAFINA BOOKS are published by

Kensington Publishing Corp.
119 West 40th Street
New York, NY 10018

All Kensington titles, imprints, and distributed lines are available at special quantity discounts for bulk purchases for sales promotion, premiums, fund-raising, and educational or institutional use.

Special book excerpts or customized printings can also be created to fit specific needs. For details, write or phone the office of the Kensington Sales Manager: Kensington Publishing Corp., 119 West 40th Street, New York, NY 10018. Attn. Sales Department. Phone: 1-800-221-2647.

Dafina and the Dafina logo Reg. U.S. Pat. & TM Off.

ISBN-13: 978-1-4967-2192-1
ISBN-10: 1-4967-2192-6
First Kensington Trade Paperback Printing: August 2019

ISBN-13: 978-1-4967-2193-8 (ebook)
ISBN-10: 1-4967-2193-4 (ebook)
First Kensington Electronic Edition: August 2019

10 9 8 7 6 5 4 3

Printed in the United States of America

To the women who raised me.

Acknowledgments

There were a few people who helped me as I went through the process of getting this book published. Thank you to Jamie, Adrienne, and K.M. for the feedback you provided over the three years it took to go from idea to final product. You ladies are fantastic! Thank you to my fabulous agent Tricia Skinner. You are my biggest hype person, and after all the uncertainty that comes with this business, I appreciate your support. Thank you to Selena James for taking a chance with my story and believing in my ability to make this book even better. I also couldn't have done this without the love and support of my family. You all have believed in me from the start, and I am truly blessed to have you in my life.

Chapter 1

The Power of Perfection.

Yvonne Cable stared at the headline and grinned. The glowing feature on her latest design made her want to do cartwheels down the hall in her office. If only she'd mastered the art of a cartwheel.

The picture below the headline was of the completed home office for her latest client. Muted blue-grey colors created a cozy and restful feel. The natural light from the picture window overlooking the home's intricate landscape brightened the room. A mixture of textures—cotton, leather, and wood—added depth and visual interest.

After clawing her way through Atlanta's cutthroat interior design community, the article in *Atlanta Life Magazine* was the coveted crown after a hard-fought battle. She created perfection for her clients. Gave them the spaces they needed to be comfortable and content, a haven in their hectic lives. Money, family, status...she didn't care. Whatever her clients needed, she was going to give them.

She put the magazine on her desk and walked over to the perfectly organized whiteboard in her downtown Atlanta office. Nine sections partitioned off. The title of her projects in blue at the top of each section. Tasks associated with each project in green. Due dates written in purple. Red checkmarks for completed tasks. The board served as a quick reference guide to where she was and what she needed to do next.

Her grin widened as she a grabbed the green dry erase marker to add the title for a new project to the ninth box. Sandra Covington Project. Or, as her assistant Bree liked to call it, the super enviable commission of every designer in Atlanta. The people who'd vied for Sandra's new home project were many, but Yvonne was the one to land it.

Sandra Covington, self-help author turned radio personality, had just announced that her radio program was going into nationwide syndication. Yvonne was familiar with Sandra's radio show. The woman's advice was quoted everywhere. Known for going deep into her readers' and clients' pasts to help them unlock the "key to their potential," her famously quoted words, Sandra kept her own personal life out of the spotlight. Yvonne didn't care about Sandra's past, all she cared about was that she'd gotten the project. Designing Sandra's house, and possibly getting a shout-out on her show, combined with the notoriety she'd gotten from her appearance on *Celebrity Housewives,* would go a long way toward increasing the demand for an original Yvonne Cable Design when someone needed decorating for their home or business.

She'd arrived. Shed the mistakes of the past and become a household name. Her mom still couldn't believe it. On most days, Yvonne couldn't believe it either.

"Yvonne, I got the fabric swatches you needed for the Tyson project, and don't forget that you've got a call with the editor of *Lady Entrepreneur* magazine in fifteen minutes."

Bree Foster, Yvonne's administrative assistant, swept into Yvonne's office with an arm full of fabric. She laid the material on the drafting table in the creative corner of Yvonne's office. Vision boards for projects adorned the walls in that corner. Sketch pads, colored pencils, and drawing notebooks littered the drafting table where Yvonne created her designs. Bree continually purchased organizers to keep Yvonne's samples in order, but when Yvonne was in the middle of the creative process, materials scattered the desk. As usual, Bree picked up the strewn color charts, pencils, post-its, and papers and put them back into their correct spots.

"Crap, I completely forgot about that call." Yvonne hurried over to her desk, in the working corner of her office. *Lady Entrepreneur* magazine wanted to start a lifestyle section which would include design tips. Yvonne wanted to be the person who supplied the articles.

Lady Entrepreneur had a wide circulation. Women all over the country subscribed to the magazine, which provided everything from tips for running a business to interviews with successful women on its pages. Of course, she wanted those same women to think of her when they thought of interior design.

"That's why I'm here," Bree said. A recent graduate of design school, they'd met when Yvonne hired Bree as an intern the summer before. After graduation, Yvonne had snatched up the brilliant designer immediately. "Besides, you've got a good excuse. I can imagine your head is elsewhere." Bree grinned and squeezed her hands together in front of her chest. Bree's curly hair was worn in a cute pixie cut and her brown eyes sparkled with excitement behind a pair of black framed glasses.

"I know. I've been busy thinking about what I need for my first meeting with Sandra Covington."

"I'm not talking about that. I mean your proposal over the weekend. The way Nathan surprised you! That was so romantic!"

Yes. The proposal. You'd think saying yes to the man she

loved after he proposed via the jumbotron at the Atlanta
Braves game wouldn't slip her mind. Honestly, she was still
getting used to the idea of being engaged. For the past six
years, she'd been a single mom and business owner. Now she
was part of a team. Of course, she would have a hard time
believing it.

Nathan Lange, home improvement television star, boy-
next-door sex symbol, and all-around good guy, was *her*
fiancé. She couldn't be happier. And if she happened to notice
that saying yes to Nathan had gotten her more congratulations
and well wishes than starting her own business, being named
business woman of the year twice, or working for a star on
Celebrity Housewives, she didn't let it bother her. Not too
much.

Marriage was a big deal. Her son, Jacob, would have a
father. She would have a man who loved and supported her.
That was worth congratulating.

She glanced at the three-carat diamond on her left hand.
"I can't wait to marry Nathan, but no, that's not what
distracted me. Now that I've got Sandra's account, I want to
make sure I don't let any other projects slip through the
crack."

"That's what you have me for," Bree said. "As your
administrative assistant, I'm determined to keep you on track.
But once you and Nathan get the television show, I may need
an assistant for all of the work that's going to come your way."

Yvonne knocked three times on the oak surface of her
desk, then crossed her fingers. "I hope so. The television show
is still up in the air."

She'd met Nathan on the set of *Celebrity Housewives,*
where he'd worked as the contractor. The disagreements and
attraction between them had sparked almost instantly. So
much so, they'd stolen every scene they were in. Their
chemistry had given Nathan's publicist the idea they could be

the new helm of a home improvement show. While Yvonne had never thought about television, she wasn't one to turn down the opportunity to grow her business even further. She'd once been forced to accept whatever scraps she could get from the person who claimed to love her. Not anymore. Neither she, nor her son, would ever be in that position again.

"You guys will get it."

"Maybe, but until then I can't forget what got me here in the first place. No matter what happens with me and Nathan, Yvonne Cable Designs is and always will be my priority. I fought too hard to build my brand to this point to let it go just because I'm getting married."

"But you will be making time to plan your wedding."

"You know it!"

"I'd expect nothing less." Bree looked at her cell phone. "Five minutes until the call. I'll leave you alone so you can get ready."

Yvonne went through the notes she'd jotted down for why she should be their go-to person for the lifestyle section. When she'd spoken with Lashon, the editor of the magazine, she'd still been considering a few other designers. This call would, hopefully, convince Lashon to go with her.

Lashon called right on time. They went through the normal pleasantries: quick stories about their kids, Lashon had two girls, and the latest good news from the magazine staffers. Then Lashon got to business.

"Look, Yvonne, I know you've gotten really busy lately."

"Not too busy to supply design tips for the readers of your magazine. I was thinking of a focus on commercial spaces. Restaurants, offices, things like that."

"Actually, I was thinking we could go in a different direction," Lashon said before Yvonne could go into the reasons why she was the right choice.

"You're no longer looking to include interior design tips?"

"No, silly. I'm surprised you haven't already figured that out," Lashon said laughing. "I want the feature to be with you *and* Nathan."

"Really?" That idea had not crossed her mind.

"It's genius, right?"

"I'm not sure I'm following along."

"*Lady Entrepreneur* is still going to focus on women business owners, but I'm thinking of expanding the lifestyle section to also tackle relationships. Doesn't that make sense?"

Not entirely, considering the magazine was supposed to be a business resource, but Yvonne never claimed to be an expert in magazine editing. "I'm intrigued by this new direction. Tell me more."

"We did a survey of our subscribers. Many of them are single women who are also struggling to find a balance between work and family. You, my friend, are now the epitome of what so many single women want. You made a successful career despite having a child."

"Despite?" A child wasn't an automatic liability.

"And even though you are a single mother, you still happened to land a great guy like Nathan Lange. We think a quarterly feature on how you balance being a wife, mother, and business owner would go a long way to giving our readers hope."

Giving the readers hope? Landing a great guy like Nathan hadn't been part of her life goals. If anything, after the disaster that was her relationship with Jacob's father, she'd never believed she would trust a man again. But she had, and yes, Nathan was great, and she was happy things worked out, but she wouldn't say her life was now defined by her engagement. Was it?

"So, what do you say?"

"Can I think about it? I really wanted to focus on Yvonne Cable Designs."

"Yes, of course, you can still mention that, but just include more information about your happy ending. You two are perfect together. Don't underestimate how much more your brand is worth now that you have him tied to it."

How much more her brand is worth? She'd thought her brand was fine as it was. Sure, people called more after she and Nathan's relationship developed on *Celebrity Housewives*. They'd done a few interviews promoting the idea of doing a show that focused on blending their styles to achieve southern sophistication, but she was more than the *Vonne* in their tentatively titled show, *Nate and Vonne*.

Or was she? She wasn't a stranger to being in this situation. Not being enough. She glanced at the *Power of Perfection* article that had given her such joy just a few minutes ago. Even that interview request had come after she and Nathan appeared on the show.

"I'll let you know about the feature with Nathan. I need to talk it over with him first."

"Great! Just think about it some more. We love what you've done and would like to work with you. Let's find a way to make that happen."

Yvonne turned over the magazine and drummed her fingers on the desk. "Sure. I'll talk to you later."

Yvonne got off the phone and leaned back in her chair. She looked around her office. The awards on the wall. The layouts for projects. Everything she'd built. Maybe Lashon had a point. Maybe people would be more drawn to her business now that she was getting married. Ignoring an angle that allowed her to expand would be ludicrous. Power couples were a big deal. Maybe that was her brand now. One half of a whole.

She took a deep breath and sat up straight. She'd come

too far to backtrack. No matter what happened, she wouldn't lose the Yvonne Cable who had overcome adversity and built a small empire. She wasn't just a master at creating fabulous interior designs. She'd spent the past six years carefully crafting her own image. Maybe it was time for another personal redesign.

Chapter 2

"You want to wait?"

Yvonne stared into Nathan's excited hazel eyes. Her fiancé. She really had to get used to calling him that. The engagement was still so new.

Nathan gripped her hand and smiled, first at their publicist, Judy Turner, sitting across from them in the conference room in her office, then back at Yvonne. "Let's set the example," he said in that sure and steady way he had. "Our relationship has always been about building a foundation of friendship first. We did that. Waiting will allow us to continue to build that foundation of love, trust, and respect."

Nathan's thumb caressed her wrist. The sensation traveled up her arm, through her nerve endings, and lit a fire low in her belly. Nine months of abstaining. Now he wanted to wait until they got married!

At first glance Nathan didn't seem like the wholesome, family values kind of guy. Long lean muscles, skin tanned from working outside, sandy brown hair just long enough to be considered unruly, and a perpetual five o'clock shadow.

Nathan had first struck her as handsome, sexy, and most likely to make her life difficult as they worked on the home renovation during the season of *Celebrity Housewives*. Contractors rarely got along with the interior designers.

He had made her job difficult, but he'd also lured her in with his calm and focused demeanor. When he'd asked her out, she hadn't thought to say no. That's when the traditional side of Nathan had come through. He was the first guy she'd dated who wanted to wait until after they got to know each other before having sex. The reality show producers caught wind of her and Nathan's budding romance and Nathan's sex after marriage ideas, and pretty soon their background role in the reality show garnered as much attention as the housewife herself.

She hadn't expected things to get this far with Nathan. Love had snuck up on her the same way her six-year-old son liked to sneak up on her in the kitchen. She was just minding her own business, then surprise! It scared her, but in a way that made her smile instead of getting startled.

"Nathan, don't you think we should talk about this some more . . ." She darted a glance at Judy. "Later?"

Like when they weren't in the middle of their publicist's office. Judy had been Nathan's publicist first and Yvonne had become her client by default now that *Nate and Vonne* was about to be a thing. Waiting longer was a big decision. Something she would have expected them to talk about more.

"Actually, I think it's a great idea," Judy said. Her blue-grey eyes sparkled with excitement.

"You do?" There was no situation in which Judy's input on Yvonne's sex life should come into play.

"You two are the latest *it* couple in the home and garden world," Judy continued, ignoring Yvonne's who-cares-what-you-think tone. "The appeal of your unconventional love means people want to know more about you."

"What does that have to do with us waiting?" Yvonne asked.

Nathan squeezed her hand again. "We're pitching our show as one that promotes simple but stylish Southern living. Our values as a couple will also play into the show."

They hadn't really discussed their values as a couple. This was more about Nathan's values becoming hers. Which she respected, she just hadn't expected it to become the focal point of their public relationship.

Judy, ever perceptive, chimed in again. "If word gets out that you two are waiting until you're married, it'll generate interest in your relationship and create a buzz for the show. Couples who wait are an anomaly today. It's no longer expected, but by doing it you both are showing a recommitment to your faith and dedication to each other."

Faith. Yeah, she'd lost a lot of her faith. Multiple disappointments early in life tended to do that to a person.

Yvonne had tried not to let people see how cynical she was about life. She'd chosen to hide her limited faith in others just as she would an unattractive feature in one of the houses she decorated. A fresh coat of I'm-an-independent-single-mother, with a few accents of let-me-roll-with-the-punches, meant most people didn't notice how bland she felt inside.

Yvonne met Nathan's gaze. Nathan had enough faith for them both. He was the one person who'd slowly made her feel it was okay to trust again. He believed good things happened to good people. He loved her and her son. He was the stable future and male role model her son needed in his life. He was the proof to never give up on finding love. But, was this a stunt just to help their show?

"Do you feel that way, too?" she asked him.

"Judy is thinking about the promotion. I'm thinking about us. I told you how I felt that first night we had dinner together."

"Which was reiterated on the episode of *Celebrity House-*

wives that had a strong undertone of your developing relationship," Judy chimed in.

Yvonne cut her eyes at the publicist. Nathan held up a hand to stop Yvonne from telling Judy to stay out of things.

"Judy, will you give us a second?" Nathan asked.

Judy looked between the two of them. Yvonne's growing frustration must have been obvious because Judy nodded and stood. After Judy walked out, Nathan reached for Yvonne. She avoided his touch and got up. She paced to the window overlooking downtown Atlanta.

"What's wrong?" Nathan asked.

Yvonne crossed her arms. "You're treating our engagement like a publicity stunt. First the big proposal on the jumbotron. Now the plan to tell the world we're going to wait until we're married just to sell the show."

This idea came a little too soon after Lashon's insistence that her readers would prefer *Nathan and Vonne*'s advice instead of just Yvonne's. One proposal, and her life was no longer hers. Was she about to lose herself, again, in a relationship when she'd promised herself to never again get swept away by a man?

She heard the shuffle of his chair a few seconds before his hands engulfed her shoulders. He slowly turned her to face him. His features were stark as worry filled his eyes.

"Yvonne, this is not about a publicity stunt. I love you and Jacob. I fell in love with you when you first came into the house and cursed me out for getting sawdust all over your fabric swatches."

"I didn't curse you out."

He grinned the signature southern-boy grin that made her heart melt. "Okay, no curse words were spoken, but you burned the hell out of my ears just the same."

Yvonne laughed at the memory. The incident that got them the attention on the reality show. One of the truly unscripted moments. She'd laid out fabric swatches in the sunroom, which he'd chosen as the perfect spot to also use a circular saw. Dust was everywhere, and Yvonne hadn't been happy.

"Next time keep the sawing outside."

Nathan's eyes crinkled as he grinned. He was so cute. Ruggedly sexy with a dash of sweet boy-next-door comfort. He was the opposite of any guy she'd dated before. She'd done that on purpose, and that decision led her to a happy ending she'd stopped wishing for long ago.

"This is why I love you. You say what's on your mind," Nathan said. "You don't hold back and are completely honest with me. I asked you to marry me because I want to spend the rest of my life with you. I did it at the Braves game because I wanted the world to know you are the woman I want to marry. I want to wait because in my heart it's the right thing to do."

Yvonne slid her arm around his waist and pressed her body against his. "You really want to wait?" She didn't feel like playing fair. Nine months was a long time to have a sexy boyfriend without any benefits.

His lids lowered. Temptation flashed in his eyes. He took a deep breath, then met her gaze again. "I've rushed into things in my past. Things that I shouldn't have done and regret doing."

"Things like what?" He'd never talked to her about having past regrets.

"I've chosen women because I let lust guide me, and I got nothing from that but shame and heartbreak. Yvonne, I'm serious about this because I want both of us to know we're in this because we love and respect each other. Not just because we want each other."

"Are you sure that's all. Nothing to do with the publicity this will bring?"

"The publicity is a bonus Judy pointed out. This is between me and you. Do you not want to do this?"

No. She didn't want to do this. She was engaged. She wanted to finally have sex with the man she was marrying. The shrewd, roll-with-the-punches, do-what's-best-to-get-to-the-next-level part of her couldn't deny the appeal of making their decision public.

They were pitching their home renovation show with a heavy undertone of good old family values. She, the hard-working single mom and interior decorator to Atlanta's rich and famous. Nathan, the down-to-Earth, family-oriented, builder-slash-woodworker. People loved Nathan's Southern boy charm and sympathized with her for being strong and independent. It was a perfect combination for the home and garden networks out there.

No one asked about her son's father, which was fine with her. He was dead to her if not dead in real life. Paying her to disappear was reason enough to consider him dead.

And why was she thinking about Jacob's father to begin with? Six years had passed. She'd taken the money and moved on. Look where she was now. About to marry the perfect guy. About to sell their traditional family values with a side of Southern city chic home renovation show to a major network. About to finally put the past behind her and celebrate the future. About to finally get over the foolish mistakes of the old Yvonne.

"Yvonne?" Nathan asked, his brows drawn together.

She lifted her chin, pushed the past out of her mind, and smiled into the eyes of her future. "We'll wait."

Yvonne's mother, Rochelle, dumped a stack of bridal magazines on the kitchen table in front of her. "I was watching one of those wedding shows," Rochelle said. "And apparently merlot, peach, and sage are perfect colors for a wedding."

Yvonne gaped at the mountain of magazines, then at her sister Valerie sitting across from her. Valerie's shoulders raised

slightly in an I-have-no-idea type of shrug before her light
brown eyes filled with laughter. Nathan had proposed a few
days ago, and her mom was already picking out colors?

Honestly, she wasn't surprised. Her mom would be sewing
the wedding dress herself if she knew where to start. Yvonne
was pretty sure Rochelle never believed her youngest daughter,
the mistake who'd ruined her first marriage and the one who'd
returned from design school alone and pregnant, would ever
get married and not to a catch like Nathan Lange. As
Rochelle had told Yvonne plenty of times since she was old
enough to understand: *"You're here because I fell for temptation
and sinned. Which means you're susceptible to the same mistakes."*

Yvonne hadn't believed her mother's mistakes would also
haunt her. Then she'd met Jacob's dad. Fallen in love.
Realized too late she'd been the secret side chick. Guess that
saying about the apple not falling far from the tree had to be
true in some situations.

Yvonne picked up one of the magazines. "Mom, what are
you talking about?"

"Merlot, peach, and sage . . . really?" Valerie said, spreading
the magazines across the oak table top. "What the hell is that,
anyway. A fruit salad?"

Her sister's reddish-brown hair formed the perfect halo of
coils around her golden-brown face. She swore her sister was
queen of the perfect wash-and-go. Yvonne, on the other
hand, had a standing appointment to get her natural curls
blown out into a sleek curtain to her shoulders.

Yvonne covered her mouth, but the effort didn't stifle her
laugher. Their mom glared at Yvonne. She pointed to her
sister. "I didn't say it."

"As I was saying," Rochelle's straight back and raised chin
matched her voice. "These colors are considered rustic, but
tasteful."

Few lines creased Rochelle's pecan-brown skin. She wore
a dark blue polo with *Word of God*, the name of her church,

stitched onto the right side and tan slacks. It was what she wore daily as part of her job as secretary for the same church.

Yvonne flipped the pages of a magazine. "So now I have to be *rustic and tasteful*."

"Of course," Rochelle exclaimed, like Yvonne was a game show contestant who'd given the right answer. "You're marrying Nathan Lange. If your show sells, you two will be the biggest hit in home renovation. You're the new charming couple that embodies contemporary southern elegance."

Yvonne barely kept herself from rolling her eyes. "Mom, you took that from the article about us in the *Journal and Constitution*." The Atlanta newspaper had done a piece on them in the style section. Further proof that *Nathan and Vonne* were a bigger hit than Just Yvonne. Since meeting on the reality show she and Nathan tag teamed on a few of the custom homes his contracting company built in southeastern Atlanta. He built the structure, she designed the inside.

Valerie cocked her head to the side. "Contemporary southern elegance?"

Yvonne waved a hand. "So long as it helps us sell this show, I'm okay with it."

She would be okay with anything that took Yvonne Cable Designs to the next level. She'd never considered pitching a television show until Nathan mentioned it after the producers of *Celebrity Housewives* were so interested in them. Honestly, she hadn't thought the idea would fly, but after the *Journal and Constitution* article and her conversation with Lashon, Yvonne was beginning to see she was better with Nathan, businesswise at least. Now they were about to take their talents to the national stage. She'd be able to give her son the life he deserved.

Rochelle pointed at Yvonne. "Which means you need to have a tasteful and sophisticated wedding. Merlot, peach, and sage are tasteful."

Why didn't her mom just come out and say what she

really meant? Don't do anything to mess this up like your last relationship. Oh, she knew why. Because Rochelle could teach a course in being passive-aggressive.

Valerie's head fell back, and she groaned. "You are killing me with this sophisticated mess. Yvonne used to be so much fun." She sat up straight. "You were the queen of late nights dancing, long weekends, and pop-up parties. Can we at least get some of that fun person back for your wedding?"

Yvonne didn't care if her wedding was the most boring in history, she just wanted to get to the day already. To become the wife of a man she could trust. To be valued for being herself, or as much of herself as she let Nathan see.

"That was the old me."

Her mom smiled with unmasked approval. Valerie's face screwed up like she smelled something old and rotten. "Old you?" Valerie asked. "There was nothing wrong with that you."

"I'm not saying anything was wrong with me," Yvonne said. Rochelle snorted. Yvonne barely stopped the flinch. Ignoring her mom, she continued talking to her sister. "But I wasn't focused."

"I miss unfocused you," Valerie grumbled, flipping through pages of a magazine.

Warmth spread in Yvonne's chest. Her sister had always been on her side. Not easy when their mom often put them against each other. Not outright, the queen of passive-aggressive wouldn't do that, but in subtle ways, like dropping reminders that Yvonne was the reason Valerie's father left. Yeah, their mom sleeping with the church deacon, getting pregnant, and having Yvonne had nothing to do with it. Sure.

"Everyone has to grow up some time," Yvonne said. "I grew up after I had Jacob. A kid ends late nights dancing, long weekends, and pop-up parties. Unless you want to hear about the two hours I spent singing and dancing with Jacob to Team Umi Zoomi the other night."

Valerie shook her head vigorously. "Please, spare me. The show is cute, but it took two hours to get one of those songs out of my head after watching with him the other week."

Jacob loved that show. Yvonne had caught herself humming the many catchy tunes even when the show wasn't on. So much so that her assistant, Bree, had told her on many occasions to stop.

Smiling, Yvonne stood and went to the kitchen window. Jacob was in her mother's backyard playing with the boy who lived next door. They tossed a foam football back and forth. Laughing and giggling, without a care in the world. Happy and safe the way all young kids should be.

"Is Jacob happy about the engagement?" Rochelle asked.

Turning away from the window, Yvonne faced her mom. She leaned her hands on the counter behind her. "He's ecstatic. In fact, he knew about it. Nathan asked Jacob if it would be okay for him to be his daddy."

Rochelle nodded approvingly. "He's such a sweet guy."

"He is," Yvonne agreed. "So, Mom, you're right about one thing. I do want this to be a classy and tasteful wedding. But before you get excited about these colors, I know that merlot will not fly."

Her mom's excitement at possibly getting her way deflated. "Why not?"

"Because Cassidy doesn't like burgundy or any color that remotely resembles it. She already told me that right after Nathan proposed."

Valerie rolled her eyes. "Who cares what Cassidy thinks?"

"I care. She's Nathan's sister and he loves her."

"Stepsister," her mom said. "Not the same."

Yvonne and Valerie exchanged a look. A wordless battle for who would take up this argument? Yvonne lost to Valerie's raised brow and eye roll.

"Stepsister is the same," Yvonne said, conceding her loss. "Blended families are normal, Mom. Nathan has known Cassidy since he was twelve years old. She's not only his sister, she's his best friend. Which means keeping her happy keeps Nathan happy."

Luckily, she and Cassidy got along well. From the start, Cassidy had supported Yvonne and Nathan's relationship. She'd folded Yvonne up in her welcoming arms and begun treating her like a sister from the jump. After Nathan proposed, she'd said it was because Nathan told her he'd believe Yvonne was *the one.*

Valerie crossed her arms and leaned back in her chair. "I still can't believe you're marrying him."

"Stranger things have happened," Rochelle said flipping through a magazine.

Yvonne bit her lip to stop an angry retort. She wasn't doomed to make her mom's mistakes anymore. Instead she'd focus on the good in her life.

"Why can't you believe we're getting married?" Yvonne tried to hide her discomfort behind a confident tone.

Valerie studied Yvonne. "I didn't think you liked him. Not seriously."

She hadn't thought they'd get to a long-term relationship, much less marriage. Yes, a part of her was marrying Nathan for stability. He was the perfect guy. Charming and sweet but also sexy and strong. A quiet leader who'd eventually won her heart.

"I love him. I never would have thought I'd be lucky enough to meet a guy like him. Much less marry him."

"Why?" Valerie asked. "You have your own gravitational pull when it comes to men."

Rochelle grunted. Valerie glared. "Mom, stop."

Yvonne shook her head. "She's not that far off. I was overly romantic and too quick to believe in happily ever after. That caused me to make mistakes."

"Mistakes like coming home early from school pregnant and alone?" her mom chimed in.

"No," Yvonne said. "I don't regret having Jacob. If anything, he's the best thing that came out of my time in Washington."

But she'd learned a lesson after that. Don't fall hard and fast. Don't believe everything a man tells you. Don't fall apart when you're tossed aside.

"Jacob taught me how strong I could be because I needed to be," she said. "I worked my interior design business until it got me here. I'm hopefully about to have one of the most anticipated shows out there. Nathan knows me and loves me, warts and all. On top of that, he's great with Jacob. He loves Jacob."

Which is more than Jacob's own father had ever given him. She pushed the thought aside. She'd been letting thoughts of Jacob's dad infiltrate her brain a lot more since the engagement.

Jacob came running into the house. "Mommy! Jamie fell and scratched his knee. Can we have a Band-Aid?"

Before Yvonne could answer, Rochelle was already jumping from her chair. She swooped over to Jacob and took his hand. "Of course, you can have a Band-Aid, baby. Gigi will get one for you."

No matter how much shade her mother threw her way, Yvonne knew Rochelle would never do the same with Jacob. She doted on her only grandchild. Regardless of Yvonne's sometimes tense relationship with her mom, she couldn't say a single bad thing about how her mom had stepped in and helped her every step of the way with Jacob. That was another reason why she chose to bite her lip and ignore the jabs at her moral character.

"Jacob, are you okay?" Yvonne asked. She did a quick visual inspection but found no outward injuries.

"I'm good."

"Of course, you are, baby," Rochelle said. "You're the toughest boy in the neighborhood. You can handle a little fall playing football." Rochelle got the bandages from the first aid kit she kept under the sink and then went outside to tend to Jamie.

"Good, now I can ask what I really want to know," Valerie said.

Yvonne breathed her own sigh of relief after her mom walked out. She wasn't ready to pick wedding colors. Hell, they didn't even have a date yet. "What's that?"

Valerie folded her hands on the table and cocked her head to the side. "Now that you're engaged are you and Nathan finally going to." She wiggled her brows. "You know?"

"God, I wish!" The exclamation was out before Yvonne could stop herself.

Valerie sat up straight. Disbelief crossed her sister's face. "You are still waiting?"

"Yes. Not my idea. It's his. He's sticking to his beliefs. I admire him for it."

Valerie raised a brow. "But . . . what if the wedding night comes and he sucks."

Yvonne laughed and went back to the table with her sister. "He won't suck. He's an excellent kisser and he's great with his hands. Believe me." She winked. "I'll be good."

Her sister held up a hand. "If you say so. I would at least want to test the waters."

She did, too. So very much. "I also respect Nathan's wishes. Besides, we've built our brand on our values. We can't go back on that just because we're engaged."

And Yvonne understood the importance of perception. She staged a room to convey whatever feeling a client wanted. Her and Nathan's public relationship was no different. They'd set the stage to make their potential viewers and clients happy.

"Ah ha!" Valerie snapped her fingers. "That's the real reason. You want to help sell the show."

She did, but that wasn't the only reason. She wanted Nathan. But she did admire and appreciate his willingness to wait. He wanted her. Not her body. She wasn't just a fun pastime. She was the woman he wanted to spend the rest of his life with.

Yvonne's chin lifted, and she smiled at Valerie. "Selling the show is a bonus. I'm going along with this because I'm worth waiting for."

She reached into her purse and pulled out her notebook and pen case. "Now, since Mom's gone through all the trouble of bringing these magazines and I do need to plan a wedding, I might as well get started. Let's go through them and—"

"Let me guess. Make a list?" Humor filled Valerie's voice.

"Yes. It's how I stay on track."

"You know, one day you're going to come across a situation that can't be fixed with a list." Valerie took one of the magazines and flipped it open.

"Doubtful. There are always pros and cons. Therefore, I will always be able to decide the right way to go."

"See, that's your problem. What happened to going with your gut?"

"Going with my gut did not get me where I am today. Now shut up, take a pen," she tossed a pink one at her sister and Valerie caught it. "And let's start writing down ideas to consider for what will be the happiest day of my life."

Chapter 3

As usual, Jacob did not want to get up and move any faster than molasses in January as Yvonne got him ready for school. As she struggled to get him out of bed, argued with him again about why it was necessary to brush his teeth daily, and said get your shoes on so many times she lost count, she once again debated the idea of hiring a nanny to help out in the mornings and afternoons. Nathan's idea.

Her interior design business had been doing remarkably well, but the recent media attention had increased her demand. The life she'd carefully orchestrated with the right balance of entrepreneur time, mommy time, and me time was becoming dramatically out of whack.

When she'd mentioned the idea of a nanny to come in and help with Jacob her mom had immediately disapproved. Her guilt trip was the reason Yvonne continued to put the idea aside. Though on mornings like this one, when Jacob moved like a stoned sloth and she had an important meeting with her new client, Sandra Covington, first thing, she yearned to have someone else there to help her in the mornings.

Nathan didn't spend the night often, and for the rest of the week he'd be working on a new project in Savannah.

She finally dropped Jacob off at school with a kiss and an I love you, glanced at her watch and swore. She was going to be late. But Atlanta's hellish traffic surprisingly cooperated with her. No major accidents and no rain to make drivers even more spastic on the road, and she arrived at Sandra's multi-million dollar newly constructed home in Buckhead's Tuxedo Park ten minutes late instead of the twenty she'd texted Bree.

She was buzzed in through the gate and parked her Audi next to Bree's Mini Cooper in the large circular drive. Grabbing her sketch pad and messenger bag filled with fabric samples, color swatches, and other materials, she hurried to the front door. Her new heels pinched her toes as she sprint-walked. She ignored the discomfort. Once upon a time she'd had a more relaxed, bohemian flair. Not a single pair of high heels in her possession. Then she'd realized designing the interiors of the homes owned by rich and privileged people meant the bohemian air had to go. She'd given up the enviable curly coils that matched her sister's for sleek straight hair, donned stylish business suits as her armor, and gotten used to heels—no higher than four inches if she wanted her knees to cooperate.

Yvonne Cable was put together, competent, and bold. At least that's what the write-up in *Southern Living* had said. She was proud of her carefully designed image. Proud of where it had gotten her. No one looked at her and saw an easy target. Not anymore.

The door was answered by an older man in a butler's uniform. "Ms. Cable?"

Yvonne nodded and tilted up her lips in a polite smile. "I am."

"Please come in. Ms. Covington is finishing up with her personal trainer. You can wait with your assistant in the study."

Yvonne thanked him and followed him into the home. Her eyes scanned the inside. The house was built to be flashy and impressive, exuding wealth and status rather than the air of a cozy, comforting retreat. The walls were the basic eggshell color given to the interior of most newly constructed homes. Typically, the builder had interior designers who worked with the homeowners to decorate while the homes were built. The Covington Home, as she'd labeled the place, had none of that. Sparsely furnished, no accents on the walls, no personal touches. A blank canvas. Her heart raced, and her fingers itched to stop and immediately begin sketching the ideas running through her head.

When they entered the study, Bree was walking around taking notes. There was furniture there; ornate, traditional furniture, that overpowered the space. With the placement of the windows and the morning light filtering in, the room deserved cleaner lines. Room to breathe.

The butler left them, and Bree came over. "She's running late."

Yvonne breathed a small sigh of relief. "She's not the only one. Sorry about that. It was a rough morning with Jacob."

Bree waved a hand. "Girl, my sister has three kids and always complains about the morning ritual. I would have had your back if she'd been on time."

That was exactly why Yvonne loved her assistant. Bree thought of the things Yvonne needed before she'd realized them herself. She matched Yvonne's style in a navy-blue business suit, but added color with a bright yellow shirt beneath that complemented her complexion.

"What are your initial impressions?" Yvonne asked.

"This house is begging for your touch. It's a clean slate. Impressive as is, but your touch will make it magnificent."

Yvonne put down her bag and flipped to an open page in her sketchbook. "Magnificent... I like the sound of that." She grabbed a few colored pencils and walked the space.

Bree fell into step with Yvonne. "Do you think you can feature the design on your show with Nathan?"

"Our show hasn't been picked up by a network, yet." But she was already thinking ahead. The house would make a great feature. She wondered if Ms. Covington would be willing to let them film a little before.

"But it's going to be." Bree's optimism flowed with every syllable of the show's full title. "*Southern Chic with Nate and Vonne*," Bree said with a flair of her hand.

Hearing the show title sent a rush of goosebumps over Yvonne's arms. She might actually have a television renovation show. She was living this life. She wanted to pinch herself but was still afraid some major jinx would happen and mess up her perfectly patterned existence.

"Judy has a few interested networks. We may even have offers by the end of the week." Yvonne stopped at the windows and started a rough sketch of the perfect drapes to frame the area.

"Nathan's proposal made you guys an even hotter topic. You were trending on Twitter the night he proposed. Usually, I'm not a fan of public proposals, but you two are so in love. You're real, you know, there aren't many couples out there who are really committed the way you and Nathan are."

Yvonne smiled and continued sketching. "It was sweet."

"And you're waiting until the wedding." Bree placed a hand over her heart. "Who does that anymore. I think it's super romantic."

Yvonne stopped sketching and turned to Bree. "How did you know we're waiting?" The decision was just made.

"It was in the statement released yesterday. Nathan and Yvonne are continuing to dedicate themselves to the values that built their relationship," Bree said, sounding like a news anchor. "They've chosen to wait until their wedding night before consummating their relationship."

"What?" A statement had gone out already? Damn, Judy.

She should have known the overeager publicist wouldn't want to wait to get the word out. Not while simultaneously trying to get the major networks to buy their show.

"I think it's admirable." A woman's voice came from the door. "We don't see many people willing to sacrifice physical pleasure to build a stronger foundation."

Yvonne ignored the burning embarrassment in her cheeks and faced the woman in the doorway. Sandra Covington, she presumed, was younger than Yvonne had expected. Probably only a few years older than her. Tall, mahogany skin, strong brown eyes and thick hair pulled back in a loose ponytail.

She walked in and held out her hand. "I'm Sandra Covington. Sorry for keeping you waiting."

Yvonne stepped forward and shook Sandra's hand. She had a firm grip. The butler said she'd been with her physical trainer, but she greeted them in a tasteful linen green suit. "Yvonne Cable. This is my assistant, Bree Foster. Thank you for allowing me to decorate your home."

Sandra slipped her hands into the pockets of her pants. Her head tilted slightly to the left. Her eyes focused on Yvonne's face. "You came highly recommended. You look just like your picture on your website."

She'd gotten odd compliments before from clients, and she hoped this was a compliment, so Yvonne kept the pleasant smile on her face. "As advertised," she said waving a hand in front of her face.

"Indeed," Sandra said still studying her. "You're...not what I expected."

"What did you expect?"

"To feel differently."

Yvonne blinked. "Differently about me?"

Sandra's head straightened, and she stepped back. "No, I'm just excited. About the house. My husband got to pick the layout and floorplan; I'm in charge of decorations. I don't know where to start."

"May I ask who referred you to me?" She liked to know who recommended her in order to send a thank you card and gift later.

"I don't remember off hand," Sandra said. "If it comes to me, I'll let you know. You're marrying Nathan Lange, right?"

"I am," Yvonne answered, unsure about the shift in questions.

"How did you manage that?"

Keeping her pleasant smile was a little harder. "I didn't manage anything. He asked, and I said yes."

"Sorry, again, I don't mean anything by that. I'm just interested in your relationship. A fairytale ending almost."

Sandra's eyes were sharp and interested as she watched Yvonne. A reminder to be careful with what she said in front of the woman. Sandra didn't engage in malicious celebrity gossip on her show. She spent most of the time counseling the callers who came to her for advice. That didn't mean she wouldn't use Yvonne's relationship with Nathan as an example of a couple to "analyze" on her show.

"Almost." Yvonne lifted her sketchbook. "Do you have ideas for the house? We can walk around, and you can tell me what you think while I take notes. Draw a few sketches, preliminary of course, then come back with more concrete ideas later."

Sandra smiled. "Sure, let's start with that."

They toured the house which was even more impressive as they went through. She and Bree took notes along the way. Instead of telling them what she'd like to see, Sandra continued to throw personal questions out to Yvonne.

"Your mother, she's from Atlanta?"

"Yes."

"What about your father?"

"Not around."

"You have one sister, correct? And you have a son, too, is that right?" Sandra asked as they walked down one of the stairs to the front of the house. "How does he feel about the engagement?"

Yvonne stopped at the bottom. She'd hidden her annoyance when she was asked about her past, but Jacob was off limits. He was her baby, and she didn't discuss him with anyone outside of her family. If this was what it would be like to work with Sandra, then maybe the job wasn't worth the effort.

"With all due respect, Sandra, I don't like to discuss my son with clients."

"I meant no disrespect. It was an innocent question."

"Still, I like to keep a line between myself and my clients. I respect your privacy and the privilege you offer by allowing me in your personal space. If you can't do the same for me, then you may need to find another interior designer."

Sandra's brows raised. "You do know that my show has a large listening audience?"

"I do." She really wanted to be known by that listening audience, but not if it meant revealing her personal life to Sandra. Between *Celebrity Housewives* and a statement about when she'll finally have sex again, her personal life had enough publicity.

"Some of the most successful and influential people in the city listen to my show and look to me for advice."

Sweat ran down Yvonne's back, but she didn't back down. The client pool she'd get from working with Sandra would make her *the* name in interior design even without the television show. But leaving Jacob out of her professional life was a hard line and one she couldn't understand why Sandra wouldn't let go.

"I do, but you also need to understand that my professional life is very public. It's about to become even more public as Nathan and I continue to work together and possibly have a television show. Keeping my son out of that spotlight is the most important thing to me."

Sandra watched her for several more seconds. Bree fidgeted

with her pencil in Yvonne's periphery. After several long seconds, Sandra relaxed and smiled.

She held out her hand. "Have it your way. But I do hope that as we work together, you'll learn to trust me. I'd like for us to become friends."

Shocked but also grateful Sandra hadn't taken offense Yvonne relaxed and shook her hand. "That would be nice."

Later that afternoon, Yvonne still couldn't get the conversation with Sandra Covington out of her mind. She didn't think she'd been rude. Typically, conversations with clients about her family were easy to keep generic. But Sandra had pushed past the superficial, or maybe she was extra sensitive after Bree mentioned the statement.

The world was about to be in her personal life. She had to keep something to herself. Still, had she pushed too far?

"Hey Bree," Yvonne called.

"Yeah," Bree called back. Her desk was right outside of Yvonne's office. They frequently had conversations via shouting across the hall.

"Can you come here for a second?"

Keys on Bree's keyboard clicked. The sound of a chair rolled against the floor before Bree stood in Yvonne's door. "What's up?"

"Was I too sensitive with Sandra and her questions this morning?"

"No. That lady was all up in your business." Bree said in a rush as if the words had been longing to come out sooner.

Yvonne nodded. "So, it wasn't just me?"

"Nah." Bree crossed her arms and leaned on the door frame. "I get the general 'are you from around here' questions, but asking about your mom, dad, and Jacob was too much. You were right to set boundaries."

"I wonder why she was like that."

"Probably so she can try and save your soul." Bree's casual reply.

Yvonne laughed at the off the wall response. "What?"

"You know those self-help types. Gotta fix everybody."

Yvonne considered it. Sandra had probably viewed her as a good conversation topic for her show. "You're right," she said. "As long as she's cool, I'll be cool. Besides, her point about making connections from her show is true."

"Why are you worried about connections? You and Nathan are about to go big time. You don't need connections."

But she'd always need her own money. Her own security net. In case Nathan tossed her aside the same way. She cut the thought short and took a deep breath. "I'm not shutting down Yvonne Cable Designs. Never hurts to keep the connections."

Yvonne's cell phone rang. "It's Judy." Bree nodded and backed out of the office. Yvonne answered the call. "Hey Judy."

"Yvonne, how are you?" Judy's voice was pleasant, as always, but something about her tone put Yvonne on edge.

"I'm good. Is everything okay with you?"

"Yes. Things are great. In fact, that's why I'm calling you. We've gotten an offer. A really generous offer."

Yvonne's concerns over Judy's tone flew out the window. She stood and walked to the window. She'd never been good at hearing important news sitting down. "That's fantastic. What network?"

"W.E.W."

The Weekend Warrior channel. Yvonne was familiar with the network that featured syndicated television shows, movies, and some instructional programming related to gardening, home remodeling, and crafts. A popular network. W.E.W. had a diverse selection of shows that pulled in a wide array of viewers.

"That's a great channel."

"I know." Judy said the words as if she hated to admit them.

Yvonne leaned against the window and shifted the phone to her other ear. "What's the problem?"

"Nothing big, it's just the owner of the network wants to meet with you before finalizing the deal."

"Oh...well, I guess that's cool. Have you talked to Nathan? When do they want to meet?"

She hadn't expected to meet with the owner of the network. Some of the executives and producers, maybe, but not the actual owner. Was that typical? She thought over what she knew about selling a show to television and only came up with the things she'd seen on television and in the movies. This was all new to her.

"No, you don't get it. The owner wants to meet with *you*. Not you and Nathan."

"What? Why?" She and Nathan were a package deal. There was no reason for the owner to meet with just her.

"I don't know. I have to ask...Yvonne, were you planning to go solo on us?"

"Really Judy? I didn't even come up with this idea, now you think I'm trying to break up my partnership with Nathan before it's even started?" Frustration tightened her fingers on her cell phone. She loved Nathan, they were a team, Judy should know that.

"Hey, I have to ask. He was insistent that he talk only to you."

"He who?" Yvonne snapped back.

"Richard Barrington. The third, not Junior. His father died about a year ago."

Yvonne's knees buckled. She placed one hand against the window. Her heart pounded like a herd of terrified elephants. Sweat slickened her face and palms until her hand slid down the window. No, her entire body was sliding down. She stumbled over to her chair and fell heavily into the leather cushion.

"Richard Barrington," she asked in a trembling voice.

"Yes. Do you know him? Do you know why he would want to meet with you?"

She did, but she couldn't tell Judy. She couldn't tell anyone that Jacob's father was suddenly back in their lives.

Chapter 4

She'd been in her second year at the Corcoran School of the Arts and Design when she'd met Richard. After an intensive round of finals, she and a few other friends had headed to a coffee house that switched into a jazz bar by night to enjoy spoken word poetry, drinks, and celebrate surviving another year. She'd noticed him almost immediately. He'd stuck out just that much. Amidst all the artists, musicians, and free spirits, a guy at the bar wearing a suit and tie, frowning into his drink, who looked like he'd just stepped over from Capitol Hill was hard to miss.

She'd been intrigued immediately. A fault of hers. Wanting to know what was going on with other people. The need to figure out how she could help if someone looked sad. Valerie said she was too nice for her own good. That her the-glass-is-half-full outlook on life made her too tenderhearted. Yvonne hadn't cared. A hot guy was at the bar and he looked like he needed a smile.

She'd slid up next to him and said hey. He'd looked up from whatever brown liquor he'd been studying. Their eyes met, and her breath got stuck somewhere between her mouth and lungs. He was handsome from a distance. Up close he was hot. In that grown man, I've-got-myself-together kind of way. Dark, dark eyes. Walnut brown skin her fingers tingled to touch. His suit was expensive and tailored, his cologne equally impressive.

Her romantic's mind had rushed to imagine an outdoor wedding, in the mountains maybe, two kids, and a cute little bungalow. Her heart had screamed you-could-marry-this-guy. Instead of blurting out that she thought they might be soul mates, she leaned her arm against the bar and smiled.

"Buy me a drink," she'd said. She'd been an unrepentant flirt. She'd reveled in the back-and-forth game of attraction. Seeing who would come out on top.

His dark eyes widened. She'd surprised him. His gaze dropped to the V-neck of her sundress then immediately popped back up. She swore embarrassment flashed in his eyes before he glanced away. Mr. I've-got-myself-together was uncomfortable with her cleavage. "I shouldn't."

He shouldn't. Not a no, and not a he didn't want to buy her a drink. Which meant he was interested. "Why?"

"Because, I'm not available to buy beautiful women drinks." He lifted the glass and took a sip of his dark drink. She'd bet it was cognac or bourbon. He looked like the type. The words had come out with regret. He wasn't happy to turn her down, but he was under some obligation to do so.

"Wife or girlfriend?" Not that she would pursue a man who was with another woman, but she had to know if he was completely off the market before succumbing to the disappointment already wrapping cold fingers around her heart.

The corner of his mouth tilted up. He had a sexy mouth. Lips evenly sized, not too big or super thin. Perfect symmetry. *Please, don't have a girlfriend,* she'd silently pleaded.

"Neither. An ex-fiancée," he said. "I broke off my engagement." He checked his watch. "Exactly two hours ago."

Yvonne hadn't known what emotion to go with. No girlfriend. Score! Literally just out of an engagement. Bummer. Either way, the cold fingers of disappointment loosened their hold.

"If you broke things off, why are you sad?"

"It just didn't feel right, you know?"

She smiled and shrugged. "Sorry, I don't. Never been engaged. Do you mean the engagement or the break up?"

The corner of his mouth kicked up again. Her stomach did a funny flip. Two minutes in and she had it bad for the guy.

He frowned into his drink. "The engagement. Everyone said we were perfect. My parents like her. Her parents like me. Our companies are merging. I've known her forever. We've dated for three years."

"But, let me guess, you didn't love her?"

"I do like many things about her. We've been friends forever. I just don't want to marry her." His dark eyes met hers. Conflicted and pleading for some type of understanding. "Does that make sense?"

Yvonne nodded. "She wasn't the one."

"The one? What does that mean?" he'd asked, sounding like a cynical businessman instead of the recently unengaged and conflicted guy he'd been a few seconds before.

"It means that if you weren't ready to marry her, then you made the right call to break things off. Who knows? Maybe the universe has something better in store for you."

"I'll try that line on my dad. He's going to be pissed when I tell him I broke off the engagement." He'd grunted and sipped his drink.

"Hey, it's your life. My philosophy is do what makes you happy. Your dad isn't the one who'd have to spend forever with her. Besides, engaged isn't married. Better to break an engagement than pay for a divorce."

The tension around his eyes and mouth melted away. "I guess you have a point."

"Of course I do." She'd drummed her hands on the bar. "So, how about you buy me that drink, and I'll try to keep you from looking like you want to drown in that...cognac?"

He'd laughed. Low and smooth and the sound warmed her body like the summer sun. "Bourbon, and I don't look like I want to drown myself."

"Yes, you do." She ordered a tequila sunrise, and they'd sat and talked. She stopped flirting and listened as he said he'd always wanted to try his hand at spoken word and that's why he'd chosen this location to have his post-breakup drink. He never told her exactly what he did, he had some big-time corporate job, family business, stressful. That's all she got. She talked about school, finishing finals, poetry.

He left without getting her number. She'd known he had baggage with a two-hour fresh breakup and conflict in his eyes. So, she'd tried to tell herself him not getting her number was for the best. Even though she'd thought about him for weeks after. Then he'd been in the bar again another night. He remembered her. They'd talked again. And before long, he showed up more, they talked more, and pretty soon, she started thinking of him as a friend and not just the hot guy who'd given her fantasies of mountain weddings and cute kids.

Now, she sat in the Atlanta W.E.W. offices and thought back on that first day, when she'd instantly been drawn to him. She still couldn't regret her decision to talk to him. After all the love, the bitter heartbreak, and the way her outlook on life was forever shattered after him, she would never regret that day. She had Jacob, and he was worth every moment.

She'd asked Judy to wait until after her meeting with

Richard to say anything to Nathan. Judy hadn't wanted to go along with it. Yvonne said she wanted to make sure Richard wasn't being a creep and trying to lure her away. If that was the case, she'd turn down the offer and they could let Nathan know afterwards. Judy reluctantly agreed. Regardless of what came of today's meeting, she was going to go back and say they needed to turn down the deal. There was no way in hell she'd let Richard anywhere near her or Jacob. Not after he tossed them aside.

"Ms. Cable, Mr. Barrington will see you now," the pleasant young receptionist said from behind her desk.

Yvonne stood, straightened her shoulders, and lifted her chin. She didn't know what kind of game Richard was playing, or why he'd chosen to play it now, when her life was finally back on track after he derailed it, but she wasn't going to put up with anything he tried to dish out.

She entered the large office. Windows took up one wall overlooking a man-made lake in the busy office park. Richard stood at the window. His back to her. When the door closed behind her, she thought she saw his broad shoulders flinch. Two heartbeats passed before he slowly turned and faced her.

A second of eye contact was all it took for a plethora of emotions to seize her. Memories flooded her brain like the Chattahoochee River after a massive rain storm. The heat of his rich dark skin. The firmness of his muscles beneath. The demand from his lips when he'd kissed her. For a fleeting moment, the happiness that used to infuse her every blood cell when she'd see him enter the bar where they'd meet and talk about books and poetry bubbled up.

"Richard," his name came out as a disbelieving whisper. He was really here. Back in front of her. Did he live in Atlanta now?

Richard's eyes were full of the wary aloofness that had made her want to slip beneath his designer suits to find the real man beneath. He wore one of those suits today, blue and tailored perfectly. The tailoring didn't really matter. His clothes always fell across his body as if they were made just to pay homage to his sex appeal.

"Hello, Yvonne." His cold, angry tone snapped her back to the present.

He'd dismissed her easily. Thrown away her love and their child for someone more *suitable*. Paid her off as if she were an escort who'd overstayed her welcome. Her heart may have fluttered at the sight of him but, judging by his icy stare, he felt nothing similar.

She shifted her weight to one foot, cocked her head to the right and gave him her best disdainful stare. "I never expected to see you again." Later today she'd have to give herself a pat on the back for sounding so unimpressed by his request to see her.

"I find that surprising." Resentment laced his deep voice.

His anger set her teeth on edge. She fought to keep her composure cool. "How's your wife? Does she know you've summoned me?" She said in a mocking tone.

Richard's jaw clenched. "My movements don't matter to her anymore. We're divorced."

She wished she were surprised. He probably thought she'd do an I–told–you–so dance. Instead, she felt empty. She'd suspected Richard wouldn't be happy with the perfect socialite he'd married. The woman he'd described to Yvonne back when they'd slowly gone from friends to lovers. Richard had rattled off the qualities of his former fiancée with a forced cheerfulness that reminded her of kids who got socks instead of a puppy for Christmas. She also remembered Richard talking more about how much his father loved his fiancée than how much he loved her. When he'd gone back to Natalie, she'd said he wouldn't be happy. After six years and a payoff for her to disappear, she couldn't muster up any feelings of satisfaction her prediction had been correct.

"I suppose that was hard on you. She was your perfect woman. More suited to your lifestyle."

"Natalie is a good woman. She just isn't the right woman for me." His gaze bore into hers. Briefly, she thought she saw some of the heat that once flared in them. So briefly, she was sure it was just her overactive imagination. The fact that she would even imagine that after all these years pissed her off.

Yvonne glared at him. "If you're here to go slumming again now that your marriage is over, forget it. Don't play with my livelihood because you're feeling lonely."

He slowly shook his head. "I never considered my relationship with you as slumming. If anything, you considered everything between us as meaningless."

He had the audacity to sound angry at her. Six years of pain stiffened her spine. Her eyes narrowed, and a hand landed on her hips. "Me! You blocked me. Sent me away like nothing but…" Yvonne took a deep breath and pressed a hand to her forehead. She wasn't this person anymore. She wasn't in love with him anymore. He didn't deserve an excess of any emotion from her. She was a businesswoman now. A mother Jacob could be proud of. Calm, poised, above the petty. "You know what, forget it." She dropped her hand and met his eye. "I don't know why you insisted on meeting with me. We both know you're not going to purchase our show. We're done. I'm done, and you get no say in my life anymore. You got what you wanted. Now that it's over, don't come back for a refund. I don't accept used returns or exchanges."

She turned to walk out of the office, not caring about whatever reason Richard thought he could tempt her to think about selling her and Nathan's show to him.

"I asked you here because of my son." The hard snap of his voice whipped across her very last let's-remain-calm nerve.

Angry and heartbroken Yvonne came roaring to the surface. She spun on her heel and wished the bite of her glare was something he could physically feel.

"Your son?" All pretense of calm was lost in the near snarl

of her voice. "Now you want him. After you made it perfectly clear you wanted nothing to do with him or me."

"What are you talking about? You kept your pregnancy a secret from me. Kept my son from me."

"The hell?" Yvonne staggered back a step. "Are you serious right now? I have the emails from your account. I saved them after all these years. I've got the words memorized. I don't want you or the kid. Get rid of it if you want. I'm starting my life and my family with the woman better suited for me." She deserved a Tony Award, hell an Oscar, for keeping the pain ripping through her chest out of her voice.

His brow crinkled, and confusion filled his eyes. "I didn't send that."

"Don't come at me with that bullshit. The email came a day after I showed up to tell you I was pregnant. Two months later your father came to me with a check for fifty grand signed by you."

"Fifty grand you took and ran with without a backwards glance."

"I did what I had to do for my son."

He took a step forward. His body rigid and gaze frigid. "You didn't even talk to me."

"You. Blocked. Me." She bit out the words. "I left voice messages and sent emails even after your hateful messages. Too stupid to realize you weren't worth it."

Bitterness crept into his expression. Richard closed his eyes and shook his head. "It wasn't me. I didn't know about our son until two days ago. The day my divorce was finalized."

"Your name was on the check. You signed it."

"I didn't know it was for you."

"Bullshit."

"Dammit, Yvonne, you know me—"

"I thought I knew you."

His nostrils flared. He ran a hand over his mouth and took

a heavy breath. "You knew me," he said slowly, deliberately. "You know I wouldn't have ignored my responsibilities."

"Which is why when your father came to me with a check, signed by you, I knew what Richard would do. He'd give me money to move on, so he could marry the woman who'd help him secure his future. I knew I'd get nothing else from you. I knew you were taking care of your responsibilities by fixing the little mess you'd made."

"I didn't know," he said quietly.

"That's what you're going to go with?" She couldn't believe his audacity. He looked sincere, but she remembered that day, remembered the bold lines of his distinct signature on the check. How could he not have known?

Richard's dark eyes shot up to hers. "I'm not going with anything. I'm telling you that I had no idea."

She took one step forward. "I came to you the day I found out. She refused to let me see you even after I told her why I was there."

Richard took a deep breath. "She told me you'd come by once. She didn't say what you wanted."

Yvonne crossed her arms over her chest. "I called you. I left voice messages. You didn't respond. You can't tell me you didn't get those either."

"I saw the messages. I never responded because I—"

"Deleted them." The two words landed between them heavy with disappointment. "That's what I thought," Yvonne's voice was flat, disappointed. "You deleted every message. I wasn't even worth that much of your time."

"I promised Natalie I'd cut all ties with you. I was marrying her. I owed that much to her."

"You owed me the right to at least be heard. But I guess what I had to say didn't matter. I was just the side piece."

His eyes snapped to hers and he stepped forward. "You were never just a side piece." Raw emotion made his voice rough. His eyes were dark with pain and regret.

Yvonne's lips parted, and she sucked in a breath. For a second, her mask crumbled. She felt the same pain, regret, longing. She wanted to believe him. Wanted so badly to know she hadn't just been a fun pastime for him. That he hadn't lied about not being engaged. That he'd actually cared. *Cared enough to not call after I cashed a check for fifty grand?* He had to have known. Even if his dad went behind his back, he should have seen the check to her. Should have had questions. Should have reached out to her.

Yvonne's resolve hardened, and she slid back. "Sorry, I guess sophisticated men like you prefer the word mistress."

The emotion in his eyes frosted over to cold anger. "She was pregnant. I wasn't going to walk away from my responsibilities."

"I was pregnant, and you walked away from me."

"How many times do I have to tell you I didn't know?"

"That's supposed to make it better?" she asked incredulously. "You deleted my emails and voice messages without even listening to them. Gave someone the ability to send hateful responses to me saying me and my kid meant nothing. Didn't even bat an eye when I cashed a check for fifty grand. I meant so little to you that even though you were doing the honorable thing with Natalie, you didn't give me enough respect to hear what I had to say. If you'd known me at all you would have realized I wouldn't reach out to you after you made your choice. Not unless I had something important to say."

His shoulders straightened. "I should have listened to your messages," he said evenly. "I'm sorry for that."

"Sorry doesn't change the past."

"Nor does it change the fact that all it took was fifty grand for you to forget about me."

His words were cool and unemotional, but they still hit Yvonne in the gut. Forget him? How could she have forgotten him. The man who'd given her the most precious child in the world and broken her heart so completely. "I didn't have many options. I'm not so noble that I'd prefer to struggle than take money to help my son's future."

He glanced around the office then back at her. "You put the money to good use."

Her eyes narrowed. "The money is in a trust for him."

His cocked brow called her a liar. She balled her hands into fists and opened her mouth to argue but he spoke before she could. "I won't let the mistakes of the past become the failures of the future. I will give your show a home. Pay you considerably well for it. You will allow me to be with my son."

Her eyes widened. Cold fear crept across her skin. "You are not taking my son from me."

"I don't want to take him from you, but I won't be an absent father. I deserve to be a part of his life."

"No. I won't let you hurt him." Not like he'd hurt her.

"I'm not going to hurt him. I'd never hurt him," he said as if her statement were ridiculous.

She brought a hand to her temple. It trembled slightly. "You said you wouldn't hurt me."

"Is that what *he* promised?" The words came out quick and razor sharp. "Is that why you're marrying him?"

Yvonne looked up. Richard's eyes were pinned to her left hand. Yvonne dropped her hand. Her right hand played with the proof of her ability to move on. To forget what Richard had done to her.

"I said yes because I wanted to. I'm very happily engaged."

Memory whispered between them. *Engaged isn't married.* When she'd spoken the words, they meant something different. She'd thought he was free. Thought she was safe opening her heart to him.

"I'm marrying a wonderful man," she said more for her benefit than his. "I will not let you try to come back and ruin everything."

Richard straightened his shoulders and stared into her eyes. Damn, if full eye contact with him didn't make her breath catch. "And I will not let you keep me from my son. If you want your show to make airtime I'd like to meet him as soon as possible. Tonight."

Her heart raced as panic set in. "No. We don't need your network. We can find other places to sell our show."

Richard shrugged as if her going someplace else meant little to him. "Fine. That doesn't change my feelings on meeting my son."

"You paid me to stay away and now you're demanding that I let you back in our lives."

"I did not pay you. Someone in my family did and believe me I will find out who did this without my knowing. I never would have turned my back on you that way."

"Except you did." She shot back without thinking. Even if he hadn't paid the money, he'd chosen to try and make things work with Natalie over being with her.

Richard looked as if he was about to argue. A spark lit up his dark eyes. His jaw shifted as if he were holding back words. He brought his fist to his nose, closed his eyes, and took a deep breath as if steadying himself. "Either tell our son the truth and set up the meeting or expect me at your doorstep unannounced."

He walked stiffly to his desk where he took a business card from a holder. His steps remained rigid as he approached her. He held out the card. "Call me when you've told him."

"He won't understand." *He's gone this long without you. He's got a new dad, someone who wants to be here.* Now she was supposed to tell Jacob his biological father was here. When he'd finally stopped asking about his father once Nathan became a staple in their life.

Nathan! What was she going to say to him? They'd never talked about Jacob's biological father. Would he understand why she'd kept that part of her life a secret? Would he understand why she'd taken the money, or would he view her the way Richard obviously did? As if she'd never cared and had only been interested in what she could get out of her time with Richard?

Richard's warm hand enveloped hers. Her body jerked. She tried to pull away. She was stunned by the reaction his touch created and the memories his touch tried to evoke. He held firm, turning her hand over in a firm, but gentle manner. He placed the card in her palm. "Then make him understand."

Chapter 5

Yvonne stopped pacing in front of her television and faced Nathan and Jacob when they came out of her kitchen. Jacob, in a pair of red pajama shorts and a white t-shirt, skipped next to Nathan. He clutched a green blanket in his hands, his blankie since he was a toddler, and laughter brightened his brown eyes. As usual, his strong resemblance to Richard took her breath away, but for the first time the resemblance made her anxious. Nervous.

Richard was back.

Jacob grinned and ran straight for her, arms raised. Yvonne bent over and placed her hands on his sides. "One, two, three, jump," she said.

Jacob jumped, and Yvonne lifted him up. Grunting because her baby was getting bigger and heavier every day. Small arms encircled her neck and he hugged her close. She ran her hand over his back. His shirt was damp. She chuckled. "Did you dry off after you got out of the tub?"

Jacob pulled back and nodded. "I did. Nathan said he'll read me a story."

That explained the damp shirt. Jacob would hurry out of the tub and barely brush himself with a towel if there was a promise of a bedtime story before bed. "Even if Nathan promised you a story you still have to dry off when you get out of the tub."

Jacob's grin didn't waver. "I will. Can you come sing to me?"

Yvonne chuckled, knowing she'd be repeating the same thing tomorrow at bedtime. "Aren't you getting too big for me to sing to?"

Jacob shook his head. "No, I'm not."

"No, you're not." Yvonne kissed his cheek. "Alright, I'll come sing to you after Nathan finishes telling you a story." She lowered him to the floor.

Nathan came over and ran his hand down her back. "Are you okay?" His concerned eyes studied her. That was the thing she loved about Nathan, he paid attention which made him attentive to her moods. He'd been her rock the past nine months. Now Richard was back, and her world was about to crack and split like a fake leather couch.

Yvonne smiled and patted his chest. "I'm good." Thankfully, her voice was even. "Just a little tired, but that's all."

His brows drew together. The concern in his eyes intensified. He looked disappointed or maybe that was her guilt. She needed to tell him.

Jacob tugged on Nathan's grey t-shirt before he could say anything else. Nathan's concern transformed into a smile. "I'm being summoned. I'll be right back." He bent and swept Jacob up and over his shoulder. "Come on, lil man."

Jacob giggled and waved at Yvonne while Nathan carried him down the hall and to his room. As soon as they were out of sight Yvonne sank down onto her couch. She pressed a hand to her temple before glancing at her watch. Five, maybe ten minutes to get her emotions in order before Nathan finished telling his story.

In the past few months Nathan had become a fixture in

Jacob's life. When they were casually dating Nathan never came to her home and hadn't met Jacob. When he told her he loved her, at a romantic candlelit dinner complete with a dozen long stem roses and champagne, he'd said he wanted to meet her son and told her there was no one else for him. That's when she first realized he'd chiseled his way through the brick wall surrounding her heart.

Since she'd introduced Nathan to Jacob, the two had gotten along quickly and easily. He'd taken Jacob fishing, shown him how to play baseball, introduced him to woodworking, and watched cartoons with him for hours. Everything a father should do.

She wanted stability for Jacob, and honestly, despite her heartbreak she wanted someone to come home to at night. Her unexpected jump into serious dating with Nathan had turned into an engagement, a set up for a television program, and the perfect father for her son.

Except, Jacob's real dad was back.

Yvonne's heart thudded. *Why, Lord, why?* After six years. After she'd finally moved on. After convincing herself she felt nothing for him and was ready to put everything concerning Richard Barrington, III, behind her, did he have to mosey his happy self right back into her life.

The sound of Jacob asking Nathan to read another story travelled up the hall. That was her cue to stop worrying about tomorrow and focus on her good life tonight. She jumped up from the couch and walked down the hall to Jacob's room. Only the bedside lamp illuminated the superhero themed room. Nathan squeezed her shoulder as he passed her on his way out. She sat on the edge of Jacob's bed and sang "Rock-a-Bye Baby," the same song she'd sung to him every night since he was a baby, then kissed his forehead. After telling him goodnight, she left his room and walked back into the living room.

Nathan sat on the couch with one arm sprawled across

the back while he flipped channels on the television. Nathan glanced up and waved her over. "Come sit down."

Typically, she wouldn't hesitate to settle in next to him on the couch. Typically, her emotions weren't a confusing jumble of barbed wire. What would he say when she told him about Richard? Would he want to bail after learning of her potential baby daddy drama? She remembered her earlier conversation with Richard. How the angry wound of broken hearts and betrayal had made the interaction tense and difficult. Not *potential* baby daddy drama, unavoidable drama.

Tonight might be her last normal night. The thought scared her more than a client hating a design she worked on all night. "I'm thirsty. I'll be right back."

She hurried into the kitchen. A few more minutes to get her thoughts under control was obviously needed. She'd tell him. She had to tell him. Just, did she have to tell him tonight?

That would be the right thing to do.

Yes. Nathan was a good man. He deserved the truth and he deserved it now. She opened the fridge to pull out a bottle of water then stopped. This day required something stronger.

Yvonne opened the freezer and pulled out a chilled bottle of peach flavored vodka. Her hands trembled as she put the bottle on the counter harder than she planned, and it made a loud thud. She was afraid to tell Nathan. Afraid of losing everything she'd finally gotten.

She jerked open the fridge and pulled out a bottle of mango cranberry juice. After getting a glass from the cupboard, she twisted open the top, poured two fingers of vodka and topped it with the juice. She lifted the glass to her lips and took a long swallow.

"Want to talk about it."

To her credit, she didn't jump. Taking a deep breath, she slowly turned and leaned against the counter. Nathan hovered at the door. He watched her steadily, expectantly.

She held the glass against her chest and tried to look more *I'm tired* and less *I'm keeping a secret*. "Just a really, really rough day."

"You know you can tell me anything. That is what married couples do." He leaned one shoulder against the frame of the door. Nathan was tall, but what really drew a woman's eye, what drew her eye even now, was his build. He worked with his hands day in and day out alongside his crews on the various homes and businesses his company was hired to work on. The work made him muscular and solid. He was solid. Honest and straightforward. He'd never lied to her—that she knew—and had never made her feel like she was just a fling. He thought she was special. Worth waiting for. Which is why she had to tell him about Richard.

She pushed away from the counter and walked over to him. "I spoke with Judy earlier today."

Some of the tension in his shoulders dissipated. "She told me about the offer from W.E.W. Network."

Of course, she did. She couldn't forget Judy had been Team Nathan before Yvonne had joined the team. "Then she told you the network owner wanted to meet me."

He pushed away from the door and crossed to her. "She did. She thinks you're going to break away from the idea of doing a joint show and focus on you."

"And what do you think?" She kept her voice even. Calm. When inside she raged and worried. If Nathan didn't trust her any more than Judy, what did that say about their relationship?

"I told her you wouldn't lie to me." His eyes asked the question. Would she lie to him?

"Richard wanted to see me because he knows me," she said in a rush.

"Richard?"

"Richard Barrington. The network owner."

Nathan shifted back slightly. He crossed his arms over his

broad chest. The muscles played beneath the soft fabric of his t-shirt. He smelled like wood. Pine and oak. She wanted to pull him close, bury her face in his chest. Hold on to his steady strength and weather the upcoming storm. "How do you know him?"

Yvonne licked her lips. "He's Jacob's father."

Nathan got so still she couldn't tell if he breathed. He took three steps back, turned and rested his hands on the counter. "His . . . father."

"Yes."

"So, Jacob's father wants to buy our television show?"

Yvonne swallowed, remembered the drink in her hand, and then took a long sip of that. "That's part of it."

Nathan faced her. One hand braced on the counter. His body stiff, wary. "What's the other part?"

"He wants to be a part of Jacob's life."

"After all this time? He had the chance to be a part of Jacob's life."

This time she turned away. "No, he didn't."

Silence filled the kitchen. She didn't want to look, but she made herself meet Nathan's eye.

"What are you talking about?"

"When I met Richard, he told me he'd just broken his engagement. We started as friends. Then one day, we were more than friends. We were together for three months, but then he told me his ex was pregnant and he had to do right by her. We split. When I found out I was pregnant, I tried to tell him, but he wouldn't return my calls, emails, anything. Finally, his dad came to me with a check for fifty thousand dollars. He said it was from Richard. My payment to disappear." Nathan shook his head. She nodded. "I took the money."

"How could you?"

"Because I was alone, pregnant, and knew he could just as easily have given me nothing," she said firmly. "Valerie's dad walked out on her and my mom the second my mom got pregnant with me. My biological father moved his family to another state and never acknowledged me. I don't even know his full name. I know you can't make a man who doesn't want to be a father act like one. I took the money so I could ensure Jacob had something from his father. Even if it was only a trust fund."

He closed his eyes. Pinched the bridge of his nose. When his lids lifted again the disappointment she'd thought was there earlier was back in full force. "Why is he back if he paid you off?"

"Because he says he didn't tell his dad to pay me off. He's divorced and just found out about Jacob."

"And you believe him?"

"No. I don't trust him." But she wanted to believe him. Wanted more than she cared to admit to believe he hadn't tossed her aside like an old can of paint.

Nathan's lips lifted in a sad smile. "You do believe him. I can see it in your eyes."

"I don't know what to think. What to do. Nathan, I thought he was gone. I thought he'd always be out of my life."

"That's why you took the money? So, you'd never have to see him again?"

"Don't say it as if I wanted to take the money."

"Are you saying you'd rather have had him than the money?"

Her mouth snapped shut. Shocked as much by the words as by the answer that had almost shot from her lips. Yes.

"I'd rather have had Jacob's father be a part of his life than have to make up reasons why his dad wouldn't be around without breaking his heart. I don't know what would have happened if Richard's dad hadn't given me the money, and you know what, I don't care." She moved forward and wrapped her arms around his waist. "The past doesn't matter.

What I do care about is moving forward. Figuring this out. You and me. Together."

He stood stiffly in her arms. His torso leaned back as if he didn't want her touch. "You should have told me, Yvonne."

Yvonne slipped her arms from around him. "I know, but I didn't know how to tell you."

"It's really easy. You open your mouth and let the truth come out. Instead you keep this secret and let it come back like this."

"I didn't want it to come back like this. We can figure out how to make things work with him and Jacob if we have to. We don't have to work with his network."

He stepped away from her. Again. "Except his network has made the best offer. They have the best distribution."

"There are other offers. Nathan, let's talk about it."

"The time for talking has passed. The time for talking was when I asked you about Jacob's dad and you said he wasn't in the picture. When I told you I love you and asked you to marry me. When Judy told you the name of the network executive who wanted to meet you." The anger in his voice rose with every word. "But you didn't talk to me, did you, Yvonne. You decided it was better to keep the secret."

She reached for him. "Nathan, please, I love you."

His eyes met hers. They were filled with hurt, and pain. "I love you, too, Yvonne. I just can't be around you right now."

Her throat thickened with tears, but her eyes stayed dry as Nathan turned and marched out of the kitchen. Every step he took was a steel toed booted kick to her heart, but she couldn't force herself to ask him to come back. Not when she'd screwed things up. Her front door opened, then slammed shut. Yvonne flinched. She had no idea how to fix this.

Chapter 6

Only Jacob's smile kept Yvonne from slamming the door after she walked into her mom's house to pick him up the next afternoon. The day had been hell, as expected. Nathan hadn't called her. She couldn't bring herself to call him. What would she say? *Please talk to me. Don't leave me and Jacob. Tell me that you do still love me.* All of that was begging, and she did not beg.

If he needed time to get his thoughts together on this, then she'd give him time. She needed time, too. She'd dreamed last night. Dreamed about good times with Richard mixed in with good times with Nathan. She wasn't sure what the dreams meant, but she didn't like that her perfectly arranged life was now completely gutted. Walls smashed, widows broken, the foundation cracked. She hadn't signed up for this. Taking that money was supposed to be the end of her dealings with Richard and everything he brought out in her.

On top of that she'd gotten a call from Lashon asking if Yvonne and Nathan had made a decision about a joint article. She'd said yes, but after the night before she wasn't sure if there would still be a *Nate and Vonne* to promote. She hoped there would be. When she'd tried pitching the idea of continuing to contribute just with her decorating tips, Lashon's response was lukewarm at best.

When had that happened? Would her own influence diminish if Nathan broke things off with her? Would all the people who she thought believed in her now abandon her? That wasn't anything new.

"Mommy!" Jacob jumped up from where he'd been playing with the new super hero action figures Valerie had gifted to him, and ran to Yvonne.

She swept Jacob up into her arms and squeezed him tight. The frustration from her argument with Nathan, fears for the future, and the mess of her life eased a bit as she cuddled her baby boy.

Yvonne pulled back to consider Jacob's smiling face. She had to protect him. She wouldn't allow Richard's return to hurt her son. "Are you being good for Grandma?"

"Mostly good," Jacob said with a cute devilish smile. "She said I couldn't go outside until you got here. Can I go out now?"

"Just in the backyard." Yvonne stood and kissed his forehead. "You can call over the fence to see if Jaden wants to come out and play."

"He's out. I heard him earlier." Jacob turned and ran toward the back of the house.

Yvonne followed more slowly. By the time she reached the kitchen, the screen door was slamming back into place behind Jacob. Her mom stood by the sink rinsing off dishes and putting them into the rack to dry. Rochelle's short hair cut was shorter and shinier, which meant today had been a salon day. She wore a *Word of God Family Day* t-shirt and jean shorts that stopped at her knees with the corner of a dish towel tucked through one of the belt loops.

"Thanks for picking him up from school today," Yvonne said. She pulled out one of the wooden chairs at the dinette table and sank into the seat. She kicked off her heels and leaned back in the chair with a heavy sigh.

"I don't mind at all," Rochelle said. She put the last dish in the rack and dried her hands on the towel through her belt loop. When she turned to Yvonne she frowned. "What's wrong with you?"

"Why can't my life work out the way I want it to?"

She'd started the sketches for the Covington home, and worked on some proposals for a few other projects today. Work had helped get her mind off the fight with Nathan and Richard's demands. She drowned herself so deeply in work she'd looked up and realized she wouldn't have been able to pick Jacob up from school on time. Which is why she'd called her mom to help.

Rochelle grunted and lifted one of her brows. "Is this about the problem you have with Nathan?"

Yvonne stiffened and met her mom's gaze. "What problem with Nathan?" She wasn't prone to freak outs, but her fight with Nathan was less than twenty-four hours ago. Her mom shouldn't know that. No one should. She hadn't even called Valerie, even though her sister would be the first person to help her list the pros and cons of her next steps.

"He came by here to drop off something for Jacob this afternoon. He didn't say much, but I got the feeling he expected something from me."

"Like what?" She sat up and leaned forward. Anticipation making her heart race. He'd come by her mom's house. Did that mean he wasn't ready to call off their engagement?

"Who knows?" Rochelle's tone was baffled. "Men only poke around when they think there's a problem." She nailed Yvonne with a stare. "What's the problem?"

"Jacob's dad is back." The words rushed out of her along with the glimmer of hope Nathan coming to her mom's house meant they weren't over. Talking this out with her mom wasn't the ideal situation, but she was about to explode under the pressure of keeping this inside. She couldn't ignore Richard or his request.

"Back? The way I see it he was never here. How can he be back?" A lip twist and eye roll accompanied Rochelle's sarcastic answer.

Yvonne quickly recounted the events of yesterday. The offer for the show, Richard making the offer, his request to see his son. "He didn't realize he was an absentee father."

Rochelle crossed her arms and gave Yvonne a don't-be-ridiculous look. "Huh?"

Yvonne took her hair out of the ponytail that held it back. A headache brewed in her temples. Her family hadn't known about the payoff. She hadn't bothered to contradict her mom's assumption she'd gotten pregnant by some asshole who wanted nothing to do with her or the baby. It had been close enough to the truth, or what she'd thought was the truth, that arguing about the details had seemed pointless. Keeping the secret was pointless now that everything was coming to a head.

She told her mom about the fifty-thousand-dollar payoff from Richard's father, and Richard's claim he had nothing to do with giving her the money.

"Well, damn," Rochelle said shaking her head. "I always wondered what was the story with Jacob's father. I knew it couldn't be good, but I didn't expect it to be this..."

Bad. Embarrassing. Stupid. Yvonne could only imagine the words her mom wanted to use. "You never asked about him."

"Because I recognized the look."

"What look?"

"The he-don't-want-me-or-my-child look." Rochelle's reply carried the weight of her failed marriage in her voice. "I wore the same look when my husband left me and then when your father moved away."

Yvonne tried to hide her shock by leaning her elbow on the table and cupping her chin in her hands. Rochelle had never hidden her disappointment about her failed marriage. She also never failed to direct the fault back at Yvonne. If she hadn't gotten pregnant with Yvonne after her husband had a vasectomy, then maybe she could have gotten away with her mistake and still be married. Especially since her ex-husband had made his first million a year after their divorce.

"I don't know if I should believe him." Yvonne brought the conversation back to her problems before Rochelle hijacked the topic. "How did he not know?"

"If he owns a network along with other businesses, then he's probably filthy rich. Fifty thousand dollars to him is like fifty cents to us."

"Do you think I should believe him?"

"I think you should find out more."

"I don't want to talk to him."

"What you want doesn't matter. The man already has access to you and the business you're trying to start with Nathan. He's already used you once, don't let him use you again. Find out what he wants. Let him help support Jacob."

"I don't want him anywhere near Jacob." Yvonne said with a slash of her hand. "We don't need him. Jacob has me and Nathan now. We know Jacob, what he likes, doesn't like, and what's best for him. Richard doesn't know me or my son."

"His son."

"Really, Mom?" Yvonne's voice rose with her disbelief.

"Well, it's the truth. He's the boy's father."

"Just because he donated a sperm doesn't mean he can come in and tell me what's best for Jacob. I can't trust him."

"I'm not telling you to trust him right off. I'm telling you to take the time to find out what he wants. He's obviously got money, maybe he can do more for Jacob."

"What about Nathan?"

"What does Nathan have to do with this?" Rochelle sounded truly confused.

"Everything. We're getting married. Jacob is starting to call him daddy."

Rochelle's searching gaze bore into Yvonne. "You and Nathan are a separate thing from Jacob and Richard. The most important thing to you should be your kid. You need to find out what Jacob's dad really wants before you let him anywhere near your son. If you figure out he really didn't know, and really only wants to be a part of his son's life, then let him. If you figure out he's back for other reasons . . ."

"Reasons like what?" Destroying Yvonne's life seemed like a good reason, but she wasn't conceited enough to believe that was his intent.

"Like getting between your legs again," Rochelle said without batting an eye.

Yvonne sputtered for a few seconds before words could form. "That's not happening."

"Easy to say when you're pretending like you can ignore him and make him go away. I don't know this Richard, but he sounds like he's used to getting what he wants. Sure, he *left* his fiancée before he met you," Rochelle make air quotes with her fingers with the word *left*. "But I doubt it. He was probably sleeping with both of you at the same time. Now he's divorced, you're a little bit famous, and he wants a piece of that pie again. Don't ruin what you have with Nathan because you get caught up in memories of old lust."

"I love Nathan."

Rochelle crossed her arms on the table. Her stare sharpened. "Do you?"

"How can you even ask me that?"

"Because I thought I loved my husband until another man came along. Then I realized I was content with being comfortable, but I wasn't in love. That's one of the reasons I slept with your dad. I thought we would both start over together. Build a new life, but in the end, he just wanted a little fun. I messed up what I had with a good man and look where it left me. Struggling to take care of two kids. Ridiculed by the people who were supposed to be my friends. Don't make the same mistakes I did."

"You always assume I'm going to mess up. I'm not. I know what I'm doing."

Rochelle grunted and tapped the table with her nail. "You knew what you were doing back in D.C. too, but you still ended up back here, pregnant, and tossed aside by the man who was supposed to love you. Don't do it again. Find out what he wants, and if it is only to be a better father, let him. With no other benefits to your reconnection."

"What if what's best for Jacob is letting Richard back in our lives."

"Then you let Jacob have a relationship with his father and you do everything in your power to make sure your relationship with Nathan is strong. Nathan is a guy you can depend on. Richard doesn't sound like he's cut from the same cloth. Don't let your body get you into trouble."

Later that evening, when Jacob asked if Nathan was coming over, Yvonne decided that was a good time to distract him by pretending to be the "Tickle Witch" and chase him around the living room. Jacob giggled as he tried to avoid her tickle fingers. Yvonne hopped around with a broomstick between her legs as she chased him to claim her tickles.

That was followed by a pillow fight. She didn't argue when he picked the yellow satin goose down accent pillow off the couch. The stitching didn't hold up past four good hits, and soon feathers flew around the living room. They were both giggling, and when the Tickle Witch tried to claim more tickles from Jacob, Yvonne slipped and fell back onto the couch. Feathers flew, and Jacob lunged onto her. The air whooshed from her lungs, but she wrapped him in her arms.

The weight of the day melted away. She breathed in the sweet mixture of bubble bath and his childish scent. She hugged him tight. No matter what happened she'd protect this. She'd make sure Jacob was always happy, giggling, and surrounded by love.

The doorbell rang. "Nathan!" Jacob cried happily.

Her heart jumped from warm and content to racing and anxious. She detangled her limbs from Jacob's. Her racing heart reached NASCAR speed levels when she saw Nathan on the other side. She barely stopped herself from clutching her chest with relief and throwing her arms around his neck after opening the door.

"I came to say goodnight to Jacob," he said.

His hair was dark, she suspected still damp from where he'd taken a shower before coming over. With the late spring sun behind him, she couldn't read his thoughts when their eyes met. His eyes were guarded, his expression neutral. Yvonne wanted to reach for him, pull him close, know they were going to be okay.

Instead she stepped back and held open the door. "He just asked about you."

The corner of Nathan's mouth lifted. Yvonne's heart clenched in her chest. That had to be good, right?

"Then I came right on time."

"I was worried you wouldn't come back," she said. "Ever."

Nathan blinked several times. He stepped in, stood close enough for her to smell the woodsy fragrance of the soap he used. "I wouldn't just disappear like that."

She wanted to believe him. "Are you sure?"

"I'm sure." His voice was low. Sincere. He brushed the back of his hand across her cheek. "We'll talk."

She nodded. She was just glad he was here. That Richard's return hadn't completely derailed her future. At least, not so far.

"I'd like that," she said.

His pulled a feather from her hair "What's this?"

"Pillow fight after a round of tickle witch."

He smiled a smile that made her heart squeeze. "Sorry I missed that."

Nathan went farther into the house. Jacob called out his name as soon as Nathan entered the living area. Yvonne grinned as she listened to Nathan greet Jacob. When she entered the living room Nathan already had Jacob up and draped over his shoulder, Jacob giggling and laughing the entire time.

They went through the bedtime routine. Yvonne cleaned up as much of the feathers as she could while Nathan read a story. She sang "Rock-A-Bye Baby." Afterwards, Yvonne took two beers out of the fridge and put them on the coffee table. She and Nathan settled on the couch with their beers after Jacob was asleep.

"You didn't call me all day," Yvonne said.

Nathan took a sip of his beer. He sighed and scratched at the label on the bottle. "I was busy today."

"Busy? You've never been too busy to call me before." Nathan called her every day during his lunch break. He said it was because he couldn't let a day pass without hearing her voice. She tried to take solace that he was here now. That the stubble on his chin meant he'd showered but didn't shave because he was in a hurry to get over to see her.

"This redevelopment project we're working on has got a lot of challenges we weren't expecting. The wiring is screwed up, the plumbing is old, and they've got termite damage in the basement."

"But that's not the reason you didn't call me," she said.

Nathan nodded slowly. "That's not the reason. I was upset about what you told me last night."

"That I met with Richard without telling you, or something else?"

He focused on the edge of the label on the bottle he continued to scratch with his thumb. "Mostly the former."

"I know I shouldn't have kept this a secret. I was in shock. I'm still in shock. I don't know how to process him being back, his claims about his family hiding Jacob from him, or what I should do about him wanting to be back in Jacob's life. I'm sorry I didn't say anything beforehand, but I had to know what he wanted. I had to make sure he wasn't dangling an offer for our show in front of us just to try and get back at me." She placed a hand on his knee. His muscles were tense beneath even though his expression revealed nothing. "Do you feel differently? Knowing the truth about my relationship with Richard?"

Nathan put the beer on the coffee table then covered her hand on his leg with his own. "It's a surprise. Everyone has a past and it wasn't as if I didn't know Jacob's father was out there somewhere." The tension slowly released from his body as he took a long breath. "Do I need to be worried?"

His eyes met hers. Eyes that usually looked at her with open trust, love, and admiration. The hesitancy in his gaze was like a pair of scissors in her chest. Sharp and painful. She didn't want to hurt him.

She shook her head and tightened her grip on his leg. "Not at all. This is only about Jacob. Richard and I are history."

"Based off what you said yesterday, if it weren't for extenuating circumstances things between you and him would have been different."

"Those circumstances don't matter anymore. We've both moved on. I made a promise to you."

His smile was sweet, but it didn't quite reach his eyes. "I can understand why you were thrown off by his offer. I just wish you would have told me immediately."

He stood and paced in front of the couch. Yvonne jumped up and stopped him from pacing by tugging on the front of his shirt. "Hey, I had to get a handle on things before I brought him up."

Nathan shifted from foot to foot; he ran a hand through his hair before he finally looked at her. "We're supposed to be a team. We're going to be a team. No more keeping secrets from me."

"I won't."

He brushed the back of his hand over her cheek then tunneled his fingers in her hair. "As long as he's good to you and Jacob then we'll work this out. I won't stand by and watch him hurt you."

She shook her head. "You won't have to." She'd eviscerate Richard if he hurt Jacob. She wouldn't let him get close enough to hurt her again.

Relief filled Nathan's eyes. The love and adoration returned. "Good." He pulled her forward and covered her mouth with his. She kissed him back and tried to forget about how to make the mismatched things in her life work together.

Chapter 7

Yvonne turned her cell phone over in her hand. Richard's business card sat stark and white in the middle of her desk. She glanced at the card, the closed door of her office, then back at the card. She'd had a day to think about it, weigh the pros and cons, toss out visceral emotions to view the situation logically, and had come to one conclusion. She had to find out what he wanted. If he really hadn't known about the payoff, or Jacob, could she trust him with her son? She couldn't ignore him, and if she remembered anything about Richard it was that when his mind was made up, he was an immovable force.

She picked up the card and dialed his cell number before she put it off any longer.

"Richard Barrington." The deep, self-assured tone sent ripples of nostalgia through her.

She let out a soft laugh despite herself. "You still answer your cell phone like you're working at a receptionist desk."

She'd always teased him about that. How he was so stiff

and serious on the phone. He'd laugh that deep sexy laugh of his that would make her body like a kitten's, soft and warm.

A beat passed before he replied. "And you still make me smile when you tease me about that."

Another laugh tried to escape. Yvonne coughed and cleared her throat. No, she was not about to pretend as if no time had passed and they were still cool with each other. "I'm free tomorrow at three." She made her tone icy, just as stiff as his had been when he first answered.

"And my son?" Her frosty reply didn't chill the warmth in his voice.

"We need to clear the air before we bring him in." She needed to make sure he was legit before agreeing to bring him into Jacob's life.

He was silent again. She could see him clearly in her mind's eye. The pinching of the bridge of his nose. The steady breaths as he tried to control his frustration. Richard was always about control. He was an arrogant businessman used to getting his way, and damn if his *I'm the boss* attitude used to make her want to straddle his waist and melt his cold exterior.

"Why are you stalling?" The frustration in his voice was barely there, but she heard it.

"Because, Richard, you barge into my life after six years and a payoff, demanding things I didn't think you wanted."

"Yvonne—"

"Look, Jacob is the most important thing to me. I'd rather us not be at each other's throats the first time he meets you. We have to lay down some ground rules, put the past behind us, before we bring him into this."

"His name is Jacob?" Wonder and disbelief filled his voice.

Yvonne's heart constricted. Richard's middle name. The only tie she'd allowed her son to have with his father. One day, when Jacob was older, she would have told him about Richard. That was more than her mom had done for her. Yvonne only knew her biological father's last name. Jones. Yeah, only about a thousand of those just in one Atlanta suburb. Good luck nailing down her real dad with those odds.

"Yes," Yvonne said to answer Richard's question.

"Yvonne—"

"Will three o'clock work?" she said in a no-nonsense voice. She heard the plea in his voice. Pain sliced through her chest like a hot knife. She didn't want to acknowledge his feelings. His feelings weren't important. Six years separated them. Six years that could never be made up. What happened between them was collateral damage. Jacob was the main priority.

"I'll clear my schedule for any time you want to meet and talk with me about this. Family is the most important thing to me."

"I know. You always choose your family."

"Jacob is my family. You're his mother and that makes you my family." He'd gone back to his authoritative confident voice. The voice that used to say he meant what he said and dared anyone to challenge him.

"I'm just your kid's mother."

"Why would you say that?" A thin layer of irritation coated his voice.

Good. He deserved to feel irritated. He was a big irritation in her life. She wouldn't make this easy for him. Not after everything between them. "Because there's no reason to make this anything deeper."

"Yvonne, it's much deeper than you just being the mother of my son."

"No, Richard, it's not. Until I know you have Jacob's best interests at heart I don't want you seeing him."

"You can't hide him from me."

"And right now, you're not on the birth certificate and

you aren't listed as any type of relative on any paperwork at his school. You show up making demands, and I'll let them know to call the police if a strange man pops up asking to see Jacob."

"You wouldn't dare."

"Try me." She stood and paced to the window. "Meet with me first. Then with me and Nathan."

"What the hell does Nathan have to do with this?"

"Everything." She wouldn't leave Nathan in the cold where this was concerned. She didn't care what her mom said. Leaving Nathan out would only make him believe he had to be worried about Richard's return. Which he didn't.

"I'll meet with you. We'll come to terms with what's best for *our* son. Then we'll figure out what to do about my network purchasing your and Nathan's show."

"We didn't agree to your deal."

"You won't get a better deal." His self-assuredness made her wish he was close, so she could knock off the smug look she was sure was all over his face.

"Why do you have to purchase our show? Is this to force me to let you see Jacob? If that's the case it won't work. I'll view this as blackmail."

"I want your show because the concept is good. And as much as I don't want to admit it, your chemistry with Nathan on camera is also good. Our network is the best place to launch and you know that. Before I realized you were the Vonne in *Nate and Vonne*, I'd already heard enough from the programming directors to be interested in purchasing. It just so happened I found out about you...and Jacob around the same time."

She didn't want to believe him, but she remembered Judy saying there was quick and early interest from W.E.W. Her life had already been on track to reconnect with Richard. She just hadn't known it.

"I didn't know you owned a network."

"My father purchased the network a few years ago. I stayed out of it and focused on our other holdings. It wasn't until the last year I became more involved."

The reminder of his father made her stomach churn. She could still see the older Richard Barrington sneering at her from across a gleaming wood table. Telling her she was just a fun pastime. The *side piece*. That his son was marrying someone better. To take the money and leave, because that's all she'd get from them.

"Tomorrow at three," she said quickly. Wanting this conversation over. "I'll text you the address. Goodbye." She hung up before he could reply. She'd spent enough time today focusing on Richard.

Yvonne left the office a few hours early and headed to Nathan's place. She'd texted to see how his afternoon was going, and when he said he was leaving his job site early and heading home she'd been surprised. Nathan typically didn't leave a job early, but she took this as a sign. She'd wanted to talk to him about her meeting with Richard without her son's sharp hearing within earshot.

Nathan lived in a renovated craftsman bungalow near Ansley Park. Every time she pulled up to his place she smiled and thought his home looked like the perfect place for a guy who loved to renovate homes. Large front porch, hardwood floors, and plantation shutters. The blue and beige colors on the outside along with the cozy landscaping gave the place a warm, welcoming feel.

Yvonne parked behind Nathan's dark grey double cab pickup truck. A bright blue Volkswagen Beetle was parked next to it. Cassidy's vehicle.

Yvonne liked Nathan's stepsister. The bubbly redhead had been quick to welcome Yvonne into the fold after she and Nathan began dating and had cheered along with the rest of the crowd when Nathan proposed. That didn't stop the kernel of annoyance from digging into Yvonne's side at the sight of Cassidy's car. She'd hoped to have this conversation with Nathan alone.

She would typically let herself in when Nathan knew she was on her way over. Whenever Cassidy was over, she preferred ringing the bell. Cassidy made Nathan's space her space, and Yvonne felt more like a visitor whenever Nathan's stepsister was at his place.

She rang the doorbell with the afternoon sun warm on her back. A few seconds later the sound of Nathan's heavy footfalls against the floor preceded him opening the door.

His grin made her feel like she was delivering him a prize. He always looked so happy when he saw her. As if he couldn't believe he'd gotten so lucky. It had been so long since a man had looked at her as if she were the greatest gift in his life. Richard used to look at her that way.

Nathan pulled her into the comfort of his embrace. She breathed in his scent, wood and the musk of his cologne. She let everything about Nathan chase away the memory of the way Richard once gave her a similar look whenever she was near.

"I'm glad you stopped by," Nathan said. "Cassidy is here. She was excited when I told her you were coming over."

She slipped out of his embrace and followed him into the house. She grabbed his arm to stop him before he could lead her to the kitchen. Where Cassidy probably waited.

"Hey, wait a second," she said.

Nathan stopped, faced her and frowned. "What's wrong?"

"Nothing. Not really. I just wanted to give you an update on that situation . . . with the show and Jacob."

Nathan's face clouded for the briefest second. Then he hid whatever his thoughts were about Richard behind a mask of I'm-here-for-you support. "Did you talk to Richard?"

"Yes. I called him this morning. I'm meeting him at three tomorrow."

Nathan immediately cupped her shoulders in his hands as if she'd fall over with a fit of vapors at just the idea of meeting with her ex.

"Do you want me there?" he asked.

She did, but not as support. She wanted Nathan there as a buffer. Tomorrow's meeting wouldn't be easy. She and Richard sparked off each other. Electricity arching through them like exposed wires. She needed someone else there to dampen the effect. Not leave her to accept all of Richard full blast. Saying so out loud would make it seem like she was afraid to be alone with him. Which she wasn't.

She shook her head. "No. I can handle this first time."

Nathan's shoulders slumped. His eyes slid away. Had she upset him?

She slipped her hand onto his waist. "I did tell him any decisions about Jacob had to include you."

Nathan's eyes brightened. The confidence back in his gaze. "You did?" He squeezed her shoulders.

She nodded feeling a tightness lift out of her chest. Nathan could not feel left out in this situation. Doing so would make it seem as if she and Richard were pushing him to the sidelines. Richard needed to know straight up that he was the sideline player. Not even that. He was just a viewer. A member of the studio audience. Standing out in the cold looking in. She and Nathan were in charge.

"Yes. You are going to be my family. I want him to understand that right from the start."

He tugged on her hand, wrapped her in his arms, and kissed her. Warmth spread through her midsection. Soft and warm like a kitten brushing against her leg. Safe and comforting.

"Come on you two. Save that for later."

Cassidy interrupted them. Yvonne smiled and broke away from Nathan. Cassidy's long red hair was twisted in a sloppy knot on the top of her head. Her blue-green eyes sparkled with mischief and her hands were propped on her curvy hips.

"I can't help it. Your brother is irresistible."

Cassidy waved her hands in front of her as if fighting a bee. "Don't go there. I'd tell you to get a room, but it would just be a waste."

Nathan draped his arm around Yvonne's shoulder. "Why is that?"

"Because you're being old-fashioned and waiting." Everything about Cassidy's tone said she thought their idea was stupid.

"It's romantic!" Yvonne said, even though she agreed with Cassidy. She was tired of waiting, but she wasn't going to throw herself at Nathan.

He had principles. He wanted to make their first time special. She had a vibrator and an endless supply of batteries.

"I don't know how you do it," Cassidy said shaking her head. "If I want a guy and he wants me, I'm going for it."

"There's nothing wrong with being traditional," Nathan said.

Cassidy rolled her eyes. "Traditional is boring. If you love someone and only want that person what's wrong with having sex with them?"

Nathan's body stiffened. His arm around Yvonne's shoulders tightened. "Cassidy let's not start that again." There was a warning in his voice.

Yvonne looked at them both. "Start what?" Had she missed the first half of this argument?

"Nothing but dear brother." Yvonne pointed at Nathan. "Seems to think I'm too liberal in my thinking when it comes to who I can and can't sleep with."

"Who do you want to sleep with?"

Cassidy crossed her arms and raised a brow. Nathan's nostrils flared. Yvonne stepped out of his embrace.

"She just met this guy." Nathan finally spit out.

Cassidy threw up her hands. "And for now, he's the guy who wants to sleep with me."

Nathan dragged his hands through his hair. He looked as if he'd rather be fighting hyenas than having this conversation. "Damn, Cassidy stop."

"Fine. You stop acting holier than the pope. Let go of all those rules. Go for what you want." Cassidy shot back.

Yvonne stepped between them and held up her hands. "Okay, let's say it's okay for Nathan to wait and for Cassidy to be with whomever she chooses."

This was also why she wasn't as comfortable at Nathan's place when Cassidy was around. She and Nathan eventually ended up at each others' throats. He disapproved of her choices. She told him to take out the rod shoved up his behind.

Personally, Yvonne agreed with Cassidy. Nathan's insistence on holding out until their wedding night was sweet and romantic, but he tended to project his beliefs on his stepsister. She wondered what he would say if he knew she thought he was being an asshole. That Cassidy could go out and sleep with whomever she wanted if no one was hurt. That he should worry less about who Cassidy was sleeping with and more about getting his fiancée in bed.

"This is why you're great," Cassidy said in a conciliatory tone. "You can deal with his old school ways."

"He's old school but not stuffy or a prude," she reminded herself. She knew what was waiting for her on her wedding night. Another reason she really had hoped to find Nathan alone. A part of her wanted, no needed, to be reminded of the heat they could generate. What she couldn't compromise in the upcoming weeks.

Nathan kissed her cheeks. "Thank you, baby."

Cassidy twisted some of her hair that escaped the bun. "Good to know he didn't lose everything."

Nathan cut his eyes at Cassidy before focusing on Yvonne. "If you're sure you don't need me tomorrow then I'd like for you to call me as soon as you're done."

Yvonne nodded, happy to move on to another topic. Even if the situation with Richard was just as volatile. "I will."

"I mean it. The second you leave him. I'll stop whatever I'm doing," he said insistently. "I want to make sure he doesn't hurt you."

"He won't hurt me." Infuriate her. Annoy her. Possibly remind her of what they once were while simultaneously making her want to cover him in honey and push him into a fire ant hill? All of that, yes, but Richard would never hurt her.

"You mean your ex who showed up out of nowhere?" Cassidy asked.

Yvonne's gaze jumped to Nathan. He'd told her? Of course, he'd told her. He'd probably gone straight to Cassidy's place after Yvonne spilled the beans about Richard.

"She's meeting him tomorrow at three," Nathan said.

"Are you going?" Cassidy asked.

Nathan shook his head. They exchanged a look. A look that asked why he wasn't going and answered I have no idea.

Yvonne started to repeat herself. She wasn't afraid of Richard and didn't need back up. Then she realized she didn't owe Cassidy any type of explanation. If Nathan had further questions or wanted to know anything else, then he could ask her his damn self.

"No, I'm going alone," she said. Her voice dared Cassidy to question her.

Taking the hint, Cassidy shrugged then smiled. "I was just finishing dinner. Come on in and eat."

She turned and sauntered down the hall. Irritation wrapped around Yvonne. She tried to pinpoint exactly when she'd gotten irritated. Nathan's disappointment at not being invited, his ridiculous fight with Cassidy, the equally ridiculous way they'd looked at each other as if Yvonne had done something wrong.

"She made salmon," Nathan said. "It's really good with a brown sugar glaze. She found the recipe online."

She shook her head. Even more exhausted than before. "You know what? I really need to go if I'm going to pick up Jacob in time. We're going by my sister's house this afternoon. I promised to help her decorate her office."

Valerie had texted earlier that day asking for assistance with the color scheme in her new office. Her sister's commercial real estate business was taking off and she wanted a posh new interior to match the clients she was bringing in. Yvonne was more than happy to help, but she knew Valerie had an ulterior motive. Mom must have told her about Richard.

"Are you sure? You just got here?"

She nodded then leaned up on her tiptoes to kiss him. "I just wanted to see you and tell you how the conversation went. I'll call you tomorrow."

He nodded. "Right after the meeting."

"Right after."

He kissed her again and she left. It wasn't until she was halfway home that she realized he hadn't sounded very eager for her to stick around.

Chapter 8

Yvonne picked up Jacob from afterschool care and went straight to Valerie's home. By the time she and Jacob pulled up at her sister's colonial duplex, after dealing with traffic and the left-over irritation from her impromptu visit with Nathan, all she wanted to do was kick off her shoes, grab a cocktail, and get Valerie's take on everything in her life.

She rang the doorbell and firmly held onto Jacob's hand to stop him from ringing the doorbell incessantly as a "fun joke" to play on auntie. She smiled at Jacob's enthusiasm, despite how exasperating his excitement about ringing a doorbell may be. How would he react when she told him about Richard? Would he be just as exuberant? Confused? Sad? He'd asked about his real dad, but with Nathan around the questions had stopped.

She would not let Richard break her son's heart. She'd do everything in her power to keep him from Jacob if tomorrow she got any hint he would cause harm to their child. She didn't care how hard she'd have to fight him. Jacob was her number one priority.

Valerie opened the door. Her cell phone was pressed to her ear. "Uh huh, I hear you. My sister is here." She waved Yvonne and Jacob inside.

"Auntie!" Jacob yelled and wrapped his arms around Valerie's legs.

Her sister stumbled back a few steps, grinned, and rubbed the top of the tight coils on his head. "Hey, Superboy!"

"You got any cookies?" Jacob asked.

"You know where to find them," Valerie replied.

"Yes!" Jacob pumped his fist and took off running down the hall toward the kitchen.

Yvonne closed the door behind her. "Who you talking to? Your boyfriend?" she teased.

Valerie rolled her eyes. "Girl, please. I don't have time for a man." Her brows drew together as she listened to whomever was on the phone. "And you shut up. I do not need to get my Bruno Mars on and make love like gorillas."

Yvonne laughed and followed her sister down the hall. "Tell Eva I said hi." Only Valerie's best friend Eva would have told Valerie to make love like gorillas.

"My sister said hi," Valerie said.

They entered the kitchen. Jacob was trying to pull a handful of cookies out of the jar Valerie kept on the kitchen table just for him.

"Oh no, mister," Yvonne said. She hurried over. Shook his wrist until the handful of cookies fell then pulled out two. "Take these."

"I'm hungry," he said pouting.

"And I'm about to order pizza."

His face brightened like a beautiful night sky. He took the cookies. "Hamburger or peperoni?"

"Hamburger, of course," she said. Jacob loved pizza with ground beef.

"Yes! I'm going to watch TV until it comes." He nearly

ran out of the kitchen. His footsteps pounded on the stairs as he made his way up to Valerie's media room.

Yvonne sat at the table and ordered pizza, wings, and a salad. She pulled a beer from the fridge and half listened as Valerie played sounding board to Eva's latest drama. More than once Valerie looked at Yvonne and either rolled her eyes, shrugged in a you-know-she's-drama fashion, or waved a fist to the sky. Each time Yvonne laughed and continued munching on cookies while scrolling through emails on her phone.

There were several from Sandra. She'd emailed a few of the preliminary sketches to her for some of the room ideas before leaving the office early. Sandra loved the designs and couldn't wait to see more. Well, at least she hadn't burned that bridge with her stay-out-of-my-personal-life stance.

"Nah, I can't come through this weekend," Valerie said into the phone. "I told you I've got to go to my dad's banquet on Saturday."

Yvonne full on listened to her sister's conversation now. After divorcing Rochelle, Valerie's dad married again and had two more kids. His disdain for Rochelle was clear whenever the two were together, but he still spent time with his daughter.

Yvonne was envious of her sister's relationship with her dad. She'd never admit it out loud, but she was. How could she not be? Dear old Deacon Jones had moved multiple states away. She had a last name and knew he moved his family to Virginia or Maryland, but that was it. She didn't cyberstalk her biological family on Facebook, though the temptation to do so was very strong even with the multiple Joneses listed in Google. She figured if he didn't want her or anything to do with her then she didn't want anything to do with him.

"Yes, the Decatur Chamber Hall of Fame banquet. They're honoring him, but you know it's just to keep him as a member." Valerie paused and listened. "Well...I mean if you want to. Aren't you hanging out with Antwan?"

More silence as Valerie listened. This time when she shrugged Yvonne tapped her watch. She was here to vent her own frustrations, not listen to her sister pacify her best friend. Valerie nodded and gave her a thumbs up.

Five minutes later, she finally got off the phone with Eva. "Girl! I'm so sorry. Eva was on a roll today." Valerie pulled out a chair at the table and sat.

"What's the deal with her today?"

"What do you think? Antwan is too busy to spend time with her. He doesn't want to be a part of a deal that could make him money. He's only interested in running for office," Valerie said in an exhausted voice. She grabbed Yvonne's beer and took a swig.

"I thought she'd be happy to be the girlfriend of an influential council member."

Yvonne didn't like to talk ill of other women, but Eva was the epitome of high maintenance. Yvonne was surprised Valerie's friend was able to find a man who met all her needs. But she always did.

"She liked the idea, but now it's sinking in that if Antwan is elected, he'll have to be a servant to the people. She's upset he's going to a community clean-up this weekend instead of taking her to the Chamber's Hall of Fame banquet."

"Yeah, I heard you mention that. So, your dad is getting an award?"

Valerie smiled. Pride on her face. "He is. That salt membrane thing he worked on. Well, a desalination company in California is buying his idea."

"That's great, Valerie. Tell him I said congrats."

Valerie's dad opened his own lab soon after the divorce. He'd worked in other labs that handled samples for various government departments and businesses, but he'd also tinkered with concocting things. Soon after, he'd begun selling some of the compounds he came up with and had made millions over the years. Their mom liked to pretend as if her ex-husband had become successful just to further rub in her face how much of a mistake she'd made. Yvonne didn't spend much time with Valerie's dad—he was nice enough to her but not exactly friendly—but in the time she was around him she knew he was over Rochelle and didn't spend half as much of his time thinking about her as she did about him.

"I will. Eva really wanted to go to the banquet and support Dad. Antwan had campaign stuff. Let the drama ensue. Not to mention Mom being upset that I'm going instead of coming with her to the church picnic."

"Why does she keep getting mad at you for spending time with your dad?" If her dad had bothered to be around, she'd want to spend time with him.

"Because she's Mom." Valerie took another sip of the beer. "She's more mad at you, though."

She didn't need to guess the reason. "She told you?"

"Richard Barrington, the third. Dang, Yvonne, why didn't you tell me?"

The doorbell rang then. The pizza arrived. Yvonne was spared immediately answering the disappointment in her sister's expression as she paid for the food. She got Jacob set up in front of the television upstairs with two slices and a bottle of water with a cherry Kool-Aid pack to sweeten it. By the time she came back down, Valerie had put the pizza and salad on plates and gotten two more beers from the fridge.

"Now, tell me why you didn't tell me Richard Barrington is Jacob's—"

"Can we not say that out loud." Yvonne looked toward the stairs. Jacob was nowhere in sight. He wouldn't be downstairs for at least another fifteen or twenty minutes. Still, she didn't want him to overhear that his dad was around until she was ready for them to meet.

"Why not?"

Yvonne pointed upstairs. Valerie sighed but nodded. "Fine. You could have told me."

"I didn't want to tell anyone." She gave the quick run-down of their history. An abbreviated CliffsNotes version that left out much of her heartbreak and focused more on the complete malice of Richard's family.

"Wow...I never would have guessed he'd be like that," Valerie said, tapping a finger on the side of her beer can. "He always seemed so...I don't know...honorable."

Yvonne slammed her beer can on the table. "You know him? How?"

"I don't *know* him know him. I met him once or twice. About two years ago when I helped his brother buy a hotel."

"What? Did he know you're my sister?"

"Honestly, family didn't come up. His brother wanted him to invest in the property with him and he came down to look. The brother, Michael, is more of a flirty, bachelor playboy kind of guy. Richard came across stiff, but nice. He had the I'm-the-responsible-one vibe, and he wanted to make sure the deal was fair and square. We barely talked to each other except to go over the things with the sale."

Yvonne fell back in the chair. Richard had been that close to her and her family. Just a few degrees of separation and their paths could have crossed earlier. Was this fate? Were they basically destined to bump into each other again?

"I'm meeting him tomorrow. I think Nathan is upset about that."

"Well, Nathan will be okay," Valerie said dismissively. "You need to get out whatever you need to get out between you two. Having Nathan there will only delay the inevitable."

"What inevitable?"

"When the huge pile of crap between you two blows up and covers everything."

Yvonne cringed. "That is not a good mental picture."

Valerie shrugged. "I'm not good at mental pictures, but I am good at telling the truth. There is a lot of stuff you two need to get out in the open before anyone else comes treading in the middle of it. Take your time. If Nathan loves you the way he says he does, he'll understand."

That's what worried her. *The way he says he does.* Wasn't there a saying about people showing their love instead of saying it? She didn't want a big gesture at a baseball game. She wanted him to understand how hard this was and be her support.

Of course, he will be supportive. He's just surprised and getting accustomed to the idea.

"You're right," she said with a smile.

"Good. Now can we look at ideas I have for the office while you tell me your game plan for meeting with R.B. tomorrow?"

"That is the real reason I'm here," she said.

"Good. I'll go get the pictures," Valerie said, standing. "And when I come back we'll start with what you're going to wear."

Yvonne laughed. "What I'm wearing?"

"Yes. Clothes set the tone. And, sister, tomorrow you're going to need a don't-mess-with-me-or-I'll-cut-you outfit."

Chapter 9

The next afternoon at three, Yvonne sat stiffly in the booth at Jacob's favorite ice cream parlor and glanced at the door. Sweet Cream was Jacob's favorite place because they hand made the ice cream in front of you. She'd picked the place because it was the least intimate location she could think of for her meeting with Richard.

Dinner implied intimacy, her home was off limits until she knew his end game, and no way in hell was she meeting him at his home or hotel. She still wasn't clear if he'd moved to Atlanta or was just here temporarily.

She stared at the empty seat across from her and jerked apart the napkin she'd gotten with her bowl of cookie dough ice cream. She'd have to get a carton of chocolate, Jacob's favorite, before leaving. Richard wouldn't know Jacob's favorite ice cream flavor. Wouldn't understand that Jacob loved watching the employees mix together the ice cream or how excited he got when they put extra gummy bears on top of his. How could he expect her to let him anywhere near her child until she was sure of his intentions? He wouldn't break her son's heart the same way he'd—

Nope. Don't go down that road again.

The bell over the door chimed. She looked up, caught Richard's eye, and straightened. A weird flutter went through her chest and she broke eye contact, swept the broken napkin into her hand and dumped the pieces into her purse. No need to provide evidence of how much this meeting unnerved her.

Richard's shadow fell over her. She took a deep breath, lifted her head, and dragged her gaze back to his. The force of his stare squeezed the air from her lungs. Valerie was right to inform her to dress in a take-no-prisoners fashion. Which is why she'd worn the custom-made dark grey business suit she pulled out for heavy hitting clients. Maybe Richard had chosen to do the same, because he had shown up looking hotter than freshly laid asphalt in the middle of August in a crisp, white button up shirt beneath an expensive looking navy suit. Six years ago, she would have teased him. Said something about how his tailored suit pants showcased his legs and other endowments better than a neon *packing dangerous heat* sign.

She exhaled slowly and steadied her shattered nerves. After everything that happened, he didn't deserve her teasing. Her smiles. Her remembering anything that was once between them. She tilted her head to the side and forced the corner of her mouth up into what she hoped was a bland smile.

"Richard." Good, her voice sounded calm.

"Hello, Yvonne," he said just as easily.

His dark gaze flicked over her quickly. Yvonne ordered her body not to fidget. That was tough, when her instinct was to make sure her hair wasn't out of place and check that she hadn't spilled ice cream on her suit. Richard was a shrewd businessman who knew how to spot weaknesses in his opponents. She couldn't give him even a hint of her inner turmoil.

He slid into the other side of the booth. "I didn't expect an ice cream parlor." He pointed to the bowl of ice cream in front of her.

"What did you expect?" She lifted the spoon and took a small bite of the ice cream.

His gaze dropped to her lips, narrowed slightly. "I don't know. Coffee maybe."

She pulled her lower lip between her teeth to get off any remaining ice cream. Released it slowly. Richard's nostrils flared before he shifted in the seat and looked around as if inspecting the place.

Her lips tilted up in a genuine smile. She still affected him, too. Good. Maybe that would make it easier to get to the point of him popping up like an unwanted zit. "I didn't want coffee. The coffee house where I typically meet clients is too much like..." The place they'd first met. "Too busy this time of day. Though they do have a poetry night. I know you like poetry."

Richard shook his head. "I don't really get into that anymore."

The admission surprised her. Poetry had been his one creative outlet when they'd been together. "I thought you'd be up on stage reading your own words by now."

"Things change. I barely have time to read poetry much less write it or read something I wrote for an audience."

"Getting on stage and reading your work was something you really wanted to do."

"There are a lot of things I wanted but couldn't have." His voice was low and full of regret. Their gazes locked.

She looked away first. They weren't here to get into past regrets or not getting things they'd wanted. This was about her son. Their son. "This is Jacob's favorite place. I thought you'd like to know that."

He clasped his hands on the table. "I want to meet him as soon as possible."

She stirred her ice cream with the plastic spoon and tried to keep the anxiety that flared from his request in check. "You just show up unexpectedly and you're making demands. You know I don't respond well to demands."

"You responded to a few of my demands well enough." His voice lowered an octave.

Just like that, her body remembered just how good Richard's demands could be. She pushed away her ice cream and glared. "Don't flatter yourself."

A flicker of uncertainty reflected on his features before his face became a hard mask. "I meant what I said. I will show up if you try to keep him from me."

"I have no intentions of keeping him from you. Once I'm sure you really mean him no harm."

"Why would I hurt my son?"

The disbelief in his voice was appalling. How could he pretend he didn't have the power to hurt? "Stop talking about him as if you care."

"I do care. If I'd known, I wouldn't have let this much time go by without being there for him or for y—"

"Why should I believe you didn't know?" She didn't want him to lie and say he would have been there for her. He'd made his choice when he refused to listen to her voice messages or read her emails.

Richard leaned forward. "Do you really think so little of me?" His voice was both surprised and concerned. "Do you honestly think that after the time we spent together I wouldn't care?"

When he looked so baffled she almost felt bad for not trusting him. Almost. "It's the only reason I took the money."

"Why would you believe I cared so little for you?"

"Because you walked away from me, from us, so easily."

"Easily? You think leaving you was easy?" He leaned back

in his seat and stared at her as if she'd spoken nonsense. "Responsibility is the only reason I went back to her. I told you why I made my choice. You didn't seem to care."

Yvonne's hand balled into a fist in her lap. "What did you want me to do, Richard? Beg you to stay? You could have been responsible and taken care of her and your child without leaving me."

"It wasn't that easy."

"No," she said with a snap of her fingers. Anger flaring hot and bright. "You did the easy thing. Leaving me was easy. Marrying the woman your dad wanted you to marry to grow your business was the easy thing to do."

"She showed up three months pregnant with my child." He said the words as if that meant she shouldn't have been hurt.

"And I respect you for wanting to step in and take care of your responsibilities, but when we met you said you broke things off with her because you didn't want to marry her. That you loved her like a friend. You said you loved me, but in the end, you walked away without a backwards glance. How am I supposed to know you weren't engaged the entire time?"

Her biggest fear. That he'd deceived her from the start. That she'd been nothing but a quick fling before his marriage.

Richard leaned forward and stared her straight in the eye. "I didn't lie about that. Natalie and I were through when I met you. I've always been honest with you. It's why I told you the minute she called and said she was pregnant."

Yvonne stirred her ice cream again. A knot loosened in her chest. She believed he hadn't lied about that. "Obviously you loved her a lot more than you let on. That's why you deleted my emails and ignored my messages. That's why it was easy for me to believe your father when he said you agreed to the payoff."

His jaw clenched. Richard took several deep breaths before

he spoke. "I didn't listen to your calls because I knew if I heard your voice, I might abandon the mother of my child," he said calmly. When his eyes met hers, they were full of regret. "Not talking to you was the only way I could stop myself from coming for you."

The words ripped a hole in the cushion of indignation she'd wrapped around herself. Damn her wounded emotions for making her want to cling to those words like someone hanging on the edge of a cliff. But too many years had passed. Now he could say all types of sweet things about how hard it was to marry Natalie and grow his fortune, but the truth was if he really wanted to reach out to her he could have. If he had cared about her just a bit, he wouldn't have ignored her.

Yvonne glanced down at the ring on her finger. She ran her hand over the diamond. Thought about Nathan. How good he was with Jacob. How good he was with her. She finally had her life together. She wasn't going to let Richard shove his way back in her life just because his marriage failed, and he suddenly decided he wanted to be a father to their child.

"Jacob is perfectly fine without knowing who you are. He's happy. We're happy. You coming now will disrupt everything."

"Everything for him, or everything for you?"

The hard edge in his voice made her head snap up. "What's that supposed to mean?"

"I mean your plans to be Nathan Lange's perfect wife." His voice held no emotion, but his body was tense as if he were preparing for a blow.

"Nathan isn't the man I'm worried about being in Jacob's life. He's been good to both of us. I can trust him, he hasn't lied to me, and he'll be a great father. I don't want to let you into Jacob's life if you're only here to play games. I still don't know if I can trust that you weren't responsible for the payoff."

"I spoke with my brother after our meeting the other

day." Richard's hands clenched into fists on the table. His shoulders rigid. "He backed up your story. He knew about what our dad did. What he and Natalie did. My dad confessed to him before he died. So much time passed. Michael didn't think it was smart to go bringing up the past."

The pain and anger in Richard's voice was as real as the pain and anger brewing between them. She'd met Richard's brother a few times and each time she hadn't believed Michael liked her. His preference for Natalie and the money and connections her family would bring to the table were clear. He would have kept any payout to her a secret.

"Why should I believe you?"

He met her eyes. "Because if I had known you were pregnant with my child, I would have given up everything."

Her lungs froze. She clenched her teeth to stop any words from coming out of her mouth. She didn't even know what she wanted to say to that. She didn't know how to process what he meant. Should she feel happy? Should she feel cheated? Should she feel vindicated? She went with the easiest emotion: anger. He couldn't come back now and say things like that. Not when she was over him. Not when her life was moving forward.

"Do you live in Atlanta?" she said stiffly. That was more important than what he would have done six years ago.

The expectation that filled his eyes was replaced with a businessman's cool demeanor. "I live in D.C., and I have no plans to move. I'm only here because of the network's interest in your show and...Natalie telling me about Jacob on the day our divorce was finalized." Anger filled his voice. He took a deep breath. "My home and family, including my daughter, is in D.C." He said softly. "She can't be that much older than Jacob."

The memory of seeing Natalie, not quite six months pregnant, when she'd tried to see Richard, slammed into Yvonne's head. The proof of her stupidity for believing

Richard ever loved her in a tasteful white and blue maternity shirt. She'd fallen in love with a man who'd gotten them both pregnant. It didn't matter that he ran a successful company, wore expensive designer suits, and had made her feel like a queen. He'd used her and tossed her aside.

"No, I guess she isn't," Yvonne said. "You did have me and Natalie at your beck and call."

"It wasn't like that."

She lifted her chin and shrugged, though the careless gesture felt stiff and wrong. "You owe me no explanation. She was your fiancée. I was just the girl you slept with during your break from her."

"Stop saying that."

"Nothing you say will change my thoughts on that. Let's get that straight right now. Look, if you want to get to know Jacob then we should clear up a few things. First, the past is over and done. We're happy now. You don't get to pop in and tell us what to do or make demands."

"I've got fifty thousand reasons why I need to know what's happening in my son's life."

Yvonne pressed her lips together. She reached into her purse and pulled out a large envelope. "This is proof that the money you gave me—"

"My father gave you."

"That *your* money is in a trust in Jacob's name." She dropped the envelope on the table. "I didn't take that money for myself. It was for him. Has been and always will be. If you want to take it back, do so knowing you're taking it from the son you suddenly decided to care about."

Yvonne watched anxiously as Richard opened the envelope. He stared at the documents that supported her claim. She'd set up the trust five years ago. He met her gaze. Her chin lifted, daring him to accuse her of taking the money for selfish reasons.

"I'm so sorry, Yvonne."

She sucked in a breath and swallowed hard, the remorse in his voice slicing her to the quick. "It's over now."

"Can we move forward?" he asked. "I want to know him. I want him to know his sister, his grandmother. I'll pay child support, cover school expenses."

Yvonne frowned. "School expenses?"

"For him to attend private school. He'll have the best education."

"You're not turning my son into another stiff copy of you. He's not going to private school."

"Are you saying you don't want what's best for him?" He tossed back.

Yvonne crossed her arms. "Of course, I do, but you can't come here and tell me what's best for our son. You don't even know him."

"I'll get to know him," he said instead of arguing the point of private school. Which meant he wasn't done with the subject. "And he'll get to know me. I'll make sure he'll have a good life."

She pointed to her chest. "*I've* made sure he has a good life. You don't get to show up and critique how I've raised him."

"But I do get an input. And before you say I don't because of this," he touched the envelope. "That was not me. I'm glad you used it to secure Jacob's future, but I didn't give it to you. My father, for whatever reasons, used a check I gave him to pay you off. Natalie approved the transaction. I had no clue about it. You can't use the payment as me giving up my rights to my child."

"I'm not asking you to give up any rights. I am asking you to realize that if you really want to be a part of his life you have to learn about him before you try to make changes."

"Nadia has been going to one of the best preparatory schools in D.C. Jacob deserves to get just as good of an education."

Her lips pressed together. "I'm sure Nadia got a lot of

things Jacob didn't have access to. That doesn't mean he isn't happy and that his experiences are less than."

"That's not what I meant." He ran a hand over his face. Frustration creeping into his features. "I want to help. I want to do something for him."

"He'll be happy just to know you."

Didn't he understand that? He didn't need to buy Jacob fancy presents or send him to an expensive private school. Jacob would be overjoyed just knowing Richard was around. So overjoyed he'd fall into the palm of Richard's hand within minutes.

Richard sat up. "Has he asked about me?"

His excited expression was so much like Jacob's she had to stare into her ice cream again. "Once or twice."

"And what did you say?"

"That his daddy was far away and couldn't be around," she said in a reassuring tone. She'd hated the way she and Richard ended, but that didn't mean she had the heart to trash him to Jacob. How could she tell her son his father didn't want him without making him wonder why?

His shoulders relaxed. "You didn't bash me to him?"

"Just because you hurt me doesn't mean I had to hurt him."

Pain flashed across his features, and he nodded. "Fine. I'll get to know him before we talk about any changes."

Which meant Richard wasn't leaving anytime soon. Which meant more meetings with him. Her heart sped up, but before she got too . . . overwhelmed by the thought she had to know what he planned. He didn't live here. Maybe he had to get back home. "How long will you be here?"

"Long enough," he said. "I can handle business from here. Especially if you and Nathan accept the offer from my network."

"We're waiting on other offers." Judy hadn't called with any other offers that were better than what W.E.W. offered, but she wasn't ready to completely intertwine her life with

Richard's again. He was pushing his way back into her personal life; him having any type of control of her business life did not seem like a good decision.

"I won't live here, but I'll visit often," he continued. "And Jacob can visit me. We'll work out a schedule as part of our joint custody."

Yvonne sat up straight. "Joint custody."

"What were you thinking?"

"Not about joint custody. Jacob will live with me and Nathan."

Businessman resolve returned to his features. "Nathan isn't a part of this decision."

"Nathan is a key part of this decision," she countered in a no-nonsense voice. "We have plans for our future. Plans that were made without a thought of you."

"That doesn't matter. I'm here now."

Her eyes widened. "Don't try to bully me about my future. You want to suddenly show up and play daddy, fine, we *might* be able to work that out, but you don't get a say in the way Nathan and I raise him."

He pointed at her chest then his. "We will raise him."

"No, Nathan and I will. You will visit."

"What does Nathan have to say about me being back?"

"He supports me and doesn't trust you." As soon as the words were out she wanted to pull them back. The tilt of his head meant he'd caught what else her words didn't say. Doesn't trust you. Maybe not trust you around me.

Richard's eyes dropped to the ring on her finger. "Are you sure about—"

She held up a hand. "You don't get to ask me that. We talk about Jacob, not my relationship with Nathan."

"As long as you understand that if your relationship with Nathan has any negative effects on our son, I will step in."

"You don't have to worry about stepping in. He's the

man Jacob views as a father. Don't worry about Nathan hurting Jacob. Just make sure you don't let him down."

"You can tell Nathan that his services are no longer needed," he replied. "I'm back, and I'm taking my place in Jacob's life. I'm his father. Don't either of you forget that."

Yvonne called Nathan after the meeting. Told him everything had gone fine and hurried off the phone, claiming to have a call from one of her clients. Instead she went to the afterschool program and picked Jacob up. They got Happy Meals at McDonald's and she let him play as long as he wanted in the play area. Afterwards, they went back to Sweet Cream and he got the biggest pile of gummy bears on his ice cream he wanted. Back at home, she helped him with homework before he took a bath and once again ran out of the bathroom with his back soaking wet because he didn't have the patience to dry off.

After his bath, the two of them sat on the floor. His favorite cartoon was on the television while they played a game of Uno. Jacob was beating her. He always beat her, but this time she wasn't throwing the game. Her mind wasn't there with Jacob enjoying her time with him.

A small hand tapped her leg. "Mommy, it's your turn."

Yvonne blinked and focused on Jacob. "Sorry, baby, I'm tired."

"Do you need to go to bed?" Jacob asked.

She smiled and ran her fingers over his soft cheek. "I do, but before we go to bed there is something I need to tell you."

She thought about what Nathan had said right before they'd gotten off the phone. *"Don't tell Jacob without me."* Immediately followed by Richard's words. *"I'm back, and I'm taking my place in Jacob's life. I'm his father."*

She looked into Jacob's deep brown eyes. For years, it had

been just the two of them. Sure, her mom and sister had been around to help out, but most of the days and nights had been like this. Her and Jacob, watching television, shopping together, eating together, making a pretty damn good life for themselves. She wanted to tell Jacob about his father and she wanted to tell him on her own terms. Just the two of them. No one else dictating how she or her son should react.

She took a deep breath. "Your father is in town. Your... real father."

The silence that followed was so deep and heavy it rivaled a black hole in its power. She focused on Jacob. He sat frozen. No movement except for the quick rise and fall of his shoulders as he sucked in air.

Yvonne reached over and placed her hand on his. "Did you hear me, Jacob? You always said you wanted to meet him."

"My dad?" he finally said. His tiny brows drew together, and he looked at her as if her words made no sense.

She guessed they didn't. Six years of "he's not around" followed by "surprise, Dad's in town" wouldn't make much sense.

"Yes." She swallowed hard and hoped she looked calm. The last thing she wanted was to freak him out or make him feel as if he had to react a certain way to the news. "He lives in Washington, D.C., but he contacted me a few days ago. He wants to meet you."

Jacob's back straightened, and his head tilted to the side. The confusion still there, but a spark of interest beneath the change. "But... if my dad is back... what about Nathan. Is he going away?"

Yvonne shook her head. "No. This changes nothing. Nathan and I are still getting married."

Jacob shifted quickly until he sat with his knees bent and his heels beneath his behind. "Where's he been? Did he stay away because he didn't want me?"

Yvonne ran her hand over Jacob's head and cupped his

cheek. "Of course, he wants you. He just...couldn't come around before."

Jacob's eyes lit up with curiosity. "Was he in jail? Jimmy's daddy is in jail and can't see him."

What the hell? She flipped through her mental files and came up with Jimmy being one of Jacob's friends from school. She'd met his mom at a school function. Guess now she knew why she hadn't met his dad. She shook her head. "No, baby, he wasn't in jail. It was just...circumstances."

Jacob's brows drew together again. "What's circumstances?"

"Things that happen that can mess up your life. Circumstances kept him away, but those things are gone now, and he wants to meet you." The simplest explanation she could think of.

Jacob got quiet and processed her words. He chewed on his lower lip and studied the carpet. Yvonne wished she could read his mind. She ran her hand up and down his tiny little back. He was so small, so fragile. Letting Richard back in his life could break him in so many ways.

"If you don't want to meet him—"

"I do." Jacob looked up and met her eyes. "I want to see my daddy."

Then he gave her a small, hopeful smile that let her know that no matter how hard it may be to have Richard in her life, she couldn't deny her son the opportunity to get to know his father. Richard better appreciate and respect the hope in their son's eyes.

The ending song for the cartoon on the television filled the room. "It's eight o'clock. Time for bed."

They went through the bedtime ritual. She expected Jacob to ask a dozen questions about his father. He didn't. Should she be happy about that or worried? Maybe a bit of both. For a kid who would randomly bring up his dad she would have thought he'd talk her ear off and refuse to go to bed.

"When will I meet him?" Jacob asked after Yvonne tucked him into bed and sang to him.

"This weekend, if you'd like."

"Okay." Then he smiled and leaned up to kiss her cheek.

Yvonne kissed him goodnight and turned off the overhead light. She left his room and went straight for the freezer. It was another night for vodka. After making her drink she went back into the living room and plopped down on the couch. Her purse sat in one corner of the sofa and she dragged it over and took out her cell phone. She'd silenced it after she and Jacob left the ice cream place.

She had one missed text from Nathan asking her to call when she left her mother's. That was the excuse she'd given for why he couldn't come straight over tonight. She didn't want to see Nathan right now. She loved him, but she was wrung dry. Seeing Richard, arguing with him, thinking about everything he said had left her twisted, tired, and through with heavy emotions. She'd text him in a few and tell him she and Jacob got home late and were going straight to bed.

She had a text from her sister asking how the day went. One from Sandra asking if they could meet next week to discuss the designs. One from Richard.

I emailed you something.

Frowning, she went to the email icon on her phone. At the top was a forwarded email from Richard. The subject: My son.

She tapped on the email. The first part was from Richard.

I know believing me may be difficult. I would
have preferred to prevent you from seeing this, but I
need you to know. I didn't agree to the payoff. It was
all my father and Natalie. I know that doesn't mean
much now. But if anything, I need you to know that I
wouldn't have done that to you.

R.

She scrolled down to the forwarded message. A chain of messages. Starting with Richard to Natalie from the other day when she'd met him in his office.

> What the hell is this I'm hearing about a payoff?
> Did you know about this?
> -Richard

Natalie's reply had come just a few hours later.

> Yes, I knew everything. Your father told me. And just like the whore I thought she was she took the money and ran. See what you pined after for years? I told you she only wanted your money.

Richard had shot back an email almost instantly.

> You lied to me for years. How could you be so heartless?

Almost twelve hours passed before Natalie replied.

> Because you lied to me, too. For six years. You never got over her. And look what you did. Ran right to her. You're pathetic.

Yvonne's hands clenched into fists. Pain tightened her chest. Anger blazed like a hot poker down her spine. She'd met Natalie once and that was all she needed to assume the woman was cold and heartless. The business mogul's daughter Richard's father wanted him to marry to make their businesses thrive together. This was proof Natalie was just as frigid as Yvonne had guessed.

She'd lied to Richard for years. Kept his father's secret.

Kept Jacob from knowing his own father. Kicked Yvonne off Richard's front porch and treated her like week-old trash. And to this day showed no signs of regret.

Yvonne went to her text messages and texted back.

I saw the emails.

Richard's reply came back in seconds. **I didn't think you'd believe me without them. I'm sorry about what she called you.**

You have no reason to be sorry.

Yes, I do. I should have answered your calls.

She started to type, yes, you should, but what would that do. Take them back down the road of what could have been. Now wasn't the time for what could have been. Obviously, they weren't meant to be together. If they were, she wouldn't have met Nathan, wouldn't have trusted herself to love him, wouldn't be getting married. She couldn't rearrange everything in her life now because what she'd believed before was a lie. Because the huge weight of the pain of what happened with her and Richard had lifted away.

She didn't know what to do now that the anger and betrayal she'd harbored for years were gone. She couldn't fill that space back up with the feelings she once had for him.

The past doesn't matter. She texted back.

We'll move forward. I told Jacob about you tonight.

What did he say?

He wants to meet you.

😊!!!!!! **Thank you! So much!**

Yvonne grinned and laughed out loud. Richard sending emojis. Who would have thought he used emojis? Warmth spread through her chest. She wished they were talking in person. That she could see the smile on his face.

And those feelings were dangerous. **I'm going to bed. We can talk tomorrow about meeting him.**

Ok. Good night, Yvonne.

She got up. Went through her nighttime routine. Slipped between the covers. Remembered she had to text Nathan. So, she did. Told him she was tired, would call him tomorrow, and that she loved him. Then navigated back to her conversation with Richard.

Good night, Richard.

Chapter 10

"You told him without me?"

Yvonne looked into Nathan's disbelieving eyes and had to hold back an angry reply. Irritation simmered beneath her skin. He acted as if she had no right to tell her son his father was back in town without having him in the room.

They were spending Friday evening having dinner at her place. Her mom had insisted on coming over once Yvonne mentioned Nathan would be there. Wedding planning discussions was her excuse. No matter that Yvonne and Nathan hadn't picked a date. Their lives had been tossed up almost immediately after he'd proposed. She wondered if Richard had seen the public proposal. Had that prompted him to return to their lives?

No, she'd read the emails. He'd forwarded more this morning. Messages where he asked both Natalie and his brother about Yvonne's allegations. His ex-wife was responsible for the messages that said Richard wanted nothing to do with her or their son. One small concession was that Richard's brother Michael hadn't known about those.

"Yes," she answered.

Yvonne opened the door of the oven and pulled out the lasagna. It was one of those frozen ones. Though she could cook, she didn't particularly like cooking. Frozen meals, takeout, and pre-made dinners from her grocery store deli usually made up her and Jacob's weeknight meals.

Nathan stopped slicing tomatoes for the salad and stared at her. "Why would you do that?"

"Because I wanted to tell him."

"I thought you wanted to tell him with me beside you."

She bristled at the way the words sounded. She didn't need Nathan to hold her hand as she delivered the news. Was the news shocking and unexpected: yes. Was it all around terrible news: Yvonne couldn't say that was the case.

"I didn't want Jacob to freak out. I wanted to tell him calmly and let him know everything would be okay."

"And you couldn't do that with me there?" Nathan put the knife on the counter and crossed his arms. "I thought we were a team, Yvonne."

"Who says we aren't a team?"

"You haven't been acting as if we are a team lately. You're meeting him without me. Keeping me out of important conversations with Jacob. Your ex is barely back and already you're pushing me aside."

"Hey, this isn't about you," she snapped. "Jacob hasn't seen his father, ever. My number one concern is making sure he's okay every step of the way in this. My feelings, Richard's feelings, and, yes, your feelings all have to take a back seat. I thought you would understand that."

Nathan ran a hand through his hair. He sighed then crossed the room to her. "I know Jacob is the most important person in this entire crazy situation. I just don't want us to get lost as Richard tries to make a place in your life."

"We won't get lost, but I also need you to understand that sometimes some things are going to be just between me and

Jacob. I'm his mom. I have to check in and make sure he's handling the transition okay. This is a big move. It's a lot for a six-year-old to take in and I wanted to be the one to handle things."

"I get that, but you also have to accept you agreed to be my wife. That means I can help you share the burden. You don't have to weather this alone." He ran his hands up and down her arms. The warmth of his touch a comfort despite her anger. "You're not a single mother anymore. We're a family."

Was that what she was doing? Still acting like she didn't have a partner in her life who was willing to share the good times and the bad? Had she been wrong for wanting to exclude Nathan from the discussion?

The back door opened, and Jacob ran in. "Grandma's here!"

Rochelle came into the door behind Jacob. Her smile brightened the second she spotted Nathan. Meeting and dating Nathan was one thing her mom universally approved of. It didn't matter that Yvonne had gotten a degree, opened a business, and had become so popular celebrities wanted to work with her. Nope, the only thing that mattered was that Yvonne had somehow snagged a good man.

"Hey Mom," Yvonne said.

"Well hello there you two love birds," Rochelle said in a crooning voice. "Nathan, sweetheart, how are you doing today? I was just telling Yvonne it's time to pick out the wedding colors. Did she tell you the combinations I came up with?"

Nathan dropped his arms from Yvonne. They exchanged a look. He knew her mother doted on him and how much it irritated her. Nathan winked and went back over to the tomatoes. "No, she didn't."

Rochelle hung her purse on the hook next to the door. "Yvonne, what is wrong with you? You should have told him."

"I've kind of had a lot of other things on my mind lately, Mom."

Rochelle waved a dismissive hand. "Nothing should come in the way of your wedding plans. You and Nathan deserve to be happy. Don't let your beautiful future get lost in all this other... nonsense."

Yvonne's brows drew together. She glanced at Nathan. He avoided her gaze and focused on the tomatoes with laser-like precision. Funny how he and her mom used almost the same wording when it came to her and Nathan. She'd known her mom would be #TeamNathan after Richard showed up. She hadn't expected Nathan to try and secure Rochelle to his side.

"I appreciate your concern, Mom, but don't worry. Nathan and I have plenty of time to pick colors."

"Do you? Because from what I remember you two haven't picked a date yet. How would I know you have plenty of time until you pick a date?"

"We just got engaged a few days ago," Yvonne countered. "Can we enjoy being engaged for a minute?"

"Your mom is right," Nathan said. "I think we should pick a date."

She spun back towards Nathan. "You do?"

He finished with the tomatoes and wiped his hands on a paper towel. "Things got a little crazy before we had the chance to talk about it."

She looked from him to her mom then back to him. "And you want to discuss it *now*?" In front of her mom who would butt her nose in their business and try to dictate everything. He had to know she wouldn't want to discuss major wedding plans in front of her mom.

"Why not now? All of the most important people are here." He pointed to Rochelle and then to Jacob, who'd plopped down at one of the kitchen chairs and was peeling a banana.

There were a ton of good reasons why not now. One, this was an ordinary Friday night and not one related to wedding discussions. Two, her sister wasn't here who was also *the* most important person Yvonne needed on her side when it came to making any wedding decisions. Three, their life had just been tossed in a paint mixer and blended into something unrecognizable. Well, maybe it wasn't that bad, but still.

As she looked at three sets of eyes, she realized she couldn't use Richard's return as an excuse to delay wedding planning.

"Okay," she said. "When were you thinking?"

"Spring," Nathan said.

Yvonne nodded. "Spring weddings are good."

"This coming spring." Nathan elaborated.

"That's less than a year to plan." Yvonne said. Summer vacation for Jacob was right around the corner.

Nathan raised an eyebrow. Gave her that smile that made her stomach tighten. "I didn't think you'd want to wait much longer than that."

Oh yeah, they were waiting. She went back to the day after he'd proposed. When she'd questioned him for wanting to wait. Where had all that urgency gone? She'd been distracted. Rightfully so, but still, maybe her mom and Nathan were right. Already she'd lost some of what she'd been feeling before Richard's unexpected arrival.

"I don't," she said firmly. "Spring it is."

"Early spring," Rochelle said emphasis on early.

Yvonne nodded. "April sound good?"

Nathan grinned. "April sounds perfect."

"Is my dad going to be in the wedding?" Jacob asked. His dark eyes were excited and expectant. His feet swung back and forth as he happily munched on his banana and stared at the adults as if his question wasn't a huge, uncomfortable elephant in the room.

Nathan's smile stiffened. Rochelle outright scowled. Leaving Yvonne to take this awkward conversation.

"Probably not," Yvonne said.

Jacob frowned. "Why not? I want him to be there. That way he can see me in my tuxedo. Grandma said I'd get to wear a tuxedo like a real man and carry your ring."

"We'll see," Yvonne said. "He may not be able to come to the wedding."

Not that she had plans to invite Richard to her wedding. Did she have to invite him now? Was that acceptable? Would he even want to come? How would Richard feel to watch her marry someone else? Would it hurt?

Why does it matter?

"You know what," Yvonne said. "Let's eat!"

She got no arguments from that. They spent the next hour eating, talking about more wedding plans, and letting Yvonne handle all mentions of Richard from Jacob. And there were a lot of mentions of Richard. Yvonne couldn't be upset about Jacob's excitement. His dad was here and wanted to meet him and Jacob was treating that fact as if the president of the United States had asked for a personal visit.

Nathan tried to be just as understanding with Jacob's enthusiasm, but Yvonne noticed how he slightly flinched whenever Jacob mentioned his father. The steady stiffening of his shoulders as the dinner wore on. The way her mom kept giving her the side eye. Richard hadn't met the rest of her family and already he was wreaking havoc.

"Jacob, how about we go out and toss the ball," Nathan finally said as they finished up the ice cream Yvonne had dished out for dessert.

"Yes!" Jacob hopped out of the chair.

Nathan grinned, the tension around his mouth easing away when faced with Jacob's exuberance. They grabbed the baseball and gloves from the mud room and went out to the backyard. Yvonne went to her kitchen window where she had a view of them and smiled. She liked watching Nathan and Jacob together. Jacob had tried so hard to be like Nathan as he'd become more of a part of their lives. The paternal influence he'd wanted and idolized.

Richard didn't play baseball. If she remembered correctly, he'd gotten a lacrosse scholarship for college. He'd played that and tennis. She'd teased him about playing what she'd called white boy sports. Mainly because she'd never met a black guy who'd played either before. He'd taken her to his local tennis league and to a lacrosse game and quickly disproved her belief that few black people played those sports. Would he teach Jacob to play them? She imagined Jacob with a kid's size tennis racquet in his hand and grinned.

"They are sweet together, aren't they?" Rochelle stood next to Yvonne. She looked out the window and smiled.

"Yes, they are." No need to mention her grin was related to thinking about what her son would learn from his biological father and not his soon to be stepfather.

Rochelle turned away from the window and eyed Yvonne. "You know you have to do better if you want to keep him."

Per usual, Yvonne's moment of joy was shot to hell thanks to a snide comment from her mom. "What are you talking about?"

"You're already letting this Richard guy mess up what you have with Nathan."

"First of all, he isn't *this Richard guy*. He's Jacob's father and he has a right to know his son." She turned away from the window and stacked the dirty ice cream bowls on the table. "Secondly, I'm not letting him mess anything up. He hasn't even met Nathan."

"Oh, he has a right to know his son now? Before, you didn't even want the man in your life. What changed?"

"We talked."

"About what?" Rochelle followed Yvonne from the window back to the table like a cloud of gnats on a scorching summer afternoon.

"What do you think we talked about, Mom? Jacob." Yvonne took the dishes off the table and dumped them in the sink with a loud clash. Thankfully none broke.

"What else? No mention of you two rekindling what you had back in D.C."

Yvonne faced her mom. She placed a hand on her hip and took a deep breath before responding. "Mom, this is not about my past relationship with Richard. This is about a father wanting to meet his son."

"Do you believe him? That he didn't know about the payout."

"Yes."

"Why?"

"Because he provided me proof," she said.

Rochelle raised a brow. Her lips twisted in a skeptical scowl. "What kind of proof?"

"Does it matter? Just know he provided proof and I believe him. He didn't know about the payoff. He didn't know about Jacob. He's honestly only here because he wants to know his son."

I should have listened to your message. The words of Richard's text to her flashed across her brain. He wished the past had been different, but that didn't mean he wished they would have stayed together. He'd already made the choice to be with Natalie. She couldn't assume he would have come back to her if he'd known she was pregnant. Or that she would have wanted him back after he'd made his choice. No, she would operate under the assumption that he would have been a presence in Jacob's life if he would have known. Nothing else.

"You just be careful. Quit meeting with him without Nathan. The more you keep Nathan in the loop of what's happening between you and Richard the better everything will be," Rochelle lectured.

"First you say keep Nathan separate from my situation with Richard, now you're telling me to bring Nathan along. What gives?" She was pretty sure whatever talk her mother had with Nathan was part of the reason.

Rochelle shrugged and looked back out of the window. "Nothing gives. I agree a child needs their father, but I don't want you to make a mistake. You're marrying a fantastic man who for some reason thinks you're the best thing next to the sun. Don't screw that up."

"Gee thanks, Mom." Yvonne didn't bother to hide her sarcasm. It wasn't as if she was a terrible catch herself. She loved Nathan and appreciated his love, but she also wasn't defined by or beholden to him because of it. Something her mom wouldn't understand or accept.

Ignoring Yvonne's tone of voice, Rochelle smiled and patted her daughter's cheek. "You're welcome, dear. Now, let's finish cleaning up and then we can go out back and watch our fellas."

Chapter 11

Yvonne got out of the car Saturday morning at the park and pulled a pair of shades from the top of her head down over her eyes to block the bright morning sunlight. She turned back to the car and grinned as Jacob jumped out of the back seat after Nathan opened the door. Jacob's arms pumped as he ran toward her. His dark eyes sparkled with excitement.

"Come on, Nathan!" Jacob waved his hand in a hurry-up fashion.

Nathan hurried forward. No outward sign he was bothered by Jacob's joy. The reason for Jacob's high spirits: They were meeting Richard.

Jacob grabbed her hand in one of his and Nathan's hand in the other then pulled them both away from the parking area and toward the park. Yvonne's pulse rushed faster with each step they took. Dozens of questions and concerns ran through her mind. Was she exposing her son to eventual heartbreak? Should she have shielded Jacob from Richard longer? Spent more time uncovering if Richard had ulterior motives?

But the excitement on Jacob's face chipped away her immediate concerns. Now that Richard and Jacob knew about each other, nothing short of an alien invasion would serve as an excuse for her to keep them apart without feeling guilty. She spotted Richard sitting on a bench near the park entrance. Richard pulled off his shades and stood. His gaze focused on Jacob. His eyes widened, a smile crept across his lips, and he placed his hand over his heart. He took one step forward, blinked several times, then stopped as if he was holding back from rushing forward.

Yvonne's eyes burned, and her steps faltered. The love and awe in Richard's gaze made her breath lodge in her chest. Richard's dark eyes left Jacob and met hers. The smile on his face softened. The look he gave her was disbelieving, joyous, overwhelmed. Her pulse jumped and the rush of pleasure that used to always creep up her spine when she saw him took over as if six years hadn't separated them.

"Yvonne?" Nathan's questioning voice.

She'd stopped walking. She tore her gaze from Richard's. Looked first at Jacob, who watched her curiously, then at Nathan, whose lips formed a tight line.

"I'm good. Just…" she trailed off. She looked back at Jacob. "I just want everything to be okay."

"It will be, Mommy," Jacob said.

Oh, the optimism of youth. She really hoped everything would be okay. Her gut feeling, however, was that after today, things would be drastically different.

The trio stopped feet away from Richard. He met her eye, nodded and smiled. There was no hint of the demanding businessman she'd seen in their previous meetings as he stood there under the sunshine wearing cargo shorts and a dark collared shirt. Her shoulders relaxed, and her lips lifted in an answering lets-see-how-this-goes grin.

She took a heavy breath then looked down. "Jacob, this is your father. Richard Barrington."

Richard lowered to his knee. Jacob watched him with guarded, wary eyes. "Hello, Jacob, I'm so happy to meet you."

Jacob looked up at Yvonne. Her hand squeezed his. She smiled her encouragement. Then he looked at Nathan who nodded.

Jacob focused back on Richard. "Nice meeting you, too," he said in a quiet voice.

His little body eased closer to hers. She placed a hand on his small shoulders. Hoped and prayed Richard never did anything to break her baby's heart.

Nathan held his hand out to Richard. "I'm Nathan Lange. Yvonne's fiancé."

Richard stood and shook his hand. "Richard Barrington."

Richard glanced at her after releasing Nathan's hand. A million things passed between them. Words they should have said. Words that needed to be said. The past and other people's arrogance that delayed this meeting by years.

"Thank you for bringing him." The pleasure in his voice made her heart squeeze.

"It's time to move forward," she said.

The happiness on Richard's face when he looked back at Jacob made him look just as young and carefree as his son. "Well, Jacob, how about we get to know each other?"

Jacob eased away from Yvonne's side. "Mommy said circumstances kept you from coming around before."

The plainly spoken statement nearly broke Yvonne's heart. Richard's responding flinch made her guess the words hit him just as hard.

"Yes," Richard said, his voice serious and solemn. He kneeled again and looked Jacob in the eye. "Circumstances did, but they won't keep me from you anymore. I can't say I'm sorry enough for not being around these past few years, but I promise you I won't go away again."

"You promise?" A glimmer of hope flashed across Jacob's face. A face that was so much like Richard's.

"I promise."

Yvonne shifted from one foot to the other. "Before we make promises—"

Richard straightened. Met her eyes. The determined, don't you dare doubt me businessman was back. "I promise." His voice challenged her to argue.

She pressed her lips together. Held back the "you've broken promises" comment that wanted to pop up. No arguing with Richard in front of Jacob. This conversation could wait until later.

He focused on Jacob. "Ask me anything or tell me if you want to play in the park. I'm up for whatever you feel like doing."

Jacob looked at Nathan and Yvonne again. Yvonne gave him a small smile and head nod. Then he grinned up at his father. "Can we go on the swings?"

Richard smiled. "The swings it is."

Yvonne tried to give Richard and Jacob some space. She didn't hover over them as they went from the swings to the slide. She also didn't go far away. She tried to stay in earshot, so she could hear everything Richard said.

"Are you okay?" Nathan asked. He ran his hand up and down her back.

This was the third time he'd asked her that. His concern didn't irritate her. Nathan was only doing what he was good at. Taking care of her. Making sure she got through this first meeting unscathed. The thing is, she wasn't sure how she felt. So far, Richard kept the conversation light. Learning about the cartoons, food, and games Jacob liked. The unmasked pleasure on his face from spending time with Jacob made her want to simultaneously clasp her hands together and twirl with delight and grab Jacob in her arms and hold him close.

To relish in the reunion and fret over what would happen next.

"I'm fine," she said to Nathan. They sat on a bench not too far from where Jacob and Richard played on the slide. Despite the awkwardness of the entire situation, Nathan was being very chill about the entire thing. This family reunion couldn't be easy for him, but he was supportive for Jacob's sake.

"Are you sure?"

"I am. Jacob is happy. Richard seems happy."

"He does, doesn't he?" Nathan sounded surprised and slightly disappointed by the observation.

"You didn't think he'd be happy?"

He shrugged and ran a hand through his hair, messing up the light strands. "I don't know what I expected."

Yvonne leaned closer and followed the same trail his fingers had taken and brought back order to his hair. She smiled at him. "You expected something. You just don't want to tell me what."

He leaned into her caress, closed his eyes for a second, before the corner of his lip raised. "Okay, I'll admit I expected him to try and spend more time getting close to you and less time getting to know Jacob."

Yvonne dropped her hand and pulled back. "I really hope you're joking because if you aren't then I'm going to be really pissed."

Why couldn't anyone understand this entire reunion was about Jacob and his father? Just because Richard was back didn't automatically mean he was out to win her back. How could she get over her own concerns if she had to deal with everyone else's doubts?

Nathan tilted his head and looked just as surprised by her annoyance as she'd been by his admission. "Why?"

"Because, I thought we already went over this. Richard's interest is in his son. Not in rekindling anything from me."

"Then why does he want to buy our show?" Nathan tossed back.

"Because it's a damn good show premise and he's the owner of a successful network. Judy mentioned W.E.W. before any other network. He told me he was already looking into purchasing our show based on what he'd heard about it before realizing I was connected to it."

She tried to keep her voice down. Being within earshot of Richard worked both ways. Richard didn't need any hint of problems between her and Nathan.

"I don't trust him." Nathan held up a hand before she could say anything. "I know you believe him when he says he didn't know about Jacob, but he hasn't convinced me."

"Don't you trust me? Do you really think I'm that gullible?"

He took her hand in his and squeezed. "Of course not, but I do think you want to make Jacob happy. You'd regret it if you tried to keep his father away especially now that you know Richard wants to know him. Until I know he isn't going to play games with you or Jacob, I'm going to be skeptical. I love you too much to sit by and let someone hurt you. Even him."

His cell phone rang before she could respond. She bit her tongue as he pulled it from his pocket and checked the screen.

"It's one of my construction managers," he said. "I need to take this call."

She nodded and watched as he stood and walked a few feet away. She looked away from him to focus on Richard and their son. Nathan's concerns were valid, but that didn't make her feel less like lashing out in defense. She wasn't being blinded by her need to save Jacob from the same daddy issues she had. Was she?

"You can call me Dad if you're comfortable with it."

Richard's words drifted over to Yvonne. That snatched

her attention immediately away from Nathan and their conversation. Call him Dad? Was he serious? He'd only been around for a few hours. Her son wasn't ready to call him Dad.

"Oh," Jacob said with a big grin that rivaled the sun for brightness. "Umm…Dad, can I ask you a question?" He skipped around to the back of the slide.

Yvonne's jaw dropped. Jacob was really okay with that? Too soon. He was getting comfortable with Richard way too soon. Maybe Nathan was right. Maybe she was being too hopeful and naive about this.

"Ask me anything," Richard answered.

Richard glanced over at Yvonne. She snapped her mouth closed but crossed her arms and legs as she watched them. No need to hide that she was actively listening to everything they said. Not after that big jump.

Jacob stopped at the bottom of the slide's ladder and looked up at Richard. "What are circumstances?"

The words punched Yvonne in the stomach. Jacob had thrown in his own get-to-know-you questions at Richard about his favorite things. This one was the first direct question about why Richard had been absent most of his life.

"Circumstances are random things that happen. Sometimes they're good. Other times they're bad. Bad circumstances kept me from knowing about you. Otherwise, I would have been here much sooner."

Jacob's dark eyes studied Richard for a few seconds before he nodded and hurried up the ladder to the top of the slide. Richard strolled to the other side and waited for Jacob to come down. He glanced at Yvonne again. A multitude of sentiments passed in that look. His lips quirked up. Not quite a smile, but also reflecting how difficult this was for him even though he was being great with Jacob.

Richard broke eye contact first. Jacob laughed as he glided down. His bright happy expression brought a smile to both her and Richard's faces.

"Can we do the swings again?" Jacob asked after he jumped off the slide again.

"Sure thing," Richard said. "You really like the swings, huh?"

"I do. It's my favorite thing. I feel like I'm flying when I go high, but Mommy won't always let me go too high. Sometimes Nathan will push me high."

"Nathan sounds like a cool guy."

The sincerity in Richard's voice surprised Yvonne. Her shoulders relaxed. She'd expected Richard to get weird whenever Jacob brought up Nathan. If he felt weird, he hid it better than Nathan did.

Nathan walked over. He slid his cell into his back pocket. "We're having a problem at the hospital expansion we're doing in Savannah. I need to get there and straighten things out before OSHA shuts us down."

Yvonne stood. "Are things that bad?"

"Not yet. It's the first crisis my new construction manager has had to deal with. I wanted to let him work things out, but I can't afford to have this job screwed up. Not so close to us getting the show picked up." He looked at Richard and Jacob jogging over to the swings. "I don't want to leave you."

She shook her head and placed a hand on his chest. "Don't even worry about it. I can handle whatever goes on with Richard."

Nathan placed his hands on her hips. His hands were warm, solid, grounding. "About earlier."

"You think I'm going to fall for some game Richard is playing."

He shook his head. "I know you're smarter than that. I don't trust him, but I do trust you. Don't forget that. I don't want you to think I don't believe in you or us."

"Good. Because you should trust me. In everything I do concerning us and Jacob."

Nathan looked over her shoulder. His body stilled. Beneath

her hand his heartbeat increased. She turned and followed his gaze. Richard looked away from them and back at Jacob.

"Hey," Nathan said.

She pulled her attention back to him. "What?"

"I don't know how long I'll be in Savannah, but I'll call you every day. I love you. Just remember that."

She sighed and leaned into him. As always, reassured by his love. "I know you love me."

"Good." His gaze darted over her shoulder again before his head lowered and he kissed her.

When Nathan kissed her a soft, slow burn usually took over her body. The burn came slower this afternoon. There were way too many witnesses. Not that anyone in the park paid special attention to them. Their show was being shopped and outside of the fans of *Celebrity Housewives* or home remodel enthusiasts, most people didn't immediately recognize her and Nathan. Jacob wasn't far away, and even though he'd seen her and Nathan kiss before, it wasn't like she made out with him in front of Jacob. Plus, she had a sinking suspicion part of this public display of affection was about a particular person watching.

She pulled back slowly. The simmer of desire in Nathan's hazel eyes cranked up her own heat. He may have kissed her to make a statement, but he'd forgotten about making a statement after putting that much effort into the kiss.

Good. All too often she'd fought with the idea she desired Nathan a little more than he desired her. Not love; she was pretty sure he loved her more. After Richard, she made sure to hold back a part of her heart to avoid any kind of similar heartbreak. But desire was a different thing. Nathan seemed completely okay with stopping before things got too hot. Whenever she caught a sign that saying no wasn't easy for him, she secretly hoped he'd break his vow to wait. She might be a terrible person for wanting him to break his promise, but what the hell, she was ready to finally make love to her boyfriend. No, fiancé.

"Drive safe and call me when you get there, okay," she said.

"I will." He kissed her again quickly.

Nathan walked over and said bye to Richard and Jacob. He picked Jacob up and gave him a big hug and promised to bring him something when he got back in town. Yvonne felt Richard's gaze on her the entire time Nathan spoke with Jacob. Yeah, she understood the subtext. Nathan was showing Richard how integral he'd made himself to Jacob's life.

How were they going to make this work? Nathan and Richard didn't know each other. Richard hadn't been around long enough to really claim any type of fatherly influence on Jacob. No matter how much she wanted to make this transition smooth, at the end of the day someone was bound to get hurt.

As long as it isn't Jacob.

Chapter 12

"Uno!" Jacob slapped down a card on the coffee table.

Yvonne looked up from her place in the dining room where she worked on a sketch for Sandra's bedroom. Piles of multi-colored Post-it notes, printed snapshots of Sandra's home, and every shade of colored pencil imaginable were spread across the table. Jacob and Richard played Uno at the coffee table in the attached living area. Jacob clutched a lone card in his hand. Richard's hand overflowed with cards. Poor guy wasn't even close to declaring Uno.

He'd come over nearly every night of the week since the park to spend time with Jacob. She'd worried that having him here, in her home with Jacob, would be awkward. That he'd take a look around her house and start questioning her life with Jacob. Evaluating the safety and comfort of their son's surroundings. Ridiculous, she knew, but she hadn't pictured this either. How easily things seemed to settle into a routine around them.

She came home, figured out something for dinner, Richard

came over and played with Jacob while she worked on sketches and other proposals. Something she usually didn't get to until after Jacob was asleep, but with Richard there, he insisted she get work done. He was there to visit Jacob, not to interfere with her. After a couple days of listening to them ask questions and watching them play cards or with the various toys Jacob had, she'd decided to get work done while being close enough to listen in and respond to any questions or comments in their conversation directed toward her.

She'd also expected to butt in a lot. To remind Richard not to make any promises, and course-correct if it seemed like Richard was getting out of line, or too demanding in his requests for Jacob's attention. Neither situation arose. Richard seemed both happy and content to just spend time doing whatever mundane activity allowed him to be with his son. Too often, she'd caught Richard just staring at Jacob with such awe and affection her chest had tightened.

"You're too good at this game," Richard said to Jacob and shook his head.

"I always beat Mommy. Sometimes I beat Nathan. Don't I?" Jacob looked at Yvonne.

Yvonne tapped her pencil on the sketch pad in front of her. "You get lucky sometimes."

The grin on Jacob's face was nothing but triumph. "I get lucky all the time."

"I don't think luck has anything to do with it," Richard said eyeing his cards. "I think you're the best Uno player I've ever come up against."

"See, Mommy, see, I told you I was the best." Jacob bounced in his seat.

"If you are, you definitely got that from me," Yvonne replied. She continued filling in the colors for the clean and simple bedroom design in soft grey with a hint of peach Sandra wanted. "I always beat your aunt Valerie at Uno when we were kids."

"Hey," Richard said with mock hurt in his voice. "I'm a pretty good Uno player myself."

Yvonne laughed and pointed her pencil at Richard. "Oh, no, you are not trying to claim that. If I recall correctly, I beat you numerous times in Uno. In fact, you never won a game against me."

Jacob's bright eyes turned to Richard. "Is she for real? She always beat you?"

Richard shrugged and rearranged his cards. The corner of his mouth lifted in a cute grin. "Not all the time."

"All the time, Jacob." Yvonne answered.

Richard's eyes met hers. Humor warmed his dark brown gaze. The smile on his full lips made her heart hiccup.

"I let you win sometimes." His deep voice slid across the room and over her like a familiar caress.

"Oh really?"

"I liked making you smile. Your smile is beautiful when you win. You wore your hair curly then. It was like this halo around your face when you laughed." The humor had faded from his voice. His eyes were serious and reflective as if he were remembering one of her victory dances whenever she had beaten him in Uno. Then the corner of his lip tilted up. "I also liked paying the price for losing."

Yvonne dropped her pencil, and she ran a hand through her straight hair. Her price had often involved a close encounter of the intimate kind. Why did he have to go and remind her of that?

Girl, like you ever forgot!

Jacob slapped down his last card. "Uno out! I win."

Yvonne blinked several times and focused on the drawing in front of her. A large four poster bed the focal point of the room. She pushed the picture aside. Time to work on the dining room area, maybe.

Jacob chatted about the other card games he liked playing. He was oblivious to the undercurrents of Richard's reminder of how good it used to be between them. Her heart still pounded as if she'd climbed Mount Everest and her lungs didn't want to cooperate with supplying oxygen to her brain. She definitely needed oxygen to clear her head.

It's been too long. You wouldn't even be feeling like this if you hadn't gone so long without sex.

"How about we celebrate with popcorn?" She slid her chair back. "I need to take a break anyway."

She didn't wait for either of them to answer before she hurried into the kitchen. She'd never been more grateful her house didn't have an open floor plan. Her escape to the kitchen meant Richard couldn't watch her from the living area as she tried to regroup.

What the hell had happened back there? Why had he even gone there? The main reason these afternoons worked was because they didn't rehash the past. No discussions about why they'd broken up. No talks about what could have been or where they messed up. Just focusing on Jacob and making sure he was okay.

She pulled a bag of popcorn out of the cupboard and placed it in the microwave. She pressed the correct time. Then pulled the band out of her pocket and put her hair into a tight ponytail. If he insisted on bringing up . . . things, then having Richard back was going to create a new set of problems.

There was a knock near the door. She jumped and swiveled. Richard looked apologetic and held up a hand. "Hey, I'm sorry about saying what I did. I shouldn't have gone there."

"No, you shouldn't have," she snapped. She wasn't angry at him. She was angry at herself for how easily he'd gotten to her. Now he had the good sense to come and apologize. Did he have to be so perfect and adult about this?

"I got carried away thinking about things . . . and, well,

I'll just say I forgot for a moment that so much time had passed. Being here with you and Jacob, it almost feels as if..."

As if this is the life they should have been living. "Look, Richard, it's going to be a transition. Jacob is obviously happy to meet you, and I want him to be happy. We can't screw that up by mixing in things that shouldn't be included."

He came into the kitchen and crossed to her. He didn't stand quite in her space, but close enough for her to smell his cologne. It was the same cologne he used to wear. Dolce & Gabbana. She hadn't forgotten that. Or forgotten how much she liked it on him.

"Things like the attraction still being there between us?" Richard said. He was so matter-of-fact about the entire thing. Not smug or creepy. All business. All let's acknowledge this and move on. Not all what-the-hell-I'm-still-attracted-to-you like she felt.

"No!" she crossed her arms. "There is no attraction. I'm engaged now."

"You being engaged doesn't have anything to do with being attracted to me. Two hours out of my engagement with Natalie didn't stop me from being attracted to you."

"That's different."

"How?" He said with a laugh.

"You're a man." Okay, that was ridiculous, but she needed something to argue. She was not like Richard. She was not feeling anything for someone else. Especially when she was engaged to the perfect man.

Richard leaned a hand against the counter. He wore a short-sleeved shirt and the muscles of his arms flexed with the movement. "Me being a man has nothing to do with attraction. I'm not saying we act on the attraction. We can work together without it becoming a problem."

Yeah, that always worked out for people. "Who said I'm working with you?"

"According to the negotiations Judy is making, I thought the signing of the deal was imminent."

"Judy is making negotiations?"

That was the first she'd heard of that. Judy mentioned a few other offers from other stations. None as good as W.E.W. When she'd conferenced with Yvonne and Nathan, who was still in Savannah, the day before, she'd suggested the deal with Richard was the one they should consider. She and Nathan had both hesitated to tell Judy to proceed. Judy didn't know Richard was Jacob's father. There definitely needed to be a discussion between her and Nathan before moving forward with the network deal.

"You didn't know that?" Richard asked.

"We haven't made up our mind about the offer."

"Any particular reason?"

Yvonne placed a hand on her hip and raised a brow. "Three guesses."

"I only need one. You're worried about working with me."

"I'm not worried about working with you. I'm concerned about your reasons. If it's good to get our lives so entangled after all this time."

He stepped forward and shrugged. He'd been working out. She didn't remember his arms being so muscled or his shoulders being so . . . broad. She jerked her eyes back to his face. She was not going to pay attention to how his body had changed. No attraction there.

"Our lives won't be entangled," Richard said. "I own the network, but creative control will remain with you and Nathan. I don't know a thing about interior design or home renovations. You won't even deal with me when it comes to the show."

"You can ax the show at any time."

"Only if the ratings are bad."

"And what if we have a fight, or you disagree with

something I'm doing with Jacob, or you and Nathan can't get along?"

His head snapped back. Confusion crossed his face. He closed his eyes and shook his head. When his lids lifted, his eyes were hard. "I wouldn't take out my personal feelings on you by going after the show. If I had a problem in any of those areas, I'd come and talk to you." He eased closer. This time the familiar scent of his cologne tickled her senses. "Yvonne, I know I messed us up, but you know me. I'm not petty, nor am I vindictive. I've always been honest and upfront with you. That wouldn't change if your show was on my network."

The thing was, she did know him. Had sensed his moods with a look. Finished his sentences when they talked. Trusted him with her fears about finishing design school and opening her own business. Richard had seen the parts of her she'd only trusted with her sister and in return he'd shown her his own hopes, fears, and insecurities. He wasn't vindictive or petty. He wouldn't use the show to bend her to his will.

"You know I'm telling the truth." The words were a statement. He'd been able to read her almost as well as she read him. He'd probably watched her come to the conclusion.

He eased forward until only a few inches separated them. Their eyes locked. The memories flowing around them. Fusing them together like an ornate luxury wallpaper in a room begging for texture. She didn't want to be glued to Richard, but she was. Would be forever because of Jacob. That's why she couldn't admit she was still attracted to him.

The doorbell rang. Yvonne put space between them. Disappointment flew across Richard's face like a wisp of smoke.

"Nathan?"

"No, he's still in Savannah." She had no clue who that could be.

She took the long way out of the kitchen. The way least

likely to result in her accidently brushing against him. So, Richard wanted to be grown up about this. Acknowledge they were still attracted to each other but pretend as if it wouldn't be a problem. Maybe it wasn't a problem with him. He had six years of marriage and a divorce behind him. He may not be ready to make his life any messier than it already was. More likely, he already had another woman in his life. He hadn't told her why he and Natalie had split. What if he'd found someone else and that's the reason for his divorce. The idea annoyed her more than it should have.

She looked through the peephole and cringed. "Damn!" she muttered. Her mom.

Every day Richard had come over she'd found a reason why her mom and sister didn't need to come by. She was blatantly and deliberately keeping them apart. Richard needed to get to know Jacob, not her family. She should have known Rochelle would show up eventually.

She opened the door and forced a smile. "Mom. What are you doing here?"

"I haven't seen my grandson all week. What other reason do I need?" Rochelle lifted up onto her toes and looked over Yvonne's shoulders. "There's a car in the yard. Do you have company?"

"I do."

"It's not Nathan." Rochelle's lips pursed in a disapproving pout.

"Nathan is in Savannah," Yvonne said, holding onto her irritation.

"So . . . who's here?"

Yvonne stepped back so her mom could enter. "Jacob's dad."

"Oh, no, Yvonne. Not while Nathan is away." Rochelle's nose scrunched up. She glanced around as if searching for signs of wrong doing.

"Nathan knows he's here. He trusts me." Her voice was confident even while her skin tingled remembering the way

Richard had reminded her of the passion that used to burn between them.

She led her mom from the entryway into the living area. Jacob's laughter met them as they entered the living room. He and Richard sat on the couch, eating popcorn, and watching Jacob's favorite cartoon. Jacob had cuddled close to Richard's side. Richard smiled down at Jacob with unmasked joy in his face.

Yvonne froze and sucked in a breath. Emotion squeezed her heart. Richard looked up then and met her eyes. The joy in his gaze softened to something else. Longing maybe. His smiled stirred up so many things she wasn't ready to sift through. Things she'd suppressed for years, things that bubbled up when she'd first seen him. Things she had no defense for in this moment, and, therefore, she couldn't stop her lips from lifting in response.

Rochelle cleared her throat. Yvonne blinked, the fantasy of the happy family she'd once pictured vanishing. Rochelle strode forward to the back of the couch.

"Jacob, darling, come give Gigi a kiss," she said in a cheerful voice.

Jacob hurried around the couch and hugged her. "Hey Grandma!"

Rochelle's face softened and she kissed the top of Jacob's head. "I missed my little man. I haven't seen you all week."

"I've been hanging out with my dad." Jacob's voice rang with pride. He pointed at Richard then grinned at his grandmother.

Rochelle's pinched look returned. "I see. So, you're the father."

Richard stood and held out his hand. His face open and friendly. "I am. You're the grandmother."

Rochelle held her hand out limply and gave a half-hearted shake. "The grandmother, the mother, and your worst nightmare if you hurt my baby."

"I have no intention of hurting Jacob," Richard said.

"He's not the only one I'm worried about." She glanced down at Jacob. "What are you still doing up, baby?"

Richard and Yvonne exchanged a look. She shrugged. Her mom was blunt. Painfully so at times. He might as well get used to that now that her mom had burst into the picture.

"Grandma, Mr. Richard...I mean Dad...likes Team Umi Zoomi, too!"

"Oh, really?" Rochelle said in a dry tone.

"My daughter loves that show," Richard replied. "I've watched it with her, too."

"I've got a sister," Jacob's voice was full of exuberance. "Isn't that cool, Grandma?"

Rochelle's eyes widened. "Yes. Very cool." Her reply was stiff and not a bit sincere. "Well, since I'm here I can tuck you into bed," Rochelle said in a more relaxed voice.

Jacob frowned at Yvonne. "I thought you said I could stay up a little longer."

Yvonne checked her watch. "You've already stayed up thirty minutes past your bedtime, Jacob. Time for bed."

Jacob sighed before looking at Richard. "Will you tuck me in tonight?" he asked in a quiet, hesitant voice.

Richard's eyes softened. "Yes, I will."

Rochelle opened her mouth, but Yvonne put a hand on her arm to stop whatever she was going to say. Her shoulder was rigid beneath her hand, but she nodded and closed her mouth. Richard didn't live here. He deserved to get to these small moments with his child.

Jacob skipped around the couch and took Richard's hand. Richard stood and they walked toward the hall.

"Oh, wait," Jacob said. He turned and ran back to Yvonne and Rochelle. He wrapped an arm around Rochelle's legs. "Good night, Grandma."

Rochelle relaxed and ran her hand over Jacob's head. "Good night, Jacob."

Jacob pulled back and looked at Yvonne. "Mommy, will you come sing to me?"

"I'll be in there soon."

Jacob ran back to Richard and they walked down the hall to his room. Rochelle sighed and glared at Yvonne.

"Richard seems to really be into playing daddy," she said with a hint of scorn.

"He's not playing daddy, Mom. He is Jacob's dad. I can't get mad at him for wanting to do what's right now."

"I'm sorry, it's just... I didn't think he'd be so comfortable with Jacob so quickly." Rochelle's head tilted to the side. "Or with you."

"I'm not comfortable with him. We're still figuring this thing out, and Jacob will talk to a brick wall. We both know that," she said by way of a paltry excuse. "I'm not too surprised he would be comfortable with Richard quickly."

Wasn't that every abandoned child's wish? For their absentee parent to come back into their lives? It had been her wish for so long. A wish she'd squashed, but couldn't deprive Jacob of now.

"As long as you don't get too comfy with him."

"What's that supposed to mean?"

Her mom stepped forward and lowered her voice. "I saw the look you two shared. Don't be stupid, Yvonne. You'll ruin things with Nathan if you keep making cow eyes at Richard."

"I'm not making cow eyes."

"Oh, should I call them how-fast-should-I-spread-my-legs eyes?" Rochelle said with a haughty air.

Yvonne closed her eyes and pressed a hand to her temple. Tension tightened her neck. "Mom, stop looking for trouble where there isn't any. Richard and I are through. We're only trying to make things work for Jacob. Stop expecting me to mess up."

"Women make dumb decisions for a good-looking man.

You've already fallen for him once. I'm going to make sure you don't fall again."

"I love Nathan."

Her mom tilted her head to the side. "Funny how you keep saying that. Who are you trying to convince? Me or yourself?"

Richard came back into the living room. Yvonne avoided eye contact. She was not in need of convincing. If she didn't love Nathan she wouldn't have said yes. Wouldn't have wished he'd been there every night to stand between her and Richard.

"I'm going to go back to my hotel now," Richard said. "Thank you for letting me spend time with him."

Yvonne nodded. "Of course. Nathan gets back tomorrow. We can talk about some type of visiting plan," she said.

Richard looked ready to argue. Rochelle cleared her throat and raised a brow. His jaw clenched. The look he threw her said they weren't done with this conversation.

"Sure," Richard said. "I'll call you tomorrow."

"Nice meeting you, Richard," Rochelle said, her tone glacial.

Richard nodded stiffly and went to the door. Yvonne glared at her mom then walked him out.

"Look, Richard, about my mom."

"Don't worry about it. I get it. I'm the guy who was absent for six years. She doesn't trust me."

"Give her time."

"I'm not worried about her." His dark eyes bored into hers. "I want you to trust me again."

She couldn't give him an answer. Not one he'd want to hear. She wasn't sure if she could trust Richard again. Not the way she once did.

He opened his mouth as if to say something, but then he shook his head. "Good night, Yvonne."

Chapter 13

"Yvonne, you've outdone yourself! I love this design." Sandra held up the sketch for her bedroom design in the light streaming in through the windows in her sunroom.

Yvonne smiled while mentally doing a fist pump. She'd stayed up past midnight to finish the design. She could have been done with the design within an hour of Jacob going to bed, but her mind had wandered and circled around the events of the evening multiple times.

Then there was the dream. Why did dreams have to be so confusing and outlandish? The dream started with her grilling hamburgers in her backyard while watching Jacob and Nathan toss the baseball. She'd been happy and content. Safe. Then in a way that only happened in dreams she'd been back in her old apartment in D.C. while Richard apologized over and over in her ear.

I'm sorry. I never should have left you. I love you.

She'd woken up crying and confused. Basically, her life was a big ole mess when just a few weeks ago it had been perfectly organized, planned and patterned.

"I wouldn't have thought I'd be okay with neutral colors, but you've made them work," Sandra continued. She was studying the paper and apparently hadn't noticed Yvonne's attention had drifted off. Again.

"The room speaks for itself," Yvonne said. "The high ceilings and those bay windows overlooking the connected stone patio are what make the room. There's no need to detract from that with an over-the-top design."

Sandra lowered the sketch to her lap. "You've done a fantastic job. I heard you were the best interior designer in Atlanta, but you've proven it. How would you like to be on my show?"

Yvonne blinked several times. "To talk about the design?"

"No, to talk about your business. How you've built an empire as a single mother and what tips you'd give for other women looking to do the same."

The offer was almost too good to be true. She'd hoped for some publicity working with Sandra. Thought maybe Sandra would recommend her to some of her colleagues in the talk show business, maybe even mention Yvonne Cable designs had handled her new home decorations, but she had not expected an offer to go onto the show.

"Me and Nathan?" she asked, remembering Lashon's insistence that readers wanted to hear from them both.

Sandra's brows drew together. "No, just you."

Yvonne relaxed. "I'd love to, but why?"

"What do you mean, why?" Sandra said as if Yvonne had asked why the ocean is salty. "I just told you why."

"What I mean is, why me? We've only been working together for a short time. I've done the sketches, but the designs aren't complete. There's still plenty of time for you to change your mind about the work."

"Are you saying your work is going to suck in some way later?"

"No. I'm very capable of completing the work, and I'm

very confident you'll be happy, but you don't know that. This is the first time we've worked together. You don't know me very well and your show reaches thousands. I'm pretty sure you don't offer your platform up to just anybody."

"You aren't just anybody," Sandra said, flinging the sketch onto the coffee table with the rest of Yvonne's preliminary designs.

Yvonne pursed her lips and watched Sandra with wary eyes. Okay, apparently, she'd hit some sort of sore spot. Not sure why, but having dealt with temperamental clients who were prone to outbursts and outlandish demands, she remained calm. Sandra hadn't shown any signs she would be that way. Yvonne suppressed a groan. She didn't need any more drama in her life.

Sandra unclenched her hands and relaxed her shoulders. "I'm sorry. I get really...upset when I hear women downplay their talents. You're right, I don't offer my platform to just anybody, but I would say you're an exception. You've built a successful business, you're sought out, you even stole the show during *Celebrity Housewives,* which led you to launch your own home renovation show with an equally successful and handsome man."

When Sandra put it like that, she did sound like a pretty good guest for her talk show. If only Sandra knew how askew her life really was, she'd be the last person sought out for advice.

Best not to bring her personal life into this. Sandra's offer was about extending her professional reach. Being on the show was a good thing. Especially since she wasn't sure if she'd be able to convince Nathan to accept the W.E.W. deal. Something else she'd thought about last night. Richard's deal was the best deal for them.

"I think your story could be a real inspiration," Sandra said.

"I don't know about inspirational, but if my story can

help another person on the way to achieving their dreams then I'm happy to share."

"Exactly! And I know you don't like getting too personal, so I won't ask any questions that are too probing. I want this to focus on you, even though people do love you and Nathan as a couple. You two are one of a kind. Deciding to wait until marriage. The love is apparent between you two whenever you're together."

Sandra watched Yvonne closely. Too closely. This must be how the guests on the show felt whenever Sandra analyzed them.

"Don't make it sound like a fairytale," Yvonne said. "We've got our struggles just like anyone else."

"But some people would say your relationship gives other women hope. You have it all. The elusive standard so many women try to achieve."

"I don't have it all," Yvonne said quickly. "Having it all is a myth. All I have is a plan I've stuck to and a whole lot of luck that got me this far. Everything I have can just as easily disappear. One decision, one wrong move, one unexpected encounter, and poof everything I have is gone."

Sandra's eyes sharpened. "Are you referring to your business, or your relationship with Nathan?"

Damn! She'd said too much. "Not one or the other," she answered carefully. "A freak accident or one bad review and my business could plummet."

"But you and Nathan seem so secure. You two just got engaged. It's too soon for trouble."

Yeah. Tell that to Richard. He had to have picked the most difficult time to pop back up. Then she remembered the elation on his and Jacob's faces and couldn't regret his return.

"You've been a talk show host for years. You know that trouble is always around the corner in relationships. All you can do is work to get through things. Nathan and I are a team and we can handle whatever comes our way."

"Because you love each other?"

Because she had to make this work. She'd made a promise to be his wife. She wanted the future he'd promised her.

What about the future you thought you'd lost?

She ignored that thought. "Of course!"

Sandra sighed and stared out of the window. "I admire what you and Nathan have. My parents were not a good example of a healthy marriage."

"Parents are people. They struggle just like we do." That was something she'd told herself over and over, whenever her mother predicted how much she or her sister would screw up their lives.

"That's very true. My mom, I love her, but she stuck with my dad despite him spreading the word," she made finger quotes, "to every woman who looked his way, if you know what I mean. I know he had at least one child outside of their marriage."

Yvonne blinked. "Oh . . . I didn't know."

Sandra waved a hand. "I don't really talk about it on my show, even though it's not like he's exceptional. Unfortunately, what he does is also done by men and women all over the world. That's why I respect what you have. I know you were raised by a single mother and you're one yourself, but you've found an exceptional man. If you listen to the so-called experts, women like you and me, from dysfunctional families or independent single mothers, will never find love."

"Those experts don't know everything," Yvonne said.

Sandra laughed. "I agree. Keep doing what you're doing. I can tell you're going to hold on to what you've got but you won't change who you are just to cling to it. You aren't someone who'll settle for less, and that's what I mean by saying you have it all. You want love, fulfillment, and happiness, but you also didn't let that stop you from getting where you are today."

She wanted stability, a father for her son, companionship.

Love—well, that had been a nice bonus. She wouldn't mind a little passion, excitement, and deep soul-stirring need. She hadn't exactly found those with Nathan, but she was sure they were there. Beneath the surface. Waiting to come out.

How many months until the wedding?

She had a flash of her dream. The confusion she'd woken up to. She sighed. April was too far away.

You aren't someone who'll settle for less.

Sandra's comment chased Yvonne like a bloodhound hunting a rabbit all afternoon. She'd never settled. She hadn't settled when her high school guidance counselor told her she was being sentimental by majoring in interior design so she could create happy spaces, and should consider engineering instead. She hadn't settled when the first three banks refused to offer her financing to start Yvonne Cable Designs. She hadn't settled when the man she'd dated before Nathan told her she was too independent, and no man would put up with her attitude and her kid. She'd pushed, worked hard, never given up, and she'd succeeded.

She'd majored in interior design. Opened her own business. Met a man who loved her and got along with her son.

So why did Sandra's words bother her so much? Why couldn't she shake the feeling that she was on the verge of settling?

Because you're ready to give up the deal of a lifetime to spare Nathan's feelings.

She stared at the multicolored scattering of Post-its, colored pencils, and fabric swatches on her desk. All blended and mixed together no matter how much Bree tried to organize them for her. Messy, disorganized, with no structure, just like her life. Her life with Jacob, her engagement to Nathan, their joint home renovation show, and Richard's return were jumbled together, but every piece still necessary. A part of her appreciated the sudden, and unexpected, change in her life. Her son would know his father. Their show could be successful.

Her cell phone rang, snapping her out of her wandering thoughts. Her sister's name was on the screen. She snatched it up and answered before the call went to voicemail.

"Mom says you're one step from ruining everything. So, I'm calling to find out what's really going on." Valerie's voice was filled with humor.

Yvonne rolled her eyes and pushed back from her desk. "I am not about to ruin anything, but listen, I'm glad you called. I need to talk something out."

"Okay, shoot."

Yvonne rapped her fingers on the desk. "Would it be weird to accept Richard's offer for our show?"

"Weird . . . no."

"But it would be . . ." She waited for her sister to continue with whatever thought she had in her mind.

"It might make things complicated."

Complicated. Okay, she could accept that. "But if I'm going to do this. If we're going to do this, shouldn't I consider the best option moving forward? If Richard wasn't involved we would have signed the deal the second it came over."

"True, but Richard is involved. You're still getting to know him again after years apart. He's still getting to know you and Jacob. Why throw in a further complication?"

"Because I want to do this. At first I was hesitant, but now I like the idea. I'm excited about the chance to grow Yvonne Cable Designs. This show could lead the way to getting my own line of home decorations in stores, more clients, and a broader reach. I've worked too hard to settle for second best just because my ex is involved."

Valerie was quiet for a moment. "Fine. I agree with you on that. But here's the big question. Is Nathan going to go for it?"

Yvonne leaned back in her chair. That was the game-winning question. Nathan didn't trust Richard. He didn't like how she'd kept her history with Richard a secret. Though he was just as eager to get their show on television, male pride could step in and make him refuse to take money from Richard. No matter how indirectly the money would come.

"I can convince him." She infused her voice with confidence.

"Mmmhmm." Valerie didn't buy it. "I was hoping to have a little excitement or drama in your relationship with Nathan. Looks like I'm going to get it."

Yvonne laughed and stood. She paced to the window. "Why would you want drama in my relationship? You detest drama. Speaking of which, I saw Eva's not quite subtle way of throwing shade at her boyfriend on Facebook. Is she trying to ruin his political career?"

"Sometimes I think she is," Valerie said. "I told her she was an idiot for putting him on blast like that. People know they're dating and are following her posts. She doesn't care. I think that will end soon."

"So why are you looking for drama on my end? You have enough with your bestie."

"My bestie is nothing but drama all the time. It's her normal. You and Nathan, on the other hand, are too perfect."

Hold up? What? That was a first from her sister. "We are not too perfect. What does that even mean anyway. If a couple is happy then they're too perfect?"

"No, but you two just fell into each other. There hasn't been an argument between you. He was super ready to step in and be your Mr. Deeds."

"My what?" Yvonne laughed.

"You know. Wesley Deeds from that *Good Deeds* movie. The guy who swooped in and saved that struggling single mother."

"He did not swoop in and save me."

"But he was super ready to be your ideal man and Jacob's daddy and, despite all your I-don't-need-a-man talk, you were super ready to settle for the picturesque life and future he painted for you two."

There was that word again. Yvonne gripped the phone with one hand and put the other on her hip. "I'm not settling for any future he painted for us. Why would you say something like that? I thought you were happy for me?"

"Hold up, I am happy for you. I'm just pointing out that you two were both more than ready to make a family."

"Well you don't sound very supportive. You sound like you're expecting something to go wrong."

"Well I'm not," Valerie said in a voice that was about as convincing as Jacob when he said he hadn't snuck an extra cookie even though it stuck out of his pocket. "You two are like this perfect couple who are bent on creating a new spin on southern sophistication, and I get that it'll help sell your show, but come on, Yvonne, we both know you aren't into putting on a front."

Bree walked past Yvonne's door. Her steps slowed. She looked in, caught Yvonne's eye, smiled, and hurried along. Yvonne crossed the room and closed the door. She hadn't told her employee about Richard. She hadn't told anyone outside of the family. She wasn't ready to put that on blast. To be honest, she wasn't sure how the admission would affect her and Nathan's image or their show. How keeping Richard's return a secret kind of played into Valerie's assumption.

"It's not a front. Nathan and I want the same things. Marriage, trust, stability. I've finally met a guy who's serious about being a grown up. He takes his responsibilities seriously and he won't bail out on me when things get tough. He's ready to stick beside me and Jacob as we figure out how to make things work with Richard."

"Look, I'm sorry if I inadvertently pissed you off. I am happy for you, and I do like Nathan. I'm just warning you that if you think Nathan is just going to roll over and say 'yes, let's take your ex-boyfriend's offer,' you might have your first disagreement on your hands."

"Nathan listens to me." And he'll understand this. Nathan was the picture of understanding. He was above the petty. No silly sense of masculine pride would convince him to take a lesser offer.

"Listening and going along with all your ideas are two different things."

"Duly noted," Yvonne said.

"When is he back in town?"

"Today," Yvonne said. "He's coming straight over when he gets back."

"And will Richard be there, too?"

"If he is we'll all make things work. This is my new family now. Everyone has to get used to it."

Valerie laughed. "Good luck with that. I would come over to see the we're-all-working-together thing in action, but I've got some work to do before I go out of town tomorrow to look at a potential property for a client."

"You gone long?"

"I'll be back early next week. But listen, for real, I am happy that you're happy."

Yvonne sighed and let go of her lingering resentment. "I know. Be careful while traveling okay. And text me as soon as you're settled."

"I will. Talk with you later."

Yvonne stared at her phone after ending the call. Of course, her sister would have concerns. She and Nathan had a whirlwind romance. From first date to engaged in less than nine months. She would prove to her mom, Valerie, and anyone else, that everything was going to work out perfectly. Just like a room with clashing colors and architectural design, she'd find a way to make everything blend together in harmony. Just like she'd convince Nathan that signing the deal with Richard's network really was the best thing for them.

Chapter 14

Yvonne's doorbell rang twenty minutes after she got home with Jacob and the eight-piece chicken dinner from the grocery store near her home.

"Jacob, don't touch that potato salad until I get back." She snatched the potato salad container out of his little hands.

"I'm hungry," Jacob said with a whine.

"And that's Nathan at the door. We'll all eat together."

Jacob's eyes brightened. "Is Dad coming, too?"

"Not for dinner."

She started to email Richard and ask him not to come over today since Nathan was coming back. Then changed her mind because there was no reason to keep Nathan and Richard apart. They were a family. They had to get used to each other. She wasn't settling for being nervous or worried about bringing the men in her life together. Because as much as she may not believe it, Richard was a man in her life now. He'd be an important part of every decision she made with Jacob from here on out.

Jacob's bright expression dimmed. "Oh."

"But he'll be over later, and aren't you glad Nathan is back?"

Jacob nodded and smiled. "Yeah. Maybe he'll toss the ball with me."

"I'm sure he'll love that." Her son's bright smile returned, and she internally breathed a sigh of relief. She didn't want Nathan to think Jacob didn't care anymore now that his dad was back, while also not wanting to censor Jacob's reactions. "Now wait until we're back in the kitchen before eating anything."

He nodded, and she walked out of the kitchen. She glanced through the peephole and the tension in her shoulders eased. When she opened the door, she held out her arms and was wrapped in Nathan's embrace.

"I missed you," he said lifting her off her feet. His lips brushed her neck, cheek, and then finally her lips.

His kisses were warm and comforting. He was back. He was happy to see her. She was back on solid ground. The doubts, concerns, frustrations, and general wavering she'd gone through while he was away settled at her feet. "I missed you, too."

He carried her over the threshold and kicked the door closed behind him. His lips found hers and he kissed her. The same type of urgent, passionate kiss that he'd given her before leaving in the park. He smelled like wood and sweat, his shoulders and body hard in the way they were whenever he'd been working a lot, and her body reacted. She loved Nathan, cared about him, wanted him, but she also felt the desperation in his kiss. His hands clung to her, pulling her closer, his lips demanding, his breathing ragged.

When he pulled back, they were both out of breath. "Wow . . . you really did miss me."

He half grinned, as if embarrassed. "Sorry. It's been a long week."

She placed her hands on his chest. "Never apologize for kissing your fiancée."

"And how long until I make you my wife?" His hand ran up and down her back.

"April of next year, but you don't have to wait that long before taking me to bed."

Nathan closed his eyes and groaned. "Don't tempt me."

Yes, tempt him. Tempt him every day. Tempt him so much that he tosses you over his shoulder and carries you to the bedroom.

She ignored the devilish voice in her head. Nathan was a man of faith and tradition. If he wanted to wait... well, she wouldn't push him at his weakest.

"In that case, let's eat. Jacob is starving and probably already halfway through the potato salad."

Nathan chuckled and slowly let her go. "You're right about that. How has he been this week?"

He followed her through the house toward the kitchen. "Really good. I got an email from his teacher saying he did well with the class assignments this week. He agreed to be in the end of the year play and is excited about that."

"How'd it go with Richard?" Nathan asked. His voice tightened on Richard's name.

"They're getting to know each other. You'll see soon enough. Richard is coming over again tonight."

She said the last quickly and right as they entered the kitchen. Maybe that was a cheap shot to keep from having a conversation about why Richard was coming over, but she didn't care. This was step one of not settling. She wanted Richard and Nathan to get along. Well, today was as good a day as any to start.

"Nathan!" Jacob exclaimed, cutting off any reply Nathan may have had for her. Jacob waved him over. "Come on, Mommy said we could eat as soon as you got here."

Nathan glanced at Yvonne. His eyes said they'd finish what she avoided later. "Mommy is right."

They settled around the table. Jacob updated Nathan on all the cool things that happened during the week. Every time Jacob focused the conversation on Richard, Nathan easily maneuvered it back to school, afterschool, or playing t-ball. Nathan had signed Jacob up for t-ball and coached his team. Jacob didn't seem to notice or care about the change of subject, but Yvonne grew a little more irritated each time Nathan did it.

She turned to Nathan as soon as Jacob ran out of the kitchen to go get his homework. He had to finish that before Nathan would go outside and throw the ball.

"Why are you doing that?" she asked.

"Doing what?" He shrugged as if he didn't know what she was talking about, but the way his eyes slid from hers told another story.

"Not letting him talk about Richard."

"I'm not doing that. I'm asking him about what's going on while I've been gone."

"Nathan, you promised to try."

"When did I promise? I said I trust you, and that I don't trust him. I never once promised to try and like the guy."

"Well how about you add that to the list of things you try and do for me," she snapped back. "He is Jacob's father. He's not going away. I want you two to get along. Especially since we're signing the contract to work with his network."

Nathan held up a hand. "Hold up? Who said we were signing the contract?"

Yeah, that was not how she planned to enter this conversation. "Richard told me Judy called back asking questions as if negotiating the contract."

"What? I didn't tell her to do that." His eyes narrowed. "Did you tell her that?"

She shook her head. Shocked and hurt by the betrayal in his voice. "Of course not. Not without talking to you first. When Richard mentioned it, I told him we weren't sure."

"It sounds like you're sure now," Nathan shot back. "You just said we were signing the contract."

"That's only because I think it's a good idea. Let's be honest, Nathan, the W.E.W. offer is the best offer. It's the best platform for our show and it's the best audience. This is exactly what we want."

"And it makes us susceptible to the whims of your ex-lover."

She clenched her teeth. He said lover as if it were dirty. What she'd had with Richard may have been a lot of things, but it wasn't dirty. She even, begrudgingly, understood why he'd gone back to Natalie after learning she was pregnant.

None of that would matter to Nathan during this conversation. None of that mattered in the long run. The past was exactly that. Past tense. She needed to look to the future and this deal was the future.

"This deal is what we both wanted. Before we even knew Richard was the head of W.E.W. we both wanted to sell the show to this network. Furthermore, we would not be susceptible to his whims. Richard isn't petty or vindictive. Anything that happens between us as a family." She pointed to Nathan then herself including him in the reference to family. "Would stay between us. The show is completely separate."

"I don't like it." He shook his head. "I don't want to work for him."

So much for not letting male pride get in the way of reason. "We'd still be working for ourselves. He owns the network, but the people with creative control and our producer are the only ones we'd be responsive to." She reached for his hand when he made a move to get up from the table. "Please, be reasonable. This is the deal we wanted. This is the move we wanted. Are we going to give up our own dreams because of your pride?"

He jerked back. "My pride?" he asked, affronted.

"Yes. Tell me this has nothing to do with my past with Richard and you having an issue with that."

He opened then closed this mouth. Red spread through his cheeks. "This has everything to do with that. You lied to me, Yvonne. Now he's suddenly back."

"I can't control the people who lied and kept him out of our life this long," she countered. "Are you saying you wouldn't have loved me or fallen in love with me if Richard had been in my life all along? That you were okay with dating a single mother as long as the baby daddy wasn't involved."

He ran a hand through his hair. This time when he stood she didn't try to stop him. Jacob ran back into the room waving a sheet of paper in his hand.

"Mommy, I already did the math. I just need to read later." He slapped the paper down on the table in front of her.

She smiled and tried to hide how much she wanted to throw something at Nathan. "Good deal, baby. Go get your ball and glove while I look over your math problems."

"Okay," he kissed her cheek, ran over and hugged Nathan's legs, then ran out of the kitchen again.

Nathan ran a hand over his mouth. His loud sigh filled the room, followed by a sardonic chuckle. Yvonne glared at him.

"What's funny?"

"Nothing. Not really. What you said is exactly what my sister said yesterday."

"You talked to her about me?" Of course, he did. She was his sister. Yvonne talked about Nathan with Valerie. The idea of Nathan talking about their relationship with Cassidy shouldn't make her feel as if Nathan was talking about her to his ex-girlfriend.

"She stopped in Savannah on her way up to Charleston," he said sounding defensive. "I can talk to my sister."

"I know. You didn't tell me she came by."

He shrugged. "It was a quick stop on her way. I didn't think it was that big a deal."

It really wasn't, so she let it drop. "What did Cassidy say that's so funny?"

"She asked if I'd be this upset if Richard had been around from the start."

At least Cassidy pointed out the same thing that worried her. "And?"

"And the answer was no . . . is no."

"So, can we move forward with signing the contract?"

Jacob ran back into the kitchen. "Got my glove."

Relief spread across Nathan's face. "Sure, buddy, let's go."

He picked Jacob up. Jacob squealed with delight and wrapped his arms around Nathan's neck. They went out the back door without a backwards glance from Nathan.

Yvonne rolled her eyes. He was just going to ignore her question, huh? Fine, she'd let him ignore it for now. They could talk more after Jacob went to bed. She wanted the W.E.W. deal. Wanted it bad, and she wasn't going to back down. If Nathan still wanted their show to be a success then he'd want this deal, too.

She put up the leftovers. Just as she finished, the doorbell rang. Her pulse jumped. Richard.

She hurried to the front door and glanced out of the peephole. He stood tall and imposing on her porch. Taking a deep breath, Yvonne opened the door.

Richard met her eyes and smiled as if his day had been made. Her mouth felt dry and she fought the urge to squirm under his scrutiny. He stepped forward and she quickly stepped back.

"Nathan's here," she blurted out.

His smile dimmed. His shoulders tensed. "I saw his car."

"He's out back with Jacob."

Richard nodded. "I'll go out back with him."

They were silent as they went through the house toward the back. She could feel Richard looking at her. She didn't meet his gaze. She wasn't sure what he thought or wanted to say. She wanted to ask him to play nice with Nathan. To be easy with him and understand this was a big adjustment for him. That Nathan may not understand things were okay between her and Richard. But saying that would make it look as if Nathan had a problem with them. He did, but Richard didn't need to know that.

She stayed on the back deck as Richard went down to hang with Jacob and Nathan. Jacob screamed "Daddy" and ran toward Richard. Richard swept Jacob up in his arms and hugged him. Nathan's face looked like a kid's who'd had his ice cream cone snatched away. By the time Richard put Jacob down and they walked back over to Nathan, he'd cleared his face and greeted Richard with a smile and handshake.

She gave them their space. Watched as they took turns tossing the ball to Jacob. Everyone on their best behavior. Everyone being extra polite to each other. They played like that for half an hour before Jacob was ready to go back inside and watch cartoons before bed.

Jacob ran inside and the three of them stood silently and awkwardly on the back deck. Nathan came over and put his hand on the small of Yvonne's back. Possessively marking his territory. Richard looked at them, raised a brow, and turned back to the backyard.

"I noticed the latch on your privacy fence was broken," Richard said.

"I'm replacing it this weekend," Nathan answered.

Yvonne bit her lip to hold back her surprise. She'd asked him two weeks ago about replacing that latch, but she let it slide. Let Nathan feel as if he were handling things.

Richard nodded. "I can take care of it tomorrow"

"No," Nathan said. "I've got it. I take care of what needs to be done around here."

Okay, time to change the subject before they started Tarzan-yelling at each other and pounding their chests. "We were talking about the deal," Yvonne said.

Nathan stiffened next to her. She didn't look at him. They needed to get this over with.

Richard turned back to them. "And what have you decided?"

Nathan spoke up before her. "We'll sign under one condition."

Richard crossed his arms and eyed Nathan. Yvonne forced herself not to look at him as if he were a stranger. Just an hour ago he was telling her that he didn't want to work for Richard. Now he had a condition.

"What's that?" Richard asked.

"We keep your connection to Yvonne a secret," Nathan said.

This time she couldn't control her expression. She did look at him as if he'd turned into a red Martian. "Why? Are you ashamed of my connection to him?"

Nathan faced her. "No, but we have an image to uphold. If it got out that Richard is your child's father and we're working for his network things would get complicated. People will ask questions and dive into your past. It could ruin our brand."

"Our brand?" Is that all he cared about? How the situation would look to other people? Didn't he understand that if they showed everyone how well they worked together that would do more for their image than pretending that Jacob's dad didn't exist?

"Fine," Richard said before Yvonne could argue.

Her head swung to him. "You're okay with that?"

At first glance, Richard's face was that of the impassive, practical businessman. Then she realized he was doing his look. The I-know-this-is-bullshit-but-I'll-go-along-with-you look. The look he'd given her when she'd told him he had to watch the four-hour-long *Pride and Prejudice* movie because it would "change his life."

"I only want to get to know my son," Richard said evenly. "I keep my personal life out of the spotlight and no one cares about me as the network owner. I have no problem with keeping my connection to Yvonne under wraps. I want your show on my network and have since the first pitch. If that's what it takes to seal the deal, then I'll do it."

"You really don't care about hiding your connection to Jacob?" And, hiding his connection with her.

He nodded and held out his hand toward Nathan. "As long as we all understand *I'm* his father regardless of what we show the world then I'm good."

Nathan hesitated a second then took Richard's hand. "So am I."

They both looked at Yvonne. Nathan's face was apologetic but determined. Richard's face was a blank slate of let's-appease-this-guy. She didn't want to agree to this. She was tired of lies. Tired of pretending as if Richard wasn't back. But she wanted this deal. They could reveal the truth later. After the show was a success and she and Nathan were married. It wouldn't matter as much then.

She met Richard's eyes and nodded. "Deal."

Chapter 15

The sound of Jacob's delighted laugh from her backyard was the first thing Yvonne heard when she got out of her car after work. Rochelle had agreed to pick up Jacob and bring him home since Yvonne had to work late.

It was the last week of school. Which meant half days at school, an afterschool program that didn't watch the kids at the end of a half day, and summer camps that wouldn't start until next week. Yvonne typically re-worked her schedule to pick up Jacob, but between Sandra's project, signing the contract with W.E.W., and making sure the expectations of her other clients were met, changing her schedule to leave early had been next to impossible.

She appreciated her mom's willingness to help with Jacob even when she didn't agree with her daughter about much of anything lately. Richard's sleek burgundy Mercedes sat in the driveway. Her mother's car wasn't there.

Yvonne slammed her car door and jogged toward the back of the house, her purse and the items she'd gotten to make dinner forgotten in the passenger seat. Maybe her mom's car was parked somewhere else. Down the street or something. There was no way she'd leave Richard here alone with Jacob.

In the weeks since Richard's return, Rochelle had run into him more often. Her hostility and suspicion hadn't gone away. She didn't like him, and even though Nathan confirmed that yes, her mom had come to him to complain about Richard, and yes he'd also told her they were all making things work, she still wasn't satisfied.

Yvonne also wasn't quite ready for Jacob to be left alone with Richard. Not that she didn't trust Richard or felt he'd hurt him. She was pretty sure Richard would step in front of a runaway train to protect Jacob. It was just, well, having Richard alone with Jacob already meant something. That they were comfortable with him. She didn't want to be completely comfortable with Richard.

She reached the backyard and stopped at the edge of the house. Richard tossed a ball to Jacob who swung the t-ball bat Nathan had given him. Jacob hit the ball and Richard cheered. Jacob ran around the makeshift bases, rocks from what she could tell, while Richard clapped and grinned. Yvonne placed a hand on her chest.

Richard looked more relaxed than she'd seen in a while. His white button-up shirt was rolled up to his elbows. He wore a pair of red and black sneakers that didn't match his shirt and dark slacks at all. A sheen of sweat covered his brow. Sweat also made the shirt cling to his chest and back. An unwanted heat rushed to parts of her body that had no business reacting the way they did.

She took her eyes off Richard, with more effort than she liked, and focused on Jacob. He had on a yellow t-shirt with Luigi's Pizza in red letters on the front and a pair of basketball shorts. His face was bright with triumph as he ran around the bases. When he got to the home plate, Richard ran over and held up both hands. Jacob gave him a high five and jumped up and down.

"I struck a home run! Can you believe it!"

"I can," Richard said with a proud laugh. "You knocked that ball to the back of the yard. You said you were a great baseball player."

"And I'm going to keep getting better. That's what Nathan says. He says I got natural talent."

Richard rubbed the top of Jacob's head and smiled at him with such joy Yvonne didn't think another billion dollars would give him the same look. "Yes, you do, son."

Yvonne couldn't handle the scene. It was too much. Too much of what she'd once wished for. How many times had she looked at Jacob and been so proud of him, wondering what Richard would say or think? She'd wanted so many times for Richard to be there for Jacob. To do exactly what he was doing now. Knowing Richard would have been there for Jacob if his father and ex-wife hadn't worked so hard to keep them apart only made the ache in her heart worse.

There's no guarantee he would have stuck around.

The pessimistic side of her chimed in. Though she tried not to listen to pessimistic Yvonne too much, she couldn't ignore the obvious. She and Richard were different. Had come from different worlds. He was worth millions. Even if they hadn't been separated, there was no guarantee they would have worked out. She shouldn't dwell on wondering what could have happened.

Yvonne took a deep breath, controlled her emotions and strolled into the backyard. "Great hit, baby."

Jacob and Richard both turned to her. Jacob's eyes lit up. Something lit in Richard's gaze too. She didn't want to dwell on that either. Jacob ran to her, distracting her from the look in Richard's eyes.

"Mommy, did you see? I hit a home run." Yvonne lowered to her knees and opened her arms. Fifty plus pounds of sweaty boy plowed into her open embrace.

"I did see, baby. Great job!"

"I'm gonna hit it just like that in the game, too."

"I know you will."

Jacob pulled back and grinned. "Dad said he'd come to my first game."

There Richard went making promises to their son she wasn't sure he would keep. "Regardless, I'll be there. And so will Grandma and Nathan."

"I will be there," Richard's deep voice intervened.

He'd walked over to them. His tall, imposing figure loomed over them in the backyard. Even sweaty and wrinkled Richard looked in control. Unwilling to let him have the advantage, Yvonne stood and met his eye. "His first game is two weeks away."

"And I will be there." Richard's voice didn't waver, didn't hold a bit of doubt.

She wanted to believe him. She'd wanted to believe him when they'd been a couple, too. That had left her with a broken heart despite the check for fifty grand. An apology check wouldn't do much to make Jacob feel better if Richard didn't show.

"We'll play this day by day," she looked down at Jacob before Richard replied. She'd seen the argument forming on his face.

"Jacob, why don't you go in and clean up while I get dinner ready?"

Jacob's eyes brightened. "What's for dinner?"

"Simple tonight, homemade pizza and home fries."

Jacob jumped up and down. The quick meal was one of his favorites. "Yay!"

"Hey, Jacob, is that you?" A voice called from the front yard. Jacob's friend Julian. "Can we come play basketball?" Julian came in the backyard.

Jacob gave her a pleading look. "Can we play ball, Mommy?"

Yvonne sighed and checked her watch. "You've got thirty

minutes. Then you need to come in, take a bath, and eat dinner."

Jacob grinned again. "I can play!"

Jacob ran over to open the fence, with its newly repaired latch, and Julian ran into the backyard with his older brother, basketball in his hands. They immediately took off for the goal on the far side of the yard.

"Friends of his?" Richard asked.

"At least twice during the week and all-day on the weekends if I'd let them. He has friends at my mom's house, too. What can I say, my son is popular."

"I see that," Richard replied.

"I'm just glad they like to come over here and play. I can watch them and make sure nothing is going on."

"That's a good thing. He's a good kid."

Of course he was a good kid. She'd done everything to make him that way. He shouldn't sound surprised about that. "He's a great kid. A happy kid who knows his family loves and supports him."

"I know, Yvonne," Richard said in a patient tone like a police officer trying to talk someone down from a ledge. Calm and collected. He'd done that before whenever he sensed her growing irritation. "You've done a great job with him. I wish I could have been here to help." He met her eyes and stood close enough for her to smell his cologne mingled with sweat from playing. The smell sent an unexpected shiver across her skin.

Yvonne took a step back from him. "Where is my mom?"

Richard rubbed the back of his neck. He eased back as well. Had he sensed her reaction? Did he need space between them, too? "She said there was an emergency at the church."

"Did Lucifer himself show up? I wouldn't think she'd leave Jacob here with you."

Richard's smile said her words hadn't hurt him. "She did mention the devil," he said with a laugh.

Yvonne's mouth curved up. They made eye contact. The shiver returned. Not good. There should be no shivers when talking to or looking at Richard. They were not attracted to each other and they were going to work together without bringing up or thinking about the way things used to be.

She wiped the smile off her face. "I'll call her later and ask about what happened."

"Just so you know she threatened to remove my intestines slowly and efficiently if I did anything to make him upset."

Yvonne laughed and shook her head. "That sounds like her."

"She sounded serious. She also said she didn't think I would hurt him. That I didn't remind her of the other assholes you've dated."

And just like that, any goodwill she had toward her mom was easily overshadowed by something she'd said. "Well, my mom is also familiar with sorry men." Her dad included, but she wasn't going there. Richard had heard her story, back when they were dating. He knew about her mother's divorce after getting pregnant with Yvonne. "Well, thank you for staying with Jacob until I got home." She turned and walked back to her car in the front.

Richard followed. "It was no trouble. I had fun playing baseball with him."

"He loves playing all types of sports."

"Really? He seemed to sneer when I mentioned playing lacrosse in college."

Yvonne laughed. "He's not familiar with lacrosse. Nathan loves baseball and his enthusiasm rubbed off on Jacob."

"Well, I'll be sure to get him acquainted with other sports as well," Richard said determination lining his voice like steel.

He said it so comfortably. As if he would be sticking around long enough to do that. And, damn if his resolve didn't make her feel warm and fuzzy inside. "Well...we'll see." She opened the back door of her car and grabbed the three plastic grocery bags out of the back.

Richard immediately came forward and took the bags out of her hand. "Let me help."

His fingers entangled with hers as he took the bag. The current of awareness shot across her skin and Yvonne tried to pull the bags back.

"I've got this. I know you have to go."

If Richard had felt the current his only indication was a smile that turned her warm and fuzzy into warm and tingly. "Who said I have to go?" He slipped the bags from her hands.

"Don't you have work to do?"

"Jacob is more important. I like spending time with him."

"You've been here almost every day for the past few weeks."

"Yvonne, please, let me stay a little longer." There was a hint of plea in his voice. His dark eyes as tempting as any Hershey bar she'd ever come across.

Damn him for making her feel something. She wasn't supposed to feel sorry for him, for the time he lost, and how desperate he must feel to make up for six years. "Fine." She pulled out her purse and went into the house.

Richard followed her into the kitchen. He unpacked the items from the plastic bags and placed them on the counters. She set aside the roll of pizza dough and jar of pizza sauce then grabbed an apron from the pantry and pulled it on over her clothes.

"Aren't you going to change and get comfortable before cooking?" Richard asked.

Yvonne shook her head. "I like to get dinner started right away so Jacob doesn't have to wait. I can change after dinner is made."

He glanced at her feet. "You cook in heels?"

She looked down, back up, and shrugged. "Sometimes. Why?"

"It's damn impressive."

Heat spread up her cheeks. "Not really." She pointed to a corner next to the door to the backyard. "I have bedroom slippers on standby."

Richard laughed. "You're amazing."

She didn't want to hear the compliment in his voice. She didn't get comfortable before making dinner because on the days she did cook she started as soon as she came through the door. She'd had to. No one else was here to help.

"I'm a mom doing what she needs to do." She kicked off the heels and slipped her feet into the slippers.

"What can I do to help?"

"I've got it."

"I'm here. I can't just do nothing and watch you cook." He pointed to the lettuce, tomatoes, and other things she'd gotten for a salad. "I'll cut the potatoes for the fries."

She couldn't keep telling him no without appearing stubborn. "Fine. If you really want to do something."

They worked in silence for a few minutes then he asked, "How was your day?"

Yvonne peered up from the pizza dough she was rolling out. "Why are you asking?"

"For conversation," he said with a patient smile.

She felt a little silly. "My day was fine."

"Are you sure? Your mom seemed a little annoyed when she came here today."

Yvonne flattened the pizza dough with extra effort. "Listen, I love her, but my mom is often annoyed."

"Why is that?"

"I'm going to mess up my life. My sister is working too much. The people at the church still treat her as if she should be wearing a scarlet letter. Her part-time job isn't giving her enough time."

"Alright, those are a lot of reasons. I don't understand the 'mess up your life' part." Richard cut the skin off the potatoes in short, swift strokes. "You're doing pretty good for yourself."

"She'd done pretty good for herself and still lost things."

"What are you going to lose?" he asked.

"Nathan." The answer was out without a second thought. She felt his eyes on her but didn't look up.

"Do you really think that'll happen? You and Nathan have good chemistry. He loves you." That last part sounded as if it were difficult for him to admit.

Good. He needed to see she could make things work with someone else. That she hadn't let his rejection close her up to relationships.

"I wouldn't be marrying him if he didn't," she replied.

Richard shifted from foot to foot. He finished the first potato and moved to the second. "People get married for a lot of reasons. Not all of them have to do with love." She wasn't sure if he was referring to her and Nathan, or his marriage to Natalie.

"Maybe so, but feeling something for the person you're marrying tends to make things easier."

"So you do feel deeply about him?" He didn't look at her when he asked.

She stopped spreading the dough. "Remember what I said the other day? You don't get to question my feelings for Nathan. That doesn't have anything to do with what you and I work out with Jacob."

His eyes finally met hers. "I'm asking because I want you to be happy," he said sincerely. "You deserve to be happy."

Her barely built up indignation fell and splattered like a tipped over paint can. Did that mean he didn't care about her being in love with someone else? Bigger question, why did the thought of him not caring pinch just a little?

Instead of answering him or focusing on her reaction, she spread the pizza sauce on the dough.

"How was the rest of your day?" Richard asked after a few minutes of working in silence. He rinsed the potatoes in the sink. She flipped the switch on the deep fryer on the counter.

She was hesitating. She didn't want to do this. Things already felt too familiar with him. As if the years hadn't passed at all. Not to mention she was hyper aware of him in her kitchen. In her space. The smell of his cologne hovered in the background. Back when they were dating she'd told him his cologne was more tempting than the smell of Sunday dinner after three hours in church.

"Good. I'm spending most of my days working on decorating Sandra Covington's home."

"Really? The radio host?" He finished washing the fries and watched her with interest.

Yvonne shrugged. "Yeah, she saw me on the Housewives show and asked me to decorate her place."

"Damn, Yvonne, I always knew you'd go far. The television show is just the icing on your cake."

She turned away, so he wouldn't see her smile. She'd finished adding the pepperoni and cheese to the pizza dough. "What's cake without icing, huh?"

"Sweet bread," he said.

They both laughed. It was like old times. Them joking and having fun together. Richard hurried over and opened the oven for her.

Yvonne put the pizza in and quickly stepped out of the way while he closed the door. "Let me check out these fries you cut."

His deep chuckle made the shivers along her skin return. "Go ahead. I knew you'd have to. You always double checked my work."

Yvonne's lips lifted in memory. "Well, you aren't exactly a wiz in the kitchen."

"No, my talents are demonstrated in other rooms."

Her breathing hitched. The sexy comeback was what he'd always said when she teased him about his limited cooking skills. She glanced over her shoulder, but he wasn't watching her. He'd walked to the back door and looked out at Jacob and his friend. Yvonne took a steady breath. Old habits were hard to break. Things were so comfortable with Richard that even their quips and teases came back with ease. Maybe he hadn't noticed. Or maybe he didn't want to make things any more awkward by acknowledging what he'd done.

The light went from red to green on the deep fryer. She put the first batch of cut potatoes in the hot grease. When she focused on him again he leaned against the backdoor jamb with a sad lift in the corner of his lips.

"Six years lost," he whispered.

He'd been wronged in this situation, too. Yes, he'd left her for Natalie, but she had known Richard. If he'd known and wanted to be a part of Jacob's life he would have. People had worked to keep them apart. He'd been hurt and had missed out on so much.

"You've got plenty of time to catch up," she said.

He looked at her. Their gazes locked. In his eyes she once again saw his promise to be there for the rest of his life. He really was back. Happiness and uncertainty formed a bubbly cocktail in her midsection.

Richard pushed away from the door and stalked towards her with undisguised intent. Her breaths stuttered. Her mind blanked of everything then raced with a dozen questions. What was going on? What was he about to say? Why was he looking at her like that? Why was it suddenly so hot in the kitchen? He stopped right in front of her. "It's not too late."

They'd been talking about Jacob, but she thought there

was more to the words. Not too late for them? He couldn't possibly mean that.

Her cell phone rang. Yvonne spun away and quickly pulled it from her purse on the table. Nathan. He must have felt a disturbance in the universe. "Hey, Nathan," she said with more enthusiasm that she felt.

"Hey, babe," Nathan said. "I'm done for the day and couldn't wait to hear your voice."

"Great," she glanced over her shoulder at Richard. He'd gone back to check the fries. "I'm making the pizza Jacob loves." She didn't want to tell him Richard was there.

"Sounds delicious. I wish I was there for dinner."

"Do you know when you'll be back in town?" He'd had to go back to Savannah the day before to make sure the expansion stayed on track.

"Early next week. I've got a couple of things I need to wrap up here."

Crap, she kinda wanted Nathan back in town as soon as possible. She didn't want to go digging around to discover all the reasons why. They talked for a few minutes more. Richard took out the fries and called in Jacob for dinner. Nathan hadn't asked her if Richard was coming over. She didn't want to dig around those reasons either.

Richard stayed for dinner. Jacob kept up enough conversation to prevent any awkward silences. The night was good, but the ease they'd found with each other before Nathan's call had shattered. That was for the best.

Jacob convinced Richard to watch television with him after dinner. That led to Richard also reading a bedtime story before Yvonne went in to sing to him. When she walked out of Jacob's room, Richard stood in the living room near the entry way.

He glanced at his watch. "I've got some work calls I need to make. I'll go back to my hotel now."

Her first instinct was to tell him he didn't have to rush off. She squashed that instinct like a bug. "I'll walk you out."

He stopped at the door and faced her. Richard softly hit the inside of the door with his fist and looked as if he wanted to say something. Her breathing stuttered. Her heart rate jumped to extreme levels. She prayed he didn't bring back up the idea of it not being too late. Finally, he let out a heavy breath and stepped out onto the porch. "Good night, Yvonne."

She ignored the disappointment in her chest. "Good night, Richard."

Chapter 16

Yvonne checked her watch and her jaw tightened. Richard had two minutes to arrive before warm-up ended and Jacob's first game started. He'd promised not to miss the first game. She knew he shouldn't have made the promise. He'd spent the entire week in D.C. Jacob hadn't been the least bit concerned about his dad being away because he was going to see him again this Thursday. Now it looked as if Richard wouldn't make it.

She looked up from her place near the dugout and scanned the crowd of proud parents, grandparents, and other family and friends who'd gathered at the baseball fields to watch their young kids play ball. Her gaze slid past a tall, handsome man running toward her then jerked back. Richard. Happiness, relief, and frustration took her heart on a wild ride.

She broke away from the crowd of parents to meet him. "You're late," she said. Though she couldn't hide the relief in her voice.

"Work," he replied, sounding exhausted. "I'm out of the

office and that makes things harder. I had to catch a later flight."

His clothes were rumpled. The sleeves of his white shirt hastily rolled up. The dark green tie askew. Tension lined his face.

"Jacob was afraid you wouldn't show." She was afraid he wouldn't show.

Richard stepped closer and placed a hand on her arm. "I'll always show up."

The no-nonsense businessman tone of voice, but his eyes were intent, sure, and begged her to believe him. Yvonne crossed her arms tight beneath her breasts. His hand fell away. She took a shallow breath and quickly licked her lips. "We'll see." She tried to sound flippant, to hide that her insides were turning warm and fluttery.

"Hey!" Jacob's voice interrupted.

Jacob ran right up to Richard. Richard kneeled to his level. Jacob opened his arms, grinned, and wrapped his arms around his dad's neck.

"You made it," Jacob said.

"Of course, I did," Richard said, giving Yvonne another dose of believe me, soulful eyes, over their son's shoulder. "I had some work to do that held me up a little."

"It's okay. We're waiting for Coach Bell to show up," Jacob said.

Richard stood and glanced at Yvonne. "Who's Coach Bell?"

"He's the assistant coach," Yvonne answered. "He agreed to help Nathan with the team, but just texted he can't make it tonight. That means Nathan has to try and keep all fifteen boys in line."

Yvonne's mouth twisted in a little grimace. As much as Nathan loved coaching the kids, she also knew he relied on the help of the assistant coach. The boys were so young and easily distracted. It took two of them to get through a game. One to actually coach, and the other to make sure the kids not playing didn't get into any trouble.

Richard glanced at Nathan surrounded by kids then back at her. He rubbed his hands together. "I'll help."

Unease swept through Yvonne. She glanced over to the other parents. Many were strangers, but some of them she recognized from Jacob's school. Strangers or not, they knew she and Nathan were engaged. If they were keeping Richard's connection to Jacob a secret, then they couldn't tell anyone here who Richard was.

She'd already prepped Jacob by telling him he had to call Richard "Mr. Richard" instead of Dad when they were in public. He'd been confused and asked why. Her only explanation was that while Mommy and Nathan were working on a television show they had to pretend as if Richard wasn't family. She'd expected a dozen more questions. Instead Jacob had asked if that was like his friend Gabby pretending as if the principal in their school wasn't her mom so the other kids wouldn't get jealous. Yvonne had immediately said it was exactly like that and Jacob had gotten excited about the idea of keeping his dad a secret from the other kids.

Nathan's condition for the television deal wasn't going to work for long. The truth would have to come out. Jacob couldn't lie forever and neither he nor Richard deserved having to keep things a secret. She hadn't told Nathan yet, but she wanted to introduce Richard as Jacob's father during the first season of the show.

"That may not be a good idea."

"Why?" Richard asked with his brows drawn together.

"The whole we aren't telling anyone what's going on," she said.

Richard's lips drew together. He ran a hand across the back of his neck. "What did you expect me to do when I got here? Sit in the back and pretend as if I don't know you?"

Well when he put it like that, of course the plan sounded ridiculous. "We don't need to draw any attention to you. People may put things together."

"Please, Mom," Jacob said grabbing her hand. "I won't tell anyone he's my dad." Jacob whispered dad.

If it were possible for Richard's jaw to tighten any more, she'd worry his teeth would fuse together. She hadn't wanted to agree to this deal in the first place. Richard made the concession because he said he wanted their show on his network, but she'd suspected one day it would really hit what they'd done.

"You said yes to this," she reminded him.

He rolled his shoulders. She noticed the play of muscles beneath the expensive white shirt. Jacob looked between them both.

Richard rubbed his mouth. Maybe to push back what he really wanted to say, then nodded. "I'd still like to help out."

Jacob jumped up and pumped his fist. "Yes!"

Nathan waved at them from the dugout. The game was about to start. "Let's get back over here for the game."

Richard fell into step behind them. She felt his gaze burning into her back. She would not feel guilty for this. He'd said yes to this before thinking things through. She'd never asked him why he'd agreed because she hadn't wanted to have the conversation. How could she defend what Nathan asked without making him appear insecure?

He was doing a damn good job of that already.

Maybe, but as his fiancée she was supposed to support him. Present a united front and not undermine him to anyone. Especially an ex.

"Jacob," Nathan said grinning when they were at the dugout. "Come on, son, we're ready to start."

Richard sucked in a breath at Nathan's use of the word son. Yvonne only heard it because he'd stopped next to her.

She wanted to reach over and take his hand. Tell him it was okay. That they could tell everyone the truth right now.

"Nathan, Mr. Richard is here, and he agreed to help coach," Jacob said beaming.

Nathan's smile stiffened. "You sure? Mr. Richard doesn't look to be dressed for baseball," Nathan said, eyeing Richard's polished shoes and rumpled suit.

"Don't worry. I can handle it. I'm a man of many talents," Richard replied confidently.

She could see the denial in Nathan's eyes. For the past few weeks he'd done a good job of making things work with Richard. Mostly by making himself scarce with the job in Savannah, but when they were together, he'd been cordial. There was no hint of cooperation in his eyes right now.

"Jacob really wants him to help," Yvonne said quickly. She followed it up with a sweet smile.

"Sure," Nathan said after a few tense seconds. "The more the merrier. Richard, you can keep the kids in line in the dugout. I've got another dad who's offered to help in the outfield." He patted Jacob's shoulder. "Okay, son, let's win this game."

"Alright!" Jacob jumped up and gave Nathan a high five.

"Good luck," Yvonne said.

Nathan nodded but didn't meet her eye. He put a hand on Jacob's shoulder and led him to the rest of the team. Richard let out a heavy breath. She slipped her hand in the back pocket of her jeans instead of following up the impulse to take Richard's hand and give it a reassuring squeeze.

"You too," she said.

Richard looked at the dugout full of chatting and laughing kids. The corner of his lips tilted up. "I'll be okay. I've got two kids remember. I'll manage."

She bit back her smile as he walked over to the kids, where Nathan introduced him to the other team members and the dad who'd volunteered to help. Richard's confidence in his ability to handle any situation was something to admire. He was a father of two, maybe he'd be okay to handle a few other rowdy boys during a quick t-ball game. As she found a spot on the bleachers to watch the game she wondered about his daughter. He didn't talk about her with Yvonne. Honestly, she'd never asked. Now she regretted not asking. She didn't want Richard's brother or mother pretending as if Jacob didn't exist. Therefore, she couldn't pretend as if Richard's daughter didn't exist. Jacob had a sister, and he deserved to get to know her.

The game started, and Richard did a pretty good job keeping the kids from wandering off or getting too distracted while their teammates were up to bat. When he got the boys to cheer in unison for the team, she had to admit he'd make a pretty good cheerleading coach. Did his daughter cheer? Maybe he'd coached one of her teams before.

"Who is that fine man helping Nathan?" Hanna Granger, the official team mom, slid down from her top spot on the bleachers to sit next to Yvonne.

Yvonne's stomach clenched. None of your business was on the tip of her tongue. She picked up the extra Gatorade she'd brought and swallowed back the response. Richard was fine, and he was a new face. The women here would be interested. She shouldn't care one bit about that.

"His name is Richard Barrington. He's a friend of Nathan's," she said casually.

"Hmm...Richard Barrington." Hanna's head tilted to the side while she studied Richard from head to toe. "Single?"

"Divorced," Yvonne answered.

"That means single. Can you introduce me after the game?"

"No," she snapped. Hanna's head swiveled to Yvonne. Her brows were drawn together. Yvonne cleared her throat and tried to smile. "I mean, he's helping with the team. If you want to meet him then go up to him and say hey. He's cool."

That seemed to satisfy Hanna because she nodded and relaxed. "Do you know what he does for a living?"

"He's an entrepreneur." Multi-millionaire business mogul was not the answer to give. Not because it might make Richard more attractive to Hanna and the other single women out there. Never that. She was protecting his privacy. His and hers. For Jacob's sake. "He kind of bounces around taking an interest in different things. He's not just involved in one specific business."

Hanna frowned. Yvonne watched as some of the interest in her eyes faded. "One of those, huh. Well, I'm not looking for husband number two. He may be fun for a few nights." She winked and elbowed Yvonne.

Yvonne swallowed hard and forced a laugh. "If you want to try that. I knew his wife and she wasn't satisfied with him in many areas."

Hanna's shoulders slumped. Yvonne ignored the kernel of guilt that tried to worm its way into her brain. This was for Richard's sake. He was here for Jacob and had just gotten out of a messy divorce. Hanna was nice enough, but the woman was pushy. She'd set her sights on Richard and before he could blink, intended to insert herself in his life. Before he knew it, he'd be engaged and re-married and Hanna would be Jacob's stepmother.

Okay, she was going off the deep end. Introducing Hanna to Richard did not mean they'd get married. She shouldn't care about Richard remarrying anyway, but she did. Only because whomever he married would have an influence on their child. Which meant, she had to take an interest in his dating life. For family's sake.

She'd barely begun convincing herself of the stretch she'd just taken when one of the kids hit the t-ball hard enough to score a home run, ending the game. Richard jumped with the rest of the team and cheered. He high-fived all the boys in the dugout and encouraged them to come out and cheer for their teammate at home plate.

Her breath caught in her throat. The smile on his face was sexy enough to melt hearts within a hundred miles. Hanna even placed a hand on her chest and sighed.

"Well," Hanna said. "Men can be taught many things. I'm going over to congratulate the team." She was up and off the bleachers in a flash.

The parents flocked over and gave high fives and congratulations. They thanked Nathan and the other dad for helping. Hanna and a few other moms personally thanked Richard for his help. He smiled graciously and shook their hands.

Yvonne ignored the way they lingered and went to Nathan's side. He took her hand and kissed her cheek. "We had a good game."

"You did."

He looked over at the women surrounding Richard. His victorious smile increased even more. "Yep, everything turned out just fine."

"Mommy, we won! Did you see?" Jacob ran over.

"I did, baby."

Yvonne kneeled and hugged Jacob. She took her mind off Richard and the numbers he was probably getting at this exact moment. It wasn't her business. She was happily engaged, and her future was set. Richard could date every woman at the baseball field. As long as he didn't tell her about it or bring any of them around Jacob, then she couldn't care less.

She caught Richard's eye over Jacob's shoulder. He lifted a shoulder in a what-can-I-say manner then smiled at her. Her chest tightened. She bit back a knowing smile. In that second, she had a feeling Richard wasn't getting any other woman's number.

★ ★ ★

"Thank you for letting me buy you both dinner."

Yvonne stopped watching Jacob run around the play area in Chick-fil-A. She shifted in her booth and faced Richard. Nathan was supposed to join them, but Cassidy called freaking out because she'd been in her attic looking for something and stepped through the ceiling creating a hole in her bedroom. Nathan, the great stepbrother that he was, had immediately run over to help her patch up the hole.

Richard hadn't made the offer to go to dinner with them until after Nathan had taken off. Jacob had asked for his favorite chicken nuggets, and before she could say anything, Richard said he'd treat. She'd been annoyed... well, not really annoyed. More like ready to escape the allure of his smile and the way it made her remember things. But she couldn't say no after seeing the eagerness in Jacob's eyes. They'd both gotten through the game pretending as if Richard was just a friend, and she didn't have the heart to not let Jacob spend some time with his dad.

"Jacob's happy," she said with a shrug. "That's what matters."

"It was difficult for him to not call me Dad a few times this afternoon," Richard said. "He almost let it slip out once."

"It's only until we finish filming this first season."

"Do you really think he'll be okay with that?"

"No." She pulled the straw out of her milkshake and licked the vanilla concoction off. The idea of making Jacob keep a secret made her feel terrible. She considered ordering three more milkshakes and drowning her feelings in sugary goodness.

Richard cleared his throat and shifted in his seat across from her. "Then we shouldn't let him."

She stabbed the thick milkshake with her straw. "You're the one who agreed to Nathan's request. I didn't want to keep it a secret anymore."

"At the time, I thought it would make him more comfortable. I didn't think about how difficult it would be in practice."

"Why would you want to make Nathan more comfortable?"

He raised a brow. "It's obvious he has a problem with me."

"He doesn't have a problem with you. He just doesn't trust you."

Richard's eyes widened. "Why not? You explained to him what happened."

"Yes, but that didn't change his mind. He's worried you'll hurt me or Jacob. He's just being protective."

"I can take care of you and Jacob," Richard shot back.

Her stomach flipped. "It's not your job to take care of us."

Richard shook his head, clearly frustrated, and shifted to sit sideways in the booth. "Then what is my job? I can't let people know I'm Jacob's father. I can't step on Nathan's toes. I can't get too close to you." Richard grimaced and rubbed his temple. "I didn't mean it like that."

Yvonne sucked in a breath. He wanted to get closer to her? She shook her head. "Look, let's not get in over our heads. We're still working out how all of us will fit together. I'll talk to Nathan and get him to understand it's hard for Jacob. He loves us. He'll understand."

Emphasis on us. Nathan did love her and Jacob. Soon he'd feel more comfortable with the situation. He'd understand and do this for them.

Richard's shoulders relaxed. "Who's Cassidy?"

"His stepsister. Why?" she hated that she sounded defensive.

"He just said Cassidy needs help and ran off. You didn't seem to mind, so I wondered who she was."

"She's family. Why would I mind. It's great that he takes care of his sister." Now she really sounded defensive.

Richard shrugged. "Very admirable of him. Nathan's a real stand up guy."

Yvonne rolled her eyes. "I know you, remember. I can hear the sarcasm in your voice."

Richard chuckled and glanced at her from the corner of his eye. "No sarcasm. He really is a great, upstanding, good guy."

She held up a hand. "Just stop. I know Nathan can be a bit... old-fashioned in his approach to things, but what's wrong with that? Too many people are willing to go with what society says they should do. Nathan stands up for what he believes in. I admire that."

Richard shifted and met her eyes. "Admire." He said the word as if considering the meaning behind it. "You *admire* a lot about Nathan."

She held up a finger. "Nope. Once again. Not discussing my relationship with him with you."

He smiled as if he'd won something and turned back to Jacob in the play area. She got a sinking suspicion she had proven something to him, but she wasn't sure what. Time to spin this conversation to something else.

"Tell me about your daughter."

He met her gaze. His eyes asked if she were sure. She nodded and waited. No more pretending as if Jacob's sister didn't exist. Nathan and Cassidy were close, and they weren't blood siblings. She wanted Jacob to have that same relationship with his sister.

Richard's face filled with pride. "She's wonderful. Smart, silly, just a little spoiled." He held up his hand with the thumb and forefinger a few centimeters apart.

Yvonne laughed and pointed at him. "And who's fault is that?"

"All mine. I can't deny it," he said placing a hand on his chest.

His smile held the same love and affection she'd seen

when she'd caught him looking at Jacob. Like then, the expression sent something fluttering in her chest. Yvonne shifted and glanced away. "Does she play any sports?"

He shook his head. "She dances. Ballet and tap. She loves it."

"I don't imagine there is as much of a chance of getting dirty at a dance recital," Yvonne said nodding toward him.

Richard looked down at the dust stains on his white shirt. The kids had also bombarded him after the game in their enthusiasm. His expensive suit was now covered in a layer of grime, but he didn't seem to care. "I don't know," Richard replied with a laugh. "I've left her recitals covered in glitter and fairy dust before." His smile slowly faded. "I'd like for Jacob to meet her."

"So would I."

His back straightened. Hope filling his expression. "Would you like to see her picture?"

Yvonne nodded. "Sure."

He slid out of his booth and over next to her. The heat of his body sizzled against her side. He seemed to take up the entire space of the booth. She didn't slide away.

Richard tapped through his cell phone and pulled up a picture. "This is her right before I left."

Yvonne leaned over to see the phone. A cute little girl with her hair in two curly puffs and a sweet smile grinned from the screen. "She's beautiful."

"I think she's kinda cute," Richard teased. He flipped through the phone to other pictures of her. "This was at her dance recital earlier this year." He pulled up one of her in an ice blue leotard and matching tutu.

"She looks happy."

"She loves to dance," he said with all the happiness of a proud father.

"You sound so proud."

"I am," he grinned at the phone. He looked at her. "I never want to break her heart."

"I don't think you'll have to worry about that." His love and devotion were written all over his face.

"I feel the same way about Jacob."

He put the phone down on the table and stretched one arm across the back of her seat. Richard shifted to his side until he faced her. The movement brought him closer. So close the air between them thinned. So close her body hummed.

"Yvonne, I thought that was you." A woman's voice.

Yikes! Yvonne looked up and met Bree's curious gaze. Richard frowned and turned around. Though the interruption was probably needed, did it have to be her ever observant assistant?

"Hey, Bree," she said brightly.

"I saw Jacob in the play area and immediately looked for you and Nathan." Her eyes landed on Richard and she raised her brows.

"Nathan had to help Cassidy with something. This is Richard. He's a friend of Nathan's."

"Mmmhmm," Bree said, not sounding convinced. She held out her hand. "Bree Foster. Yvonne's assistant."

Richard shook her hand. "Nice to meet you."

"Likewise." Bree dropped his hand and glanced at Yvonne. A hundred questions in her gaze. The most prominent was who-is-this-man and why-are-you-sharing-a-booth? "Don't forget you and Nathan have the interview with Southern Living tomorrow. They called today, and the reporter said she couldn't wait to hear from home improvement's newest *it* couple."

Richard's body tensed. He slid away from Yvonne. She pretended she didn't miss his closeness.

"I remember, Bree. Thank you," she said, with a dose of please move along.

Bree sighed, but got the message. "Well, I guess I'll see you tomorrow. Hope to see you again, Richard."

"You will," was Richard's confident reply.

Bree lifted a brow and grinned before striding off.

"Southern Living wants to meet the new *it* couple," Richard said tightly.

"Yep," she said happily. "Which is great you know. It means more publicity before the show airs. Now that we've signed with W.E.W., Judy has set up a big press tour."

He nodded and drummed his fingers on the table. "You and the man you respect and admire."

His eyes met hers. A challenge in his gaze she wasn't ready to face. "Richard don't. This is good. For all of us."

Their hands were next to each other in the seat of the booth. Richard softly brushed his fingers over the back of her hand. "If you say so, Yvonne."

He got the look in his eye that said he was going along with her bullshit again. Along with a look that said he wasn't going to go along with it for long. Richard was going to push eventually. Instead of making her angry, the idea sent a rush of exhilaration through her.

Yvonne snatched her hand away. "Whatever, Richard. Let's get Jacob home and in bed."

He slid over and out of the booth and stepped back so she could get up. "I'll get him from the playground and tell him it's time to go home," he said.

Only after he walked away did she realize when she'd said home, she'd thought of him being there with her and Jacob, and that her hand still tingled from where he'd brushed against it.

Chapter 17

"Who was that man and don't tell me it was Nathan's friend."

Bree hit Yvonne up two minutes after she got in the office. Yvonne knew this was coming. Not only was Bree always straightforward, she was a big fan of Yvonne and Nathan.

"He's the head of the W.E.W. Network." Yvonne said, sipping her coffee. At least Bree had waited until Yvonne had coffee in her hand before bombarding her with questions.

The answer was obviously not what Bree expected because she seemed to deflate a little. "Oh."

"Who did you expect me to say he was?" Yvonne asked.

Going with a part of the truth was better than going through with a lie. Later, when she Nathan and Richard decided on the best way to release Richard's real relationship with Jacob, then she'd deal with explaining more to Bree. For now, she had too much to straighten out on her own without getting grilled by her admin. Once again, she'd dreamed last night. Once again, she'd woken up with memories of being in Richard's arms flooding her system.

Bree crossed her arms. "Well, I don't know. From the way he looked at you."

"He was showing me pictures of his daughter. I was talking about Jacob. That's all that was going on."

Bree pulled on her ear. "Alright, I'm sorry. I saw him and you and you both looked kind of . . . I don't know. Into each other, and I got worried."

"Why would you worry? You know I'm engaged to Nathan."

"I know, and you two are great together."

"But?" She definitely heard a "but" in that statement.

Bree shrugged. "But nothing. I was being silly. So, did he say anything new about the show?"

"Just that he's excited to work with me and Nathan. After you left, we talked about the interview with *Southern Living* this afternoon. He said he can't wait to read the article."

Bree seemed relieved. "Good. Sorry if I made it weird when I popped over."

"You didn't make it weird because nothing weird was going on," Yvonne said confidently.

Bree nodded and uncrossed her arms. "Right. Do you need anything from me this morning? I've got a meeting with Nancy Harmon about her guest house. Were you okay with the final design?"

"Yes, you did a good job incorporating her recycled artwork. She should be excited about the concept."

"Thank you! Hey, look, again sorry about yesterday. I shouldn't have even implied anything was going on there. I know you love Nathan. You two are perfect together."

Yvonne forced herself to smile. Bree hadn't been out of line. There was something there. The old attraction Richard brought up and tried to get her to discuss before. The attraction she wanted to look the other way and ignore. She and Nathan were perfect. Everyone kept saying they were.

Everyone could see it. They were role models. A couple people could look up to.

"Don't worry about it."

Bree left, and Yvonne lost herself in work. She worked on a few projects, returned phone calls and emails, and set up a few meetings for the following week. Business continued to pick up thanks to the news of the upcoming television show. The network was currently looking for potential homes for her and Nathan to renovate for the show. They had a meeting with the producers in a few weeks to go over details of prospects. Yvonne sifted through a few of her current clients who'd mentioned possible renovations in the future. She may tap into that arena to see if there was any interest.

The morning went by quickly, and before she knew it the time to leave and meet Nathan and the reporter for the interview had come. They were doing it at Nathan's house. A good way to show off the work he'd done and get a feel for them in a comfortable environment.

Her cell phone chimed just as she was shutting things down and getting ready to leave. A text message from Richard.

Good luck with the interview.

He remembered. She smiled. He'd always been that way. Remembering when she had something important coming up.

Thanks. She texted back.

She waited for more. Nothing else came, but her smile remained as she left the office.

Nathan ran his hand down her back. "You okay?"

She jumped and heat spread across her cheeks. She felt guilty and she hadn't even done anything. Well, she'd been thinking about the little things Richard used to do when she'd been nervous or excited about something upcoming. The flowers he'd sent her the afternoon after a brutal exam. The note he'd left on her car that said, "I love you and you got this" the morning when she'd had an interview with a designer she wanted to work for. When he'd called to check and make sure everything was okay when she'd had to fly to Atlanta for the weekend because her mom was sick.

One stupid text message and she remembered some of the good things about them being together. She was being an idiot. One text message shouldn't have her looking back with rose colored glasses.

"I'm fine, just distracted. It was a long morning."

He kissed her temple. "Try to focus. She may try to find a weakness to exploit," he whispered in her ear.

Yvonne pulled away. "Do we have a weakness to exploit?"

Nathan's neck and face reddened. "No!" he said quickly. His eyes darting away.

What the hell was that about? Then it hit her. Richard was their weakness. She may be distracted, but she wasn't going to be so unfocused as to bring up her history with Richard.

The reporter, Robin Ellis, walked over to them. She'd been strolling around Nathan's backyard, capturing photos of the gazebo he'd built along with pictures of them.

"This place is amazing," Robin said, grinning. "Nathan, you really are handy."

"Thank you," Nathan said easily. "I love working with my hands. Luckily, I was able to make a living doing just that."

They settled around the glass table on Nathan's patio. Robin put a recording device on the table between them and used a stylus to take notes on her tablet. "Will you two live here after the wedding?"

Yvonne was shaking her head when Nathan answered. "Yes. I want to start my life with Yvonne right here in the home I renovated for my family."

Robin's eyes lit up. She beamed at Yvonne. "Are you excited about moving into Nathan's home?"

She hadn't thought about moving into Nathan's home, because they hadn't discussed it. She loved her place. It was close to her mom which made picking up Jacob from school easier for her mom. Moving would mean she'd lose that convenience and Jacob would be forced to change schools.

"I'm excited about our future together. No matter where we live," she said. Not wanting to contradict Nathan in front of the reporter.

He rubbed her back again. When she looked at him there was an apology in his eyes. He knew he'd spoken out of turn. She relaxed a little. They could discuss this later.

"Now that you have an offer with W.E.W. do you have plans to delay the wedding?"

"Why would we?" Nathan answered. "The television show is just another aspect of our jobs. We wouldn't let our work delay our wedding, therefore the show shouldn't either. In fact, our fans may get a treat and catch glimpses of our wedding during the show."

"Oh really! That would be great," Robin said taking frantic notes.

Another news flash for Yvonne. She didn't want the media anywhere near their wedding. She wanted things to be private between them. So much of their relationship had been public. Their introduction, courtship, and even their sex life. Their wedding should be a private affair between them and their families.

"That's not set in stone, yet," Yvonne chimed in. "We're still debating that. I do like the idea of keeping the ceremony itself private."

"I can understand that," Robin agreed. "You both have been instant sensations since you met on the set of *Celebrity Housewives*. Your attraction was instant, and yet your relationship is viewed as a sweet exception to the rule in today's hypersexual society. What do you say to that?"

"We want to be role models," Nathan said instantly. "To

show people it's important to build a foundation before rushing into anything."

"Oh, really?" Robin said.

"Mostly it was our personal choice," Yvonne replied. "Nathan is a man who believes in traditions and building a strong base in everything he does. I've chosen to respect his decision."

"Are you saying you don't want to wait?" Robin asked eagerly.

Nathan took her hand in his. "We both are committed to this. It wasn't one of us pushing our beliefs on the other. We talked about this and we both wanted to build a friendship first. Yvonne has a son and we wanted to set a good example for him of what real love is about."

"Real love?" Robin raised a brow. "Are you saying people who chose to do differently than you aren't really in love?"

"I'm saying emotions and desires can lead people to make hasty decisions they regret later," Nathan answered. "We were very deliberate about our relationship. Yvonne knows I am with her because I love her. Not just because I lust for her. I won't abandon her, and she won't have to worry about me leaving her because I fell for someone else. She knows I'm a man of character and a man of my word." He looked Yvonne in her eye. "I'm not like the other men who've hurt her in the past."

"Well, sounds like you're saying you're better than the men she's known before," Robin prompted.

Nathan's smile was full of cocky swagger. A look she'd never seen on him before, and one she wasn't sure she liked. "Well if the shoe fits."

Robin laughed. Nathan joined. Yvonne tried to force a smile but couldn't. She slipped her hand away from his.

"Nathan isn't like the other men I've dated, but that doesn't make him better or worse. We've all had disappointments in our past. Just because one person disappointed or hurt you doesn't necessarily make them a bad person. Things happen that can be out of our control. How we bounce back after a tough relationship is what's really important."

"Good point," Robin said. "But you have to admit you're happier with Nathan. He is the man you're marrying."

Was she happier with Nathan? He looked at her with worry in his eyes. Her heart did a jackhammer impersonation. He was the man she was marrying. She had to be happier with him.

"Yes," she said in a rush. "I am."

Nathan relaxed next to her. Robin glanced at him quickly then took notes. Damn, that couldn't be good. She expected a follow up question, but instead Robin took the conversation back to the show and their plans for it. She and Nathan relaxed into easy conversation once they talked about their creative hopes and the earlier awkwardness was forgotten. By the time Robin left, Yvonne felt confident the interview had gone pretty good, but there were some things she and Nathan needed to get straight.

"Nathan, you never told me you wanted us to move in here with you," she said after Robin was gone and they sat on his couch.

"Where else would we stay?" he said as if the idea of staying at her place, or anywhere else for that matter, was as foreign a concept as mermaids on the moon.

"I thought we'd find a place together. Somewhere we both felt comfortable."

"You don't feel comfortable here?"

"I do, but it's not my home. Jacob would have to change schools. My mom wouldn't be as close."

"I thought that would be a plus," he said grinning.

Any other time she'd agree, but having her mother's help wasn't a small deal. Nathan's parents lived in Portland. They were great and had treated Jacob sweetly, but they weren't here. Nathan didn't understand how helpful having a reliable grandparent nearby could be.

"Nathan, I'm serious. My mom helps out a lot with Jacob."

"You won't need her help after we're married. I can pick him up, and we can hire a live-in nanny. Picking Jacob up from school can be part of her job."

"I don't want a nanny picking him up from school or living here taking care of him."

"Yvonne, we'll be traveling a lot. Not just for the show but also with my job. A nanny will be helpful when we're busy and when we have our own children."

"First of all, Jacob is our child. If we have more kids, they all will be our children."

He rubbed the back of her neck. "I didn't mean it that way. You know I love Jacob and consider him my family."

Yvonne relaxed a little. She'd once been sure of that. "Jacob won't understand if suddenly I'm out of the picture and a nanny takes over. My mom dotes on Jacob. I want him to always be surrounded by love."

"You're acting like I'm asking you to send him off to boarding school. It's just a nanny, Yvonne." He stood and dragged his fingers through his hair.

"Maybe to you, but to me it's my preference. I prefer not to have a live-in nanny. I prefer to take Jacob to school and pick him up. I prefer having my mom pick him up from school if I can't. Why can't you understand that?"

"I'm trying to make things easier for you. You've worked so hard for so long. Let me help."

She stood and placed her hand on his hip. "This isn't something I need help with. It's not a part of my life I'm struggling with. We're supposed to be a partnership, but so far everything has been your way."

"What are you talking about? I've put up with Richard coming back."

She stepped away from him. "Put up with him? How about helping me deal with a major change in my and Jacob's life."

Nathan sighed and reached for her. He pulled her into his arms. "Hey, I'm sorry. I didn't mean it like that."

"Then how do you mean it?" She didn't pull out of his arms. She needed to feel them around her. She needed reassurance that they were okay.

"I am here for you, and I want you to be happy in this. Nothing's set in stone. We've got time to decide what we do next." He kissed her forehead. "I'm sorry. I love you. Things have been busy. We haven't spent a lot of time alone together. I made assumptions, but this is why we're talking. Why we built a friendship. We can work together to figure everything out." He leaned back to meet her eyes. "Will you forgive me?"

His eyes were so apologetic. His body warm and steady. Some of her concerns drifted away. "As long as you agree there are still things we need to decide."

He kissed her. Softly and slowly and perfectly. She tasted the apology on his lips. Felt his need to move past this argument and get back to being the couple everyone loved. She would have typically felt comforted by his kiss. Right now, she wondered if it was a ploy.

"I'm sorry. I love you." He said against her lips.

Her resolve weakened. April was still a long time away. They had plenty of time to work out the details. Nathan would come around because he loved her.

She nodded, squeezed him tight, and melted into the kiss. "I love you, too."

Chapter 18

"I'm thinking of having a July fourth cookout," Yvonne said to her mom and sister the next afternoon.

Valerie looked up from scrolling through her phone. Her sister had come over to talk about the design of her office. She liked the ideas Yvonne had given her and now she was ready to start making purchases. As soon as their mom found out she and Valerie were hanging out she'd decided to come over as well.

"Why?" Rochelle asked. "Shouldn't you be focused on making wedding plans?"

"I have plenty of time to make wedding plans," Yvonne replied. "I think it will be a good time to get everyone together."

Valerie set her phone down and gave Yvonne her full attention. "Everyone like who?"

"Us, Nathan, and Richard," she said brightly.

"No." Rochelle said with a wave of her hand. "Absolutely not."

Yvonne had thought this through and decided the time

had come. Richard had mentioned offhand that she and Jacob should come to D.C. for the holiday. Nathan suggested grilling at his place or going to the beach. Her mom wanted them to go to the church social. Basically, whomever Yvonne chose to spend the holiday with would cause problems with someone else. The solution: host the holiday at her home.

"Absolutely, yes!" Valerie said sitting up straight. "I'm here all day if you're going to have a family cookout with both Richard and Nathan here."

Yvonne appreciated her sister's support, even if she was there for the potential drama. "Richard and Nathan should spend more time together."

"Have you been hit with a stupid stick?" Rochelle exclaimed. "You don't need to keep bringing those two men together. You need to keep them separate. They are different parts of your life that don't need to cross."

"I disagree," Valerie said calmly. She held up a hand in a give-me-a-second gesture when Rochelle looked affronted. "If Yvonne is marrying Nathan and Richard is going to continue to be a part of Jacob's life, getting them together makes sense. These will be the two most influential men in his life and he should see they can get along."

"Thank you!" Yvonne said. "I don't want them to walk on eggshells around each other or feel as if I'm picking sides."

"But you have to pick a side," her mom said. "You can't treat them equally. Like it or not, Nathan will be your husband and that gives him a leg up on Richard."

"How so?" Valerie asked. "He doesn't own or control her."

"Maybe not, but he is the man she's chosen to spend the rest of her life with," Rochelle said with a haughty lift of her chin. "That could be fifty or more years. Until death do them part. Meaning, if you want to make it to forever with your husband, then you got to be willing to put in the work to make your marriage successful. Another man's feelings don't count for anything." Rochelle's head tilted to the side and she considered Yvonne with a critical look. "Your feelings for another man don't count for anything. Not if you want to keep your husband."

"I want to keep Nathan, but I don't want to discount Richard's feelings. He is Jacob's father. He will always be a part of our lives and I want him to feel comfortable."

Rochelle shook her head. "That's where you're messing up. He shouldn't feel comfortable in your home because it isn't *his* place to feel comfortable." Rochelle slapped her hands together with the words. "Your home won't be your home anymore. It'll be your and Nathan's home. He can be a guest in your place but that is it. Never comfortable. As soon as you make another man feel comfortable in your home, then he feels as if he has a right to have a say in what goes on within those walls. And a right to other things in your house." Rochelle pursed her lips and looked Yvonne up and down as if she were the *other* things Richard would feel owed to him.

Heat shot up Yvonne's face. "That won't be the case if we have boundaries. He will have a say in what happens with Jacob because he's his father. If we can all get along now then making decisions together later will be easier."

Rochelle rolled her eyes. Valerie sighed and shrugged. "I hear what you're saying, Yvonne, and I agree with you." She pointed a finger when Yvonne opened her mouth to thank her sister. "But I also see Mom's point. While I don't believe you're offering anything else to Richard, I do agree you have to make it clear early on that while Richard might be welcome in your home, he shouldn't get too comfortable."

"He's not too comfortable now."

Valerie grimaced. "I don't know. He's there almost every night when he's in town. He's tucking Jacob into bed. He's helping you make dinner."

"He's what?" Rochelle looked at Yvonne as if her head rotated three hundred degrees.

Yvonne returned her mother's glare. "Only on the day

you left him alone with Jacob. Talk about making someone feel welcome."

"There was an emergency at the church," Rochelle replied. Her eyes fluttered away from Yvonne's.

"What kind of emergency? You are not a member of the Richard fan club so I'm surprised you felt comfortable leaving him there with Jacob."

"I know the man isn't going to hurt him," Rochelle defended. "He's crazy about Jacob, which is his one redeeming quality."

At least her mom gave Richard that much credit. "You still haven't answered what was going on at the church that was so important."

Rochelle shifted in the chair, patted her hair and brushed at her pants leg. Yvonne and Valerie exchanged confused looks. That had to have been some emergency.

Valerie waved her fingers in the come-on fashion. "Spill it."

"Spill what?" Rochelle asked.

"You're acting way too weird about a church emergency," Valerie said. "Any other time you'd be happy to tell us what's going on over there."

"There was a board meeting," Rochelle said. "As the church secretary, I had to be there."

Oh no, there was more to that story. Yvonne wasn't buying it. "Mom, you've skipped board meetings before or been late. Now will you just tell us what's going on."

"Fine," Rochelle said with a heavy sigh. She met Yvonne's eye. "Your dad was back in town. He wanted to meet with some of his old friends from the church. He may come back as a guest pastor during our August revival."

Yvonne felt as if her mom had kicked the chair out from under her. The air rushed out of her lungs. Her body hurt. Indignation rose up with anger. "Why didn't you tell me?"

"You didn't need to know," Rochelle said with such firm assurance that for a second Yvonne felt unsure for even asking.

A quick second. "I didn't need to know? Mom, you couldn't tell me my dad was in town? What if I wanted to see him?"

"He didn't want to see you. I know because I asked him. He has his own family, and as he told me in the nicest way possible, let's not go stirring up dust that's settled."

Dust that's settled? Is that all she was to her dad? Dust settled into the hidden corners of his life that weren't to be disturbed?

"See," Rochelle said shaking her head. "This is why I didn't want to tell you. Now you're looking all sick and hurt. Get over it, child. Your dad was good at two things, preaching and getting women into bed with him. I fell for his slick lines and lost everything." Rochelle's hand balled into a fist on the table. "I could be living the life Linda has. I could be going to the fancy banquets and taking the expensive vacations. Not working as a church secretary and watching my daughter make the same mistakes I did."

Yvonne bit her lip, refusing to follow her mom down the road of self-pity. She wanted to point out that if Rochelle had never fallen for a slick guy's lines she wouldn't be here. Valerie picked up her phone and started scrolling. She tended to clam up whenever Rochelle brought up her dad. Valerie was stuck in the hard place between the two. They both knew there was nothing they could say that would make Rochelle feel better or accept the mistakes of her past.

Rochelle deflated after her outburst and her daughter's refusal to engage. She checked her watch. "I've got to get to the grocery store before it's too late." She stood and snatched up her purse. "I'll say goodbye to Jacob on my way out. You have your cookout if you want. Don't listen to what I have to say. It's your life to screw up however you want. But believe me when I tell you that even though Richard may say all the right things, and start to look like a chance at something you don't have with Nathan, he left you once and he'll leave you again."

Yvonne dropped her head into her hands after her mom left. "She's so ..."

"I know," Valerie said. "I think if Dad would have become a bum, she'd be okay with what happened."

Yvonne hated to admit it, but Valerie was right. Rochelle didn't miss her ex-husband's love. She missed the money and security that came with the success he'd found after their divorce.

"I can make this work between Nathan and Richard," she said firmly.

Valerie's smile was a mixture of support and good luck. "We're going to make this the best cookout ever."

"Can you invite Eva and her boyfriend?"

Valerie frowned. "Why would you want that drama there?"

"More people. The more people who are there the easier it'll be for people to get along and less likely to make a scene."

"Mmmm, I don't think it works like that. You ever been to a club? Lots of people and fights tend to break out."

Yvonne nodded and got more excited about the idea. "Yeah ... that's the key. More people there."

"One problem, more people means more people who are likely to make the connection between you and Richard. We are keeping that a secret, right?"

Yvonne deflated. "We are. Fine, we'll make it work with just family. Everything will be fine, and we'll prove to Mom we can all get along."

Valerie nodded in solidarity. "Yep. It'll be like a Disney movie." Then Valerie laughed. "You ever noticed how someone usually dies in those fairytales?"

Yvonne glared. Flashes of Bambi's mom, Mufasa, and Princess Tiana's father filtered through her mind. She shook her head. "Shut up. No one will die. It'll be perfect."

Chapter 19

The doorbell rang early on July fourth and Yvonne's stomach was a mess of unnatural flutters, nervous clenching, and good old-fashioned nausea. She took a deep breath and stared at her front door. She crossed her fingers and looked skyward.

Please let today go well.

"Mommy, answer the door." Jacob ran past her to the door.

She jerked her gaze off the ceiling and focused on Jacob. He bounced on the balls of his feet. An excited grin split his cute face. When Richard asked if his family could come she couldn't think of a reason to say no. Jacob had another grandmother, a sister, and an uncle. He couldn't wait to meet them and had talked non-stop about getting to play with his sister when she came to town.

"I'm going to answer the door," she said, trying to hide her nerves with a smile.

"I can't wait to see Dad. I've got to tell him how much better I got at t-ball."

"I think he knows," she said with a genuine laugh. Jacob

insisted on video chatting with Richard whenever he was back in D.C. She'd expected the routine to eventually stop, but Richard looked forward to hearing Jacob's stories about what happened in his day almost as much as Jacob loved telling them.

Jacob unlocked and opened the door before she could. Clearly, he was not in the mood to wait for his mommy to get her act together. Yvonne hurried forward to greet her guests.

Richard stood on the porch in a grey crew neck shirt and dark shorts. Which made her notice the width of his shoulders and the length of his legs. Their eyes connected. He gave her a nervous smile. They shared a moment of solidarity that made her own nerves settle. They could do this.

She recognized his brother Michael. They'd met once or twice before when she and Richard were together. He and Richard were similar in height and build except Michael's dark eyes sparkled with mischief. The playboy younger brother, as Valerie described him.

She'd never met his mom, but the resemblance was there in her brown eyes and direct measuring stare. His mom's hair was dreaded with goddess locks she'd pulled back into an intricate twist at the back of her neck. Her tasteful light green linen shirt and shorts perfectly complemented her golden-brown skin. Her hands rested almost protectively on the shoulders of a little girl. Nadia.

Yvonne smiled at Richard's daughter. The girl's big bright eyes were the color of honey and her curly hair was collected in a cute puff at the top of her head. She studied Yvonne warily with one finger in her mouth as she leaned back against her grandmother.

"Hey," Richard said. "I hope we're not too early."

"Not at all," Yvonne answered. "I was just about to get the grill started. Come in."

She waved everyone inside. Jacob was unexpectedly quiet

when faced with everyone. He grabbed Yvonne's hand and watched his new family members enter the home with wide, curious eyes. Once in the living room, Richard proceeded with the introductions.

He stepped forward and waved Jacob to him. "Jacob, this is your Grandmother Sharon, Uncle Michael, and your sister Nadia."

Jacob didn't let go of Yvonne as he slid his small hand in Richard's. Yvonne gave his hand a reassuring squeeze. "Hi," he said in a small, nervous voice.

"Hey, little man. Nice to meet you," Michael said in a friendly voice. "You think you can help me and your dad on the grill today?"

Jacob relaxed and nodded. "Mommy said I can carry out the hamburgers," Jacob said proudly.

Michael gave him a thumbs up. "I knew you looked like a man with a plan."

Jacob grinned up at Yvonne then back at his uncle. Yvonne let out a long breath. Michael hadn't been a fan of hers. He'd thought Richard should have stayed with Natalie because of the ties her family's business brought to theirs. She'd worried he wouldn't be friendly with Jacob.

Sharon stepped forward next. Her eyes were bright, and she blinked several times. Yvonne was shocked to see the woman holding back tears.

"It's so great to meet you, Jacob," she said, emotion thick in her voice. "I can't wait to get to know you better."

Jacob nodded and eased a little closer to Richard. "Dad says you make really great cookies."

Sharon smiled with pride. "The best, and I brought some for you."

Jacob bounced on his feet. Yvonne wasn't sure how involved Sharon had been in hiding things from Richard. The emotion she barely suppressed made it seem as if she hadn't known or deeply regretted keeping the secret. She'd give

Sharon the chance to prove herself before trusting her. This introduction wouldn't have had to be delayed for years if Richard's family hadn't been so willing to block her out.

"Nadia?" Richard held out his hand to her.

Nadia took Richard's hand. She looked at Jacob with unveiled interest. "I'm Nadia."

Yvonne squeezed Jacob's hand again. He wasn't a big fan of girls, but he had been interested in the idea of having a sister. "Hey. Do you play t-ball?"

"I can play anything," Nadia said with confidence that had to have been inherited from her dad.

Jacob loved a challenge. "Well, come on then."

Nadia looked at her dad who nodded and then the two kids ran out the back door to play.

"Well, that was easy," Yvonne said to Richard.

He slid closer to her. "Things are always easier with kids. It's us adults who mess everything up."

Something in his voice hit her. Regret and yearning. Not obvious, but a subtle undercurrent in his words. "That's why we're trying to fix those mistakes."

"So, Yvonne," Michael interrupted. "Long time no see."

She jerked her attention from Richard and back to his brother. "Michael, good seeing you again," Yvonne said politely. Friendly but not necessarily genuine.

"Especially when we didn't think we'd see each other again," Michael said.

Yvonne's jaw hardened. "No, I guess we didn't."

Sharon slapped the back of Michael's head. "Stop being a smarty pants. This situation is already difficult without you making it worse." She looked at Yvonne apologetically.

The doorbell rang again. "I'll get that!" Yvonne hurried back to the door. "Richard, there are drinks in the cooler out back. You all go out and get settled."

Valerie was at the door. "Thank God you're here!" Yvonne said.

Valerie grinned, held up a six pack of beer and crossed the threshold. "I figured he'd show up early and I'm here for moral support."

Yvonne wrapped her arms around her sister. She took the beer when she pulled back. "I owe you for this."

"I know. That's why you're designing my new office. Mom is coming later. She's nosey as hell to meet Richard's family, but coming early would make it look like she approves of this blending. Is Nathan here yet?"

"He's coming later. He's bringing Cassidy, and apparently she won't be ready until after one." She tried not to sound annoyed.

"Really?" Valerie asked, letting her own annoyance show. "He couldn't come over and be here when you greeted Richard's family? Some united front."

"Cassidy needs a ride. Her car is acting up. It's no big deal."

Except it was a big deal. She'd wanted Nathan at her side from the very beginning. She'd even asked him to spend the night to make sure he'd be there. Except he'd gotten back late from Savannah and then his sister needed the ride. Thank goodness for great sisters who came through.

They went to the back porch. Richard was already at the grill with his brother lighting the coals. His mom had started spreading out the placemats Yvonne had put on the patio table and opened the umbrella. All things Yvonne had planned to do herself. A wave of appreciation went through her. They didn't have to step in and get things started, but she appreciated that they did.

"Damn," Valerie said looking at Richard and Michael. "Nathan better get in here quick, because Richard has already made himself at home in your house."

Sharon caught Yvonne in the kitchen just as Richard and Michael were putting the ribs and chicken on the grill. She'd been nice. A lot nicer than Yvonne had expected. Valerie had given Yvonne a thumbs up after talking to her. Michael was being okay, as well. If he still didn't like her, he wasn't showing it.

Yvonne went into the kitchen to make tea and lemonade while Valerie talked to Michael about the property she'd sold him a few years before. She was in the middle of texting Nathan to see how much longer he'd be when Sharon came into the kitchen.

"Jacob is a sweet boy," Sharon said. "You did a great job with him."

"I tried my best. Thankfully, my mom and sister stepped in to help me. Even if that included spoiling him."

Her mom was on the way. She'd called Yvonne a few minutes earlier to let her know that, and to find out who was there. As soon as Yvonne said Jacob's other grandmother was there, she'd practically smelled the burning rubber of her mom's car tires in her haste to get over here.

Sharon leaned against the counter near Yvonne. "That's what family is for, I guess. Try not to hold it against me when I spoil him, too. I always wished I would have had more kids, but after I got pregnant with Michael so quickly after Richard, I felt overwhelmed and didn't think I'd want more. When they hit the teenage years, I immediately regretted my decision. Now I look forward to lots of grandchildren."

Yvonne tried to imagine Jacob as a teenager and had a mini panic attack. Her baby was only six, but those six years had gone by so quickly. She'd blink and another ten will have passed. She hadn't thought about having more kids while she'd been in the throes of raising Jacob. She knew Nathan wanted kids, and she did too. "I can understand that."

"I don't know why my husband decided to keep you and Jacob hidden from me," Sharon said in a sad, angry voice.

Yvonne stopped in the middle of stirring sugar into the lemonade. She'd assumed the entire family had wanted to save Richard from her so that he could marry someone more influential. Seeing the delight, and sadness, on Sharon's face when she'd first met Jacob had made Yvonne doubt Sharon would have wanted to be kept away.

"You had no idea?" Yvonne asked.

Sharon shook her head. One of her hands balled into a fist that she pressed against her abdomen. "I learned a lot of things about my husband after he died. How much he tried to *protect* us from things. He was a proud man who only thought about legacy and money regardless of how his aim at meeting those goals affected the other members of his family. When Richard told me about Jacob... when he accused me of knowing." Sharon shook her head. "I never would have kept my son away from his child. Regardless of how I may have felt about that child's mother."

"If your husband knew how much you wanted grandkids maybe telling you would have meant keeping me in Richard's life. We both know he didn't want that."

Sharon sighed and wiped at the corner of her eye. "I'll be honest, when I first heard Richard broke things off with Natalie, I thought it was cold feet. Especially, when his dad expressed concerns that he'd moved on too quickly afterwards."

"I can't say I disagree. Richard and I got together too soon after his breakup." Yvonne tasted the lemonade. The tangy sweetness similar to her thoughts about her past relationship with Richard.

Sharon pushed away from the counter and shook her head. "I don't think so. I saw the difference in him after he and Natalie got back together. I look back now and realize he wasn't happy, but he was doing what he thought was right. I thought he did the right thing. It wasn't until later that I realized he shouldn't have married Natalie."

"But he did," Yvonne said, hardening her heart against the feelings his mother's words stirred up. She tried not to be mad about Richard going back to Natalie anymore. Of course, he'd tried to do the right thing. The second he'd said Natalie was pregnant she'd known she'd lost him forever. She'd been the one to fan the flames of hope that he'd answer her calls and come back to her after learning she was pregnant. When that hope burned out, the scar tissue ran deep.

"I don't think he would have married her if he'd known about you," Sharon said.

"If he'd wanted to know he could have. But none of that matters. He knows now. Jacob is thrilled and that's all that matters to me."

"Richard is thrilled, too," Sharon said. "Jacob is ninety percent of that, but I think there's a little bit of excitement about you, too."

Her heart was not beating faster. She did not care. "Well, we're both trying to make things work. For Jacob's sake."

Sharon nodded and smiled, but that didn't hide the disappointment in her eyes. "I just want my son to be happy. So, where is this fiancé of yours?"

Yvonne heard the front door opening, followed by Nathan calling. "Hello!"

"That's him now," she said cheerily. She excused herself and hurried to the front of the house.

Nathan and Cassidy met her halfway, bags of groceries in their hands. "Hey, what's all this?"

Nathan leaned over and kissed her cheek. "Just a few things for the cookout."

"What kind of things?" Yvonne took a few bags from Cassidy who thanked her.

"Burgers, hot dogs, steaks, and ribs," Nathan answered as they made their way into the kitchen.

Sharon stepped out of the way as they entered and put down the items Nathan brought. When all the bags were down Nathan glanced at Sharon, then at Yvonne curiously.

"Nathan, this is Richard's mom Sharon." She walked over

and wrapped an arm around Nathan's waist. "Sharon, this is the fiancé you've been asking about, and his sister, Cassidy."

Sharon and Nathan shook hands. "I hope you have a lot more people coming because that is a lot of food."

"Plenty of to-go plates," Yvonne said.

Nathan gave her a curious glance. "I told you I had the meat."

"I know, but I wanted to get started early. I knew you were in Savannah yesterday and didn't want you to worry. Richard and his brother Michael are already grilling chicken."

Nathan's body went rigid beneath her arms. "Richard is on the grill?"

She slid her arm away from him. What was he upset about? Did he expect her to just wait for him to finally arrive with Cassidy hours after she planned to start cooking?

"Yes, Valerie is out there with them, too. Mom is on the way."

Nathan grunted. "Nice." He smiled, but there wasn't a hint of happiness in his eyes.

The sound of a beer can being opened interrupted whatever Yvonne would have said. They all turned to Cassidy, who lifted the can in her hand.

"Here's to a day of fun and family," she took a long sip. "I'm going out to say hello." She strolled out of the kitchen and onto the back porch.

Sharon's brows drew together. "I think I'll join her."

"What's up with Cassidy?" Yvonne asked when they were alone.

Nathan ran a hand through his hair. "The guy I warned her about turned out to be just as much of an asshole as I told her he would be. She's already tipsy."

"Already?" Yvonne looked at the clock. Yep, it was only two.

"I've got to keep an eye on her. I guess it's a good thing Richard is already handling the grill for me."

"He's not handling the grill for you. He's helping me out. He got here early."

"With his entire family." Nathan said sarcastically.

"I told you his family was coming," she shot back. "Why are you upset?"

Nathan shook his head. "It's nothing... Cassidy put me in a mood." He came over and kissed her forehead. "Forget it. I'll play nice." He looked out of the window and frowned. "Starting by keeping your ex's brother off my sister."

Nathan spun away and rushed out of the house. Yvonne looked out the window. Michael and Cassidy were talking. Cassidy was running her hand over Michael's shirt. Yvonne slapped a hand to her forehead. Why the hell had she thought a big family cookout was a good idea?

Chapter 20

Her mom had been right. Yvonne hated to admit it, but about an hour after everyone arrived she realized that dumping everyone together in the hopes that things would work themselves out may not have been the best plan. Not because anyone was outright rude or anything, but the tension between Richard and Nathan was obvious and palpable.

When Nathan commented on how "helpful" Richard was being by working the grill, Richard had offered to give up the spot if it would make Nathan feel better. Which resulted in Nathan telling Richard to keep at it instead of looking as if he were uncomfortable with Richard on the grill.

Nathan was also being more touchy-feely with Yvonne. He held her hand constantly. From one end of the yard to the other. If they were in each other's vicinity, Nathan had her hand in his. She was pretty sure her fingers would shrivel up like prunes from the sweat the constant clasping created.

When Nathan wasn't trying to show that he and Yvonne

were a couple, he watched and frowned at Cassidy. Yvonne wasn't sure if Cassidy was genuinely attracted to Michael, or if she was coming on to him because of her recent breakup and to get a rise out of her brother. Whatever her reasons were, it was working. Michael's interest was definitely sparked if the flirty gleam in his eye meant anything, and Nathan's face turned red with anger every time he spotted the two of them together.

He needed a distraction, and Yvonne did not want her cookout ruined by him and Cassidy eventually fighting in front of everyone.

Yvonne tugged on Nathan's hand. He pulled his attention away from where Cassidy and Michael played Cornhole with Nadia and Jacob. Michael was partnered with Nadia and Cassidy with Jacob and their trash talking was punctuated with a lot of sly touches, long looks, and flirty smiles.

"Valerie is starting a game of cards." She pointed to where her sister sat on the patio with Richard and Sharon. Valerie held up the deck and waved them over. "Want to play?"

Nathan's hold on her tightened slightly. "What are they playing?"

"Let's go find out." She pulled on his hand.

He hesitated a second before following. He glanced over his shoulder at Cassidy and Michael again. Yvonne couldn't stop herself from rolling her eyes.

"Hey, will you give it a rest already," she said.

Nathan stopped and faced her. "Give what a rest?"

"Stop hovering over Cassidy and judging everything she's doing. You're acting more like a jealous boyfriend than a concerned brother."

His head jerked back. His face flushed, and he shook his head. "Sorry, it's just." He sighed. "She's been drinking, and I know she's upset. I don't want her falling into bed with Richard's brother because she's in a low place."

He said Richard's brother as if Cassidy would be falling in

bed with a troll. While she wouldn't have considered hooking Cassidy up with Michael, as it would be too close to home to have Nathan's sister dating her ex's brother, she wouldn't have discouraged her either. Michael may not have liked her much back then, but as far as she knew he wasn't a complete asshole.

"Cassidy is an adult and can make her own decisions. We'll both watch and if it looks like she's had too much to drink you can take her home. For now, it's just harmless flirting. Can we please move on, so you can relax and help me get through this afternoon?"

Nathan relaxed and cupped her cheek in his hand. "Yes. I'm sorry." He smiled and kissed her quickly.

He glanced over his shoulder again as they continued toward Valerie. Yvonne pretended not to notice. She'd known he was old-fashioned and conservative in his values back when they'd gone on their first date. She couldn't act surprised now when his sister was popping beer cans every half hour and flirting with the brother of the man he felt threatened by.

No, Nathan was not threatened by Richard. Where had that thought come from? He didn't trust Richard, that was different. She met Richard's eye as they approached. He kept his expression neutral, but she recognized the question in his eye. The what's-up-with-your-man question. She looked away before he read her answer—he's being overprotective and stupid—in her own gaze.

"You guys ready to lose at spades?" Valerie asked.

Richard laughed and tugged on the front of his shirt. "Oh, you're already talking trash. I see it runs in the family."

Yvonne pulled her hand from Nathan's and held it to her chest. "I know you're not talking about me because I don't talk trash, I speak the truth."

"Okay!" Valerie held up her hand, and Yvonne gave her a high five.

Richard waved his hand back and forth in front of his

neck. "Nah, don't even come at me with that. Sit down and take this beating."

Yvonne grinned as she sat in the chair next to Richard. Completely caught up in the rush of his competitiveness. Getting the best of Richard was something she'd never been able to resist. Watching the always composed and professional businessman let loose whenever they were together used to be the highlight of her day. Something she'd known he hadn't been able to do with anyone else.

"How about I sit down, and me and my sister can deliver you this beating."

Richard put his hand on the back of her chair and met her eyes. "You know you can't beat me." His voice lowered with his determination.

Yvonne leaned closer to him. "How much you want to bet?"

His stare lowered to her lips. The corner of his mouth tilted up wistfully. When he met her gaze again heat flashed in his eyes. "You can't pay my price."

The fire that rushed through her veins was swift and intense. Her pulse quickened. Her breathing hitched. His wistful smile melted away. His eyes remained focused, searching, encouraged.

Nathan placed his hands on Yvonne's shoulders. "You know what. I don't think it's fair to put Yvonne and Valerie on the same team. They're sisters and I've seen them play together. They cheat." He squeezed Yvonne's shoulders. "How about me and you partner up, baby. Let Richard play with Valerie."

Yvonne jerked her gaze away from Richard. Her sister's face was blank. Too blank. Sharon hid a smile behind her hand. Rochelle looked like her head was about to explode.

"Yes," Rochelle said nodding frantically. "That's a very good idea."

Heat rushed up Yvonne's face. She placed her hand over

Nathan's. "Sure. Let's show them what we've got." Her voice sounded reedy and thin.

Nathan squeezed her again then dropped his hands. "Good." He went to the other side of the table and sat next to Valerie.

Yvonne kept her eyes off Richard as he leaned back in his chair and picked up the deck of cards. "I'll shuffle."

An air of awkwardness fell over the table as Richard shuffled the cards. Okay, she hadn't meant to flirt with Richard. It just kind of happened. Richard was like an old couch. Familiar, comfortable, and hard to let go of even though it no longer fit the décor. Except, she wasn't supposed to hold onto Richard. She'd let him go years ago. Painfully. Now she was ready to just…what? Fall back into what they'd had before? She couldn't. She was engaged.

"Okay, Richard, don't hold me back," Valerie said. "I will drag you for the rest of the day if you mess up this game."

"Don't worry," Richard said. "I know what I'm doing. You just bring your game today."

Yvonne relaxed and gave Valerie a grateful look. Valerie winked and lifted her chin. Awkward silence broken. The game started, and the trash talk commenced. Nathan hadn't played spades often, but he was a decent player. Just not good enough to match up against her sister and Richard. She and Yvonne played similarly, so Richard easily picked up on her style and they beat the crap out of her and Nathan.

Nathan's mood deteriorated with each lost book. Yvonne tried to keep up his spirits, but Cassidy and Michael came over to watch the game while the kids went inside to play video games. Sharon and Rochelle quickly hurried to follow the kids and get away from the brewing storm of disappointment on the back porch.

Cassidy's tipsy flirtation with Michael didn't do much to lighten the mood. By the end of the game, Yvonne tried to remain upbeat and laugh at the ridiculous claims of glory

Valerie and Richard spewed; they were funny, but Nathan's simmering silence made it hard for her to enjoy the game.

"That was fun," Yvonne said with false cheer when they lost.

Nathan slid his card across the table. "A hoot," he said in a bitter voice.

Cassidy sat on the arm of the chair Michael relaxed in. She placed a hand on his shoulder and leaned in to him. "Want to drive me home?"

Valerie's eyes widened, and she looked back and forth from Cassidy to Nathan to Yvonne with blatant interest. She pointed at Cassidy and mouthed "Is she serious?" to Yvonne.

"Where do you live?" Michael asked with a flirtatious smile.

Nathan stood. "I'll take you home."

Yvonne jumped up. "You're leaving?"

"I didn't ask you to take me home," Cassidy shot back to Nathan. When she got to her feet she wobbled. Apparently, Cassidy was a little more than tipsy.

"I didn't ask you to come here and act like this, either." Nathan's voice was hard. "What is wrong with you?"

She pointed a finger at him. "You know good and damn well what's wrong with me."

Yvonne rushed over to Cassidy. Maybe she could defuse the situation before it got further out of hand. "Hey, I can make you some coffee and you can lie down in my room for a little bit. You'll be fine."

"Oh, now you're on my case too. Nathan's little miss perfect. You're not perfect. We know you aren't." Cassidy's finger swung from Nathan to Yvonne. "You're sexing your ex-boyfriend with your eyes. See that, Nathan. Yvonne likes sex, too."

Yvonne sucked in a breath. Valerie jumped up from her seat. Yvonne held up a hand. She knew her sister was about to jump in and curse Cassidy out. Yvonne bit her tongue to keep from doing it herself. Cassidy was drunk and heartbroken. People did dumb crap when those two situations were combined. But that didn't mean she had to put up with it.

"You know what, Nathan," she said slowly, suppressing the anger rising in her. "I think it is time for you to take Cassidy home."

Nathan ran a hand over his face. When he walked over, he ran his hand down her back. "Yvonne, don't listen to her."

She stepped back. "Please, just sober her up. We can clear the air later."

Cassidy brought a hand to her mouth. Her eyes brimmed with tears. "Yvonne, I'm sorry. I didn't mean..."

"We'll talk later, Cassidy," she said.

Nathan put his arm around Cassidy's waist. "I'll come back by later after I get her settled."

Yvonne nodded. They all were silent as Nathan took Cassidy into the house. Yvonne couldn't look at Richard. What Cassidy said was rude, but true. What was wrong with her? Was she bound to mess up her own life the same way her mom had?

"In-laws," Michael said, throwing up his hands.

Yvonne couldn't help it, a laugh bubbled up. "She's usually not that bad."

"Is he always that...fatherly?" Michael asked with a raised brow.

She nodded and laughed harder. The ridiculousness of Nathan's overprotective relationship with Cassidy seemed even more over-the-top after this little scene. "Sometimes worse."

Michael and Valerie joined in with the laughter. Yvonne's humor died when she noticed Richard wasn't laughing. Hell, he hadn't even cracked a smile. He watched her. That same intense look he'd given her before the game.

"I think it's time to go," Richard said. "Michael, will you tell Nadia and mom."

Michael leaned back on his heels. He watched them like a bookie considering the odds of a race. "Sure."

"I'll go with you," Valerie said quickly.

Yvonne raised a brow at her sister. Valerie gave her a thumbs up and mouthed "I like him." She pointed at Richard.

What the hell? Was her sister encouraging her to choose Richard? Was it even a choice?

"You should fix a plate or something before leaving," she said, after Valerie and Michael left. "I'll go start."

She tried to go past him. His hand shot out and gently clasped her arm right above the elbow. He eased her closer to him until her shoulder brushed his chest.

"Richard, look, about earlier."

"I don't care about earlier. I care about you admitting how you feel about me." He said it easily. As if he were telling a subordinate they needed to turn in a report by the end of the day. As if his words weren't to be ignored.

"I'm marrying Nathan. What I feel about you is just affection for what we once were to each other."

"That can't be all," he said incredulously.

She swallowed hard. "It is all." That's all it had to be.

He took several deep breaths. "But you don't love him."

Her eyes narrowed, and her head jerked up so she could glare at him. "I'm marrying him. Everything between us was great until you showed up. Don't even try to tell me what I'm feeling."

His nearness sent sparks across her skin. Yvonne sucked in a breath but didn't back away.

"If you loved him," he said in a low, rumbling voice. His hand lifted, and his fingers lightly traced her bottom lip. "You wouldn't look at me like that."

Yvonne jerked back. She drew her lower lip into her mouth. The fleeting touch echoed throughout her body. In the erratic beat of her heart, the desire spreading through her system like a virus. The flare of triumph in his eyes made her want to wipe the smug smile off his face.

"The way you used to look at me," she said. "Right before you went back to Natalie. Your dad may have lied about Jacob, but you made your choice long before he made that decision. Don't talk to me about love. Not when you never loved me in the first place."

The pain on his face mirrored the pain ripping through her heart. Fighting back the need to push him for stirring things up, she hurried past him and went into the house. Richard had broken her heart once. She wouldn't let him break it again.

The knock on her door later that night wasn't unexpected. Yvonne expected Nathan to show up and apologize for earlier. He'd texted and said Cassidy felt horrible, she wasn't in a good place, and he was going to stay the night with her. She'd secretly hoped he would find a way to break away and come see her.

She needed to see Nathan. Kiss him. Touch him. Be reminded of all the things they were before Richard had come back and mixed up her life.

After everyone left, she'd showered, watched television with Jacob—who talked nonstop about how cool his sister was, for a girl—then settled on the couch with a glass of wine after he'd gone to bed. She was half-heartedly watching a horror movie on Netflix. No romance for her. Her love life was almost as screwed up as the people onscreen. She didn't need that.

She opened her door and bit her lip. Richard stood on her porch. He hadn't changed like she had. The dark shirt and shorts hugging his perfect body. His gaze slid over her then darkened. Her stomach flipped, and she quickly crossed her arms over her chest.

"What are you doing here, Richard?" she'd thought her
words would have kept him away longer. She needed him to
stay away longer.

"We need to talk." His voice was calm. Even. His
corporate voice.

"You can't just pop up like this. What if Nathan were
here?"

"I would have kept driving if I saw his car. This
conversation needs to be between me and you. No one else.
It's time to clear the air."

She wanted to deny him. Send him packing with the
accusation she'd tossed out earlier. Instead she stepped back.
They did need to set some things straight. "Fine."

He followed her into the living room. They'd been alone
in here before in the days he'd visited Jacob. Today felt
different. His presence consumed the room. The faint smell of
his cologne hung in the air, surrounding her. The attraction
he'd mentioned weeks ago hung out between them. Anxious
and bouncing to be acknowledged like a smart kid in school
with their hand raised.

Talking this out had been a bad idea.

Yvonne headed toward the dining room table. He took
her elbow. The feel of his strong grip sent fissures of heat up
her arm and down into the depths of her.

"We're not treating this discussion like a business meeting,"
he said in a firm voice. "We'll sit on the couch."

"We don't have to be cozy," she snapped.

The corner of his lips lifted. "Are you afraid of me?"

Scared out of her mind. Not of him, but of the way he
made her feel. Vulnerable, breathless, sexually aware. She slid
her arm out of his grasp.

"No." Belatedly she realized she sounded like a petulant
teenager who refused to admit to any type of fear.

"Then we'll sit on the couch."

Richard settled on one end. Yvonne didn't care that he

smiled when she tucked herself into the other corner. Well, maybe a little. Her arms crossed tightly, and she glared.

"Talk."

Richard rubbed his jaw and sighed. "I need to talk to you about Natalie."

Her head drew back. That wasn't what she expected. She had zero interest in hearing about Natalie. In fact, she'd rather sit through a lecture on the structure of concrete than talk about his ex-wife.

"That's unnecessary," Yvonne said.

"I need to. The way she lied about you was uncalled for, but there's more to the story."

Yvonne held up her hand. "As much as I hate what she did, a part of me gets it." She didn't like Natalie, really didn't like her, but she could understand her resentment, too. "I was the other woman. It doesn't matter that you'd broken up with her. We met the same day. She had a right to be upset."

"She didn't have a right to hide our child from me."

Yvonne stood and paced across the room. "No, she didn't, but me coming back would've ruined things with you two. Resentment makes people do crazy things."

"Our engagement wasn't because we loved each other. It was a business arrangement." Richard said in his cool, corporate voice. "We both knew marriage would convince her father to merge with my family's business. I cared about her, but I didn't love her."

She forced herself to face him and say what she'd never admitted out loud before. "You say that now, but you had to have loved her a little to ask her."

"My brother loves to pick up a new woman every month and have fun, but I hate everything about dating. The awkward dinners, uncomfortable first kisses, and the whole get-to-know-you back and forth. Natalie and I were already comfortable with each other. Marrying her to secure our business also kept my parents off my case about settling down and stopped Michael from dragging me to bars." His voice was matter-of-fact. "I'm not proud of my reasons for asking her, but you have to understand love wasn't part of it. I thought everything in my life would go well after that, but in my heart I knew I couldn't go through with it. Then I met you right after we split, and everything changed. All my plans for a nice, easy future were shattered the second I heard you laugh. I thought maybe I'd been hasty, so I didn't cut communication when Natalie kept calling me. Possible reconciliation always hovered in the background, but I couldn't get you out of my mind."

Her pulse pounded like wild horses in her veins. "You make it sound like I stole you from her."

"From the second I broke the engagement, I wasn't hers to steal. Why do you think I came back to that coffee house?"

"Because you like poetry."

"Because I hoped you would be there. You teased me about my suits. Didn't laugh at my bad attempts to write a poem. Gave me something to look forward to after a long day. I was happy."

"I know the rest of this story, Richard. I didn't like it the first time and I don't want to relive it." She didn't want to think about how happy they'd once been. That happiness hadn't lasted.

He stood abruptly. "The thing is, because Natalie and I remained friends after we split, she didn't like it when she learned about you. When she realized she was pregnant, that's when she made the ultimatum. Her and my child or you. I couldn't walk away from my child. But even though I made my choice, she saw I couldn't get you out of my mind. She's still angry. On the day of our divorce, she accused me of planning to run back to you, and you know what, even if there hadn't been Jacob, I knew I wouldn't have been able to not look you up."

Yvonne turned away from him. "You ignored me, told me to go away—"

"Do you know how hard it is to walk away from the only woman you love because of obligation?"

The words pounded into her resolve. She took a deep breath, forced herself to stroll casually over to the pictures of Jacob hanging on her wall. To not let his words make her believe they could forget everything and go back. He could hurt her so much. She never wanted to feel that pain again.

"I don't know, Richard, how hard is it?" She forced sarcasm into her voice. "Is it as hard as having the father of the man you love pay you to stay away?"

He moved closer to her. He smelled faintly of the smoke from the grill along with his own unique scent. His nearness made her burn as if she were sitting by a fire.

"That was a mistake I want to make up for." He took a deep breath. "I want you back."

She shook her head. Not wanting to hear the words or feel the jump in her pulse the words created. "I told you there is no going back."

"Then let's move forward." He eased even closer.

Sparks shot across her skin. Her pulse increased in anticipation. Yvonne held up a hand. "Richard, we didn't work before and we won't work now. This is just old attraction stirring up. Not something worth breaking up our lives over." She needed to remember that. Believe that.

The words didn't lessen the determination in his eyes. "Circumstances and bad decisions broke us last time. What we felt for each other wasn't a lie and it wasn't frivolous. We can get that back."

"I don't want that back. I don't want to feel that way again. It hurts too much when it goes away, and let's face it, Richard, you'll go away."

Long fingers wrapped around her elbow. He caressed her

cheek with his fingertips. "I thought of you nearly every day for the past five years. No matter how hard I tried to move on I couldn't forget you, or our time together. If I get you back, Yvonne, believe me when I say I won't let you go so easily."

His voice was deep, determined, and so damn sexy. His head lowered and his lips brushed hers. The familiar shock of his kiss was like an arrow of nostalgia to her chest. The memories and need so acute she was seconds from falling back into old habits.

She broke away from him. Turned her back and tried to catch her breath. Tried to think when all she wanted was for him to wrap his arms around her again.

Richard eased her back against him. One of his hands lifted and pushed the hair behind her ear. "Do you know how hard it is having you back in my life and not being able to be as close to you as I once was?"

"We can't do this." So why wasn't she pulling away?

"Stop running away from me." His voice trembled.

Yvonne's breath stuttered. She had to pull away. But, damn, he felt so good against her. She tried unscrambling her brain for reason. "I'm not running. I'm being sensible." Protecting her heart.

"There's nothing sensible about us."

"Why? Because you're rich Richard Barrington and what you say goes?" Her sarcasm would work a lot better if her voice wasn't so breathless.

"Because after all these years I still love you, Yvonne, and after all these years I can't figure out a way to stop that."

Yvonne squeezed her eyes shut to stop the tears. Tears! Of all things. She didn't want to cry, but Richard's admission broke through everything. The pain, fear, and insecurity of her feelings for him. The need to run hit her like a train. Maybe he sensed it, because his body tensed and then his lips pressed against her neck.

Pleasure rumbled in her mid-section. He gently nipped at

the sensitive skin there and her knees nearly buckled. His voice broke when he spoke again. "I still love you."

She shook her head and kept her eyes squeezed shut. "Don't say that."

"Why?"

"Because I don't feel the same." The words struggled to come out.

His hand left her waist and pressed into her stomach. "But you feel something."

She did feel something. Something she didn't want to admit. Something that would ruin everything. Something that would destroy the designs for her future: perfect husband, perfect job, perfect family. Everything she hadn't had growing up, but was finally able to give Jacob. Something Richard tried to snatch away with his words of regret and love. Words that were six years too late but tempted her to forget every promise she'd made to Nathan.

Panic rushed in her bloodstream, quick and sharp. She used her entire body to push back. Richard stumbled back and let her go.

"Yvonne?" he reached for her.

She pointed to the door. She kept her eyes away from him. "You need to go. Richard, I can't go back there with you." She ran her fingers over her face. The light glinted off the ring on her finger. "You're free to do this. You're divorced, and ready to start over. You've found the woman you once loved, your son, and you're ready to jump in and make a nice and neat little family again. But I'm not free to do this." She tapped her chest. "Regardless of whether you think I love Nathan or not, I do respect him. I won't hurt him. I won't cheat myself out of being happy just because we're still attracted to each other. I came into your life at the time you needed to justify your decision to break things off with Natalie. I wanted you, so I ignored my better judgment to get involved with you when you were still conflicted, but never to prove you would choose me over her. I respected your decision to be with her enough for that. Don't you dare come here and not respect me the same." Her insides still reeled from his brief kiss, his touch, but her voice was firm. Her brain had to run this show.

"You'd really marry him knowing there's still something between us?

Her heart iced over. "Did you hear a word I said?"

"If what you have to say is that we should ignore what's between us because of a guy you don't love, then no, I don't want to hear it."

She glared at him. Wished she could wipe the knowing, this-is-what's-best-for-us look off his face. "This is your problem, Richard. You think you know everything. That you can just snap your fingers and things go the way you want them to. You aren't going to control me."

"I'm not trying to control you," he said evenly. "I don't stand for weak excuses. You don't love him. You're hiding behind that ring to avoid facing the truth."

"Even without this ring I wouldn't go back to you. I was silly and lovestruck six years ago, but I'm not now. I would have overlooked the fact that you're a control freak and hoped one day you'd take the stick out of your behind."

"The stick?" He pointed to his chest. "What about your upstanding Nathan. The guy you won't even be yourself around."

"I am myself around him."

"No, you're not. You're his peacemaker. You defer to him. Let him speak for you both instead of speaking for yourself. You may want to call what you had with me as being silly and lovestruck, but at least it was real. I never asked you to be different."

His words hit a sore spot she didn't know she had. Angry heat flooded her face. "You don't know what you're talking about. You're searching for excuses to ignore what you don't want to hear. I don't know why I would expect you to listen to me. You didn't listen to me then, why would you listen to me now?"

He rubbed the bridge of his nose. "Yvonne, don't compare this conversation to what I did before."

"I'm going to compare everything you do to what you did before, because you showed me once who you really are. Even without this ring I won't let myself fall in love with you again. I won't set myself up to be hurt like that ever again."

Richard walked to her. The regret in his eyes made her want to fall back into his arms. "Give me time to show you who I am now. I never lied to you. I never asked you to be someone, or anything, other than yourself. Don't lie to me or yourself now. Don't go back to Nathan unless you're sure he's the person you really want to spend every day by your side. I made that decision six years ago, and I know how much I regretted it. Don't waste years of your life because you're afraid to trust me again."

He stepped forward as if to touch her. She slid away. "Please just...go."

Richard dropped his hand. "I won't force this. But marry him knowing that no matter what happens between us or with Jacob, I still love you, and I'll never abandon you and Jacob again."

Chapter 21

"Do not tell him!" Valerie's eyes practically exploded out of her head after Yvonne told her what happened the night before.

Valerie jumped up from Yvonne's kitchen table and went to the fridge. She opened it and pulled out the bottle of sparkling wine sitting in the door and the orange juice off the top shelf.

"What are you doing?" Yvonne asked.

"We're going to need alcohol for the rest of this story. Actually, we needed alcohol before you started." Valerie grabbed two glasses out of the cabinet and dumped everything on the table.

She started to tell her sister to forget it, but changed her mind. She needed something after last night. She'd texted Valerie at five in the morning saying she had an emergency and needed to talk as soon as she woke up. Valerie was at her door at six. Jacob was still asleep. Yvonne was forever grateful he wasn't one of those kids who popped up before the sun rose on weekends.

"I have to tell him," Yvonne said, taking the hastily made

mimosa her sister slid her way. "I can't keep this a secret." And she'd taken too long to finally push him away.

"You can keep this a secret and you will keep this damn secret until the day you die."

"Are you crazy? I'm marrying him. I can't go into the marriage with something like this on my conscience."

Valerie turned her chair around and straddled it. "Yes, the hell you can." She said vehemently. "Unless ... you don't want to marry Nathan."

"What? No! Of course I want to marry Nathan. He's the perfect guy."

Valerie rolled her eyes. "There you go again with that perfect guy mess. No one is perfect."

"He's been the perfect guy for me. Where else am I going to find someone like him? He's not obsessed with getting me in bed. He's great with Jacob. He's handy and can fix anything. We're doing a television show together."

"Okay," Valerie said pursing her lips. "He's also not the guy who kissed you last night." She sipped her drink and eyed Yvonne over the rim.

Yvonne's face burned. Her entire body burned. She slapped a hand over her face. "It was barely a kiss. Over before it even started."

"But he also admitted he still loved you. You loved him once. You really want to tell Nathan all that?"

Yvonne closed her eyes. She pressed the cool glass to her hot cheeks. Richard had broken up with her. He'd moved on. He'd married someone else. He'd ignored her calls and opened the door for his dad to lie to her.

She'd held on to that for years, but the grip on her anger was loosening. "I loved him six years ago. I do love Nathan. He is great, and I will be happy with him."

"But will you be happier with Richard?"

"I don't know. I can't think about what we were like before. We were young and didn't think things through. It was a different place in my life. Now I'm building something with Nathan."

"And are you holding onto that because Nathan was so eager to build something with you after you thought Richard didn't want to build anything with you?"

She glared at her sister over her glass. "Okay Dr. Phil. You can stop trying to give me television therapy."

Her sister shrugged. "I'm trying to get you to think about things you don't want to think about. Richard's dad was an asshole, and his ex-wife doesn't sound very pleasant either. But he seems like a decent guy. His love for Jacob is obvious. The way he feels about you is apparent whenever he looks at you. I know you love Nathan, but I saw the way you looked at Richard and I'm not surprised about what happened between you two. So, either suck it up and break up with Nathan or keep this buried and march down that aisle without giving Nathan any reason to doubt how you feel."

"But isn't that wrong? He may not want me after hearing about this."

"If that's true you lose him either way. Both of which open the door for Richard to try to slide back in."

"Damn," she mumbled and gulped the drink. She didn't want Richard to slide back in. Wouldn't it be ridiculous to go back to the ex-boyfriend after all these years? Wouldn't it be ridiculous to believe him when he'd said he was still in love with her? Except, he'd looked very serious when he said it.

"Yeah," was Valerie's unhelpful response.

The doorbell rang. Both she and Valerie sat up straight, their eyes wide as they silently asked the question: was Richard back?

Yvonne pushed her chair back. "It's not him."

"If it is him, I'm all the way team Richard."

She waved off her sister and hurried to the door. Valerie's footsteps followed eagerly behind. Yvonne's nerves heightened with each step she took toward the door. If it was Richard, she would send him away. She needed time to think. Time to figure out why she had taken so long to push him away.

She swung open the door ready to tell Richard to leave her alone. Nathan swept her up into his arms and squeezed her tight.

"Nathan? I didn't expect you today," she said. She looked at Valerie for answers, but her sister cringed and walked away.

Nathan's eyes were bright with excitement. "Apologies should be given in person." He picked her up by the waist and pulled her body against his.

Yvonne shrieked with surprised. "Apology accep—"

He cut her off with a kiss as passionate and exuberant as he appeared. Yvonne's first impulse was to pull back. Confess everything. She ignored instinct and kissed him back. Maybe, just maybe, she'd be hit with the same desire and urgency she'd felt last night. At least some of those feelings. Enough to prove that last night with Richard was an anomaly. Nathan was a good kisser, and she focused until she lost herself in the kiss.

When he pulled back, he grinned at her as if she were sunshine and he'd been in darkness forever. Guilt pierced her heart like a dull blade. Ragged and angry. "Nathan, I need to tell you—"

"No, I need to tell you something first. Cassidy." He shook his head. "I'm not going back and forth with her anymore. I'm not fighting with her anymore. You are my future. We are going to build something that is perfect and sweet and pure. I don't care about Richard being back because I know what type of woman you are. I can trust you and you won't lead me astray. I asked you to marry me because I knew you were special. That hasn't changed."

"Nathan…" Tears burned her eyes. Flashes of memory: Richard's kiss. The touch of his hands on her. He didn't deserve this. "Nathan, you can do so much better than me."

He took her face in his hands. "There is no one better.

That's why I'm here. Let's get out of here for the rest of the weekend. Just the two of us. We've let other people get in the way of what we both knew was right from the moment I asked you. Let's focus on us and come back ready to face the world."

She couldn't go out of town with him. How could she face him knowing what happened? The guilt would crush her heart.

She shook her head. "I can't. Nathan I—"

"I'll watch Jacob," Valerie chimed in quickly.

Nathan jumped and faced Valerie. Surprise on his face. Valerie shrugged and smiled. "Hey, Nathan, I came over early. Guy trouble. Needed to talk to my sister."

"Don't you have things to do this weekend?" Yvonne said.

Valerie shook her head. "Nope. I think it's a *great* idea for you and Nathan to spend some time alone. Reconnect. Get some clarity on your future."

She knew what her sister was up to. Going out of town with Nathan wasn't the answer. If anything, it would make things more confusing.

"Thank you, Valerie," Nathan said.

Before Yvonne could deny her sister's "gracious" offer, Jacob came into the entryway. "Why is everyone over here? Mommy, have you made breakfast?"

Nathan laughed and kissed Yvonne's cheek. His excitement was almost scary. He seemed desperate to get her out of town and now relieved that they were leaving. "I've got breakfast. Come on, Jacob, tell me what you want."

He swept Jacob up into his arms and carried him into the kitchen. Yvonne rushed over and slapped her sister's arm. "What the hell? I can't go out of town with him."

"You can, and you will. Let Nathan get you off and then come home and make the decision."

"I have to tell him."

"You have to go and figure out if you really want a future with him. Richard's cards are on the table. He wants you back. Don't ruin things with Nathan before you know you're really ready to be single and get rid of the only real defense you have against going back to Richard."

Sex! That's exactly what she needed. And not just any old sex with anybody. She needed sex with Nathan. Sex of the hot, sweat-out-my-perm, can't-breathe-or-sit-down, rock-my-world variety.

Yvonne was sure of it. If she could get Nathan to lay it down and show her unequivocally that their connection was of mind, body, and soul then she'd know for sure. She understood sex wasn't everything in a relationship, but it was also a very important part. No matter what people may try to say. She was comparing everything she had with Richard to what she had with Nathan, and she didn't have everything with Nathan. She only had the friendship they'd built. She was sure the sex would be out of this world and then she'd be completely sure about marrying him.

She was not as sure about telling him. She understood her sister's reasoning, but the guilt was killing her. Every time Nathan looked at her as if she were the answer to his prayers, she felt a sharp pain in her chest.

She was going to tell him. She had to tell him. As soon as they had sex. Unfortunately, Nathan was being very good at not having sex with her. He'd brought her to Helena, Georgia, where he had a cabin in the mountains. He also had every moment of their day planned. Fishing, hiking in the Chattahoochee National Forest, visiting the Bavarian-style buildings in the town, and viewing the Raven Cliff Waterfalls. He kept them so busy during the day that they both collapsed in exhaustion when they got back to his cabin.

A part of her wondered if he was tiring her out on

purpose. He seemed even more hands off with her than usual. Typically, Nathan was eager to kiss, touch and do everything but have sex. This weekend he was exceptionally chaste. Quick kisses, brief caresses and only holding her hand.

They were on their last night for the quick weekend and Yvonne was not going to be deterred. She'd made coffee, drank two cups and pulled out the red lace teddy she'd packed before leaving. She fluffed her hair and took in her reflection in the bathroom mirror. The panties were crotchless and her breasts practically spilled out of the lacy top. She was going to have sex with her fiancé if it was the last thing she did.

"Baby," Nathan called from the bedroom. "Are you done in there? I'm going to shower and go to bed early. We have to leave early tomorrow."

Yvonne grinned and went to the door. Now or never. She swung open the door and rested her hand against the frame. "All done."

Nathan's jaw dropped. He took her in from head to toe, then licked his lips. "What's this for?"

So far so good. She sauntered across the room and placed her hands on his chest. His heart beat rapidly beneath her hands. Another good sign.

"It's for you." She lifted on her toes and brushed his lips with hers.

Nathan gripped her hips. Her heart jumped in anticipation. She waited for him to pull her closer. He pushed her back. "You look...fantastic."

She wrapped her arms around his neck and pressed her breasts against him. "I'll look even better when you take this off me."

She kissed him. He hesitated then kissed her back. She walked him backwards toward the bed and they fell onto it in a tangle of limbs. Yvonne pulled on the edge of his t-shirt and he let her drag it over his head. Yes! Even better. Her hands went to his waistband. She was going to make this happen.

Nathan grabbed her wrist and stopped her. "What are you doing?"

She grinned. "What do you think?"

"We shouldn't push things."

She pulled back. "Push things? We've pushed things in the past."

Nathan rolled away from her and sat on the edge of the bed. "I know. That was my fault. I don't want to push anymore."

"What does that mean?"

"It means no more going too far. We said we'd wait and that's what we're going to do. No sex of any kind until the wedding day. If we're more disciplined, then..." He dragged his fingers through his hair.

"Then what?"

"We'll make better role models. It'll be good for the show. People will love it."

They were back to this? She pushed off the bed and marched around to stand in front of him. "You said this wasn't about ratings or the show."

"It's not."

"Then who cares what the public thinks? Nathan, we're engaged. If you want to wait...fine, I'll wait, but don't tell me now you're suddenly putting everything off the table and the only reason you're giving me is because it'll make us better role models. I don't care about being role models to people we don't know. I care about making sure we make it. That you want me."

He ran his hands over his face. "I do want you, Yvonne. I do. I don't deserve you, but somehow, I found you, and we're making this work. I don't want to mess things up."

Tears burned her eyes. He didn't want to mess things up? She was the one who'd already messed things up. She was the one who, despite all her efforts to get Nathan in bed this weekend, couldn't get Richard's kiss out of her mind.

"Nathan, there's something I need to tell you."

Nathan's cell phone vibrated. Yvonne looked to the ceiling and threw up her hands. Really? Her confession interrupted by a phone.

Nathan jumped up and snatched his phone off the dresser. Almost as if he dreaded hearing whatever she had to say as much as she dreaded saying it.

"Who is it?"

"It's a text from Judy. Have you seen this?" He mumbled reading the words on the screen. "There's a link."

Yvonne went over to him. "What's the link to?"

Nathan clicked on the link. On his screen was a picture of Yvonne and Richard and the headline "Home Renovation's Latest It Couple Sells Show to Yvonne Cable's Baby Daddy."

Chapter 22

Yvonne hadn't appreciated how much being a mini celebrity sucked until she and Nathan got back to Atlanta. Paparazzi hovered around his home trying to catch a picture of them. Until then, she'd enjoyed her minor celebrity status. The clients who'd come to her company because they'd heard of her, or the rare person who recognized her in the grocery store. Even when she'd agreed to pursue a show, she hadn't thought she would be swarmed by the media. Sure, there was interest in the lives of the hosts on the cooking and home improvement shows, but they weren't the ones on the cover of every tabloid and magazine in the grocery store.

Now, with the photographers camped out in front of Nathan's place and her place based on what Valerie had seen when she'd driven by, she wasn't so sure she wanted to do the show anymore.

Nathan pulled his car through the crowd and into the back of his house. They quickly went in through the back door. Judy was already there waiting on them. Nathan wouldn't look at Yvonne. She'd deal with that after talking to her mom to see if she was willing to watch Jacob for her until things died down.

"Well, this is good!" Judy said, after Yvonne got off the phone with her mom and joined her and Nathan in the living room.

Nathan turned away from the window. He'd been peering through the curtains at the group outside. His brows drew together, and he looked at Judy as if she'd just grown another arm. "How is this good?"

"For publicity," Judy said. Her eyes were bright with the possibilities as she looked between Yvonne and Nathan. "I'll admit the way it was announced could have been better, but we can spin this."

"Spin it how?" Yvonne asked. From what she'd read, the article not only spilled all the tea about her and Richard's prior relationship and child, it also insinuated that the reason Richard's network made the offer to sign their show was because of lingering affections between him and Yvonne.

"We'll make it a family thing. Say that you two were trying to be very private about your family life, but you've always worked together for the good of Jacob. With the image you've cultivated the public will eat up the idea of you all coming together to be one big happy, blended family."

Nathan shook his head. "It won't work."

"It will," Judy said sternly. "If you two want to continue to hold your golden glow then you need to get ahead of this. You do want to keep your golden glow . . . don't you?"

Yvonne looked at Nathan. She couldn't answer. He wouldn't even talk to her. She'd kissed Richard. Well, Richard kissed her, but she'd taken way too long to push him away. None of that meant she didn't love Nathan, or that she didn't want the future they talked about.

But are you still in love with Richard?

"You're right," Nathan said nodding. His jaw set with

determination. "We need to stay the course. We'll get ahead of this. Control the story."

Yvonne stepped closer to him. "Are you sure?" He still hadn't met her eye.

When he looked at her there was resolve in his gaze, but not the sweet affection he typically had. "I'm sure. We've worked too hard to let this come between us."

Not quite the words she wanted to hear. Her cell phone rang. She pulled it from her back pocket expecting a call from her mom or sister. Richard's number is what she saw instead.

"It's Richard."

Nathan snorted. "Typical. Ask him why he decided to release this story."

"We don't know Richard did this," Yvonne said quickly. "He agreed to the terms."

"I don't think he cares very much about respecting boundaries." Nathan's voice was hard and nasty before he turned and marched out of the living room.

Judy held up a hand. "Answer that. Tell him the plan. I'll calm Nathan down." She followed Nathan out.

Yvonne took a deep, restorative breath before answering the call. She hadn't spoken to Richard since he'd kissed her. He had to know she'd gone out of town with Nathan the next day. That shouldn't bother her. Nathan was her fiancé. That didn't stop the nerves from fluttering in her stomach.

"Richard, did you do this?"

"No. This was Natalie." He sounded like a man who'd already gone nine rounds in a boxing ring and was prepping himself to go one more.

"Natalie?"

"She still has an interest in the company. She didn't know about us purchasing your show. When she found out she was...upset. Words were spoken and the next thing I know, the story was released."

Words were spoken. No wonder he sounded as if he'd been through a fight. If what he said was true, and Natalie had known he'd still cared about Yvonne, then she could imagine the hell Natalie must have put Richard through. "Does this mean the deal is off?"

"No. We're trying to think of damage control. I still want you."

Yvonne sucked in a breath. He may be implying the show, but there was another meaning in the warm tone of his voice. Guilt warred with something else. A feeling that made her press a hand into her stomach. Why did her body still react to him like this?

"You want me and Nathan. For the show."

There was several seconds of silence. "I think you made your choice very clear."

"What choice?"

"You went out of town for a romantic weekend."

"I did."

They were both silent. Both calculating what this meant. She wasn't sure about her choice. She'd been so sure of what she was going to do before. So sure that she and Nathan were the right choice. But now, hearing Richard's voice. Still feeling everything he'd done to her flowing through her body. Was it lust, or was it more? Was she being foolish?

"Then there's nothing left to say about that," he said with resignation. "Now it's on to damage control."

He'd given up. The realization was like an unexpectedly disappointing ending to a movie. She'd gone out of town with Nathan to reinforce their relationship, and Richard had accepted he wasn't the one chosen. This was good. She was free to move forward and take Valerie's advice. This was not another example of Richard not following through on the things he said.

"We've already discussed damage control," Yvonne said. "We're going to go with the story, but say we've all been working together from the start. We're one big happy blended family."

"Your idea?"

She hesitated, not wanting to admit she was doing what Nathan wanted. "Yes."

"That could work. I'll be in Atlanta tomorrow. We can talk about it then."

"Sure, we'll come by your office. Just let me know when you're in town."

"I will. I'll talk with you later." Richard ended the call.

"Why are we going by his office?" Nathan asked.

She swung around and faced him. "He likes Judy's idea. Apparently, Natalie, his ex-wife, leaked the story. He'd like to discuss how we do damage control."

"I need to go back to Savannah tomorrow."

Oh, now he was leaving? "You can't postpone it by one day?" Her voice was razor sharp.

"It's important."

"So is this. Or do I need to repeat what Judy asked? Do you even want to fight for us anymore?"

For the briefest second, she saw no in his expression. Then he ran a hand over his face, the look of affection returned, and he walked over and wrapped her in his arms. "You're right. I'll be here tomorrow for the meeting."

"Thank you," she said, hugging him back, but she didn't feel any relief. What would he have said if she hadn't gone along with the plan to paint over the cracks in their ideal relationship?

Chapter 23

Yvonne left Nathan's place with Judy and spent the night at Valerie's. After giving her sister the rundown of how the weekend with Nathan had gone, Valerie had sent her to bed with one question.

"Are you sure you and Nathan should get married?"

She hadn't answered, but she'd stayed up all night thinking about what her sister said. When Nathan asked her to marry him, she'd been shocked. They'd only been dating a few months and while they'd both wanted the same things, a loving committed relationship, they'd only talked about marriage in the abstract. She'd known she loved him, but if asked if she was head over heels in love, she would have said no. Nathan's wants didn't always align with hers, and she hadn't thought they'd be together forever.

When he'd asked her to marry him in the middle of a large stadium full of fans, their picture on the jumbotron, and him confessing to the entire world how much he loved her and wanted to spend the rest of his life with her, something inside of her had given way. Something she hadn't realized had been attached to her for years. The idea that she wasn't wanted. She was the accidental child. The other woman. The independent single mom. The high-maintenance chick. All the things she'd accepted whenever someone gave her a new label. Then Nathan came along. Sweet, conservative, loving Nathan, standing there, saying he loved her and wanted to marry her in front of thousands of people. She couldn't say no to that. Before she could take the time to really consider the ramifications, Richard returned, making things even more confusing.

Had she fought too hard to make her and Nathan work, only because she wanted to belong somewhere?

That's the question that still bounced around her head as she rode the elevator up to Richard's office the next afternoon. Her cell phone buzzed as she got off on the top floor.

Emergency. I can't make it.

She stopped abruptly in front of the receptionist's desk. Nathan couldn't make it? What kind of emergency was he dealing with? This meeting was supposed to be about all of their futures.

Her fingers flew over the letters on the screen. **What's going on?**

Three bubbles flashed in the conversation letting her know he was typing. The bubbles stopped and started a few times. Yvonne tapped her foot. If it was really an emergency, he shouldn't have to think about what he was sending.

Finally, his answer came.

Savannah job imploding. Not literally. I have to go. Ask Richard if we can meet later. I already called Judy.

Yvonne gripped the phone to keep from throwing it. The hospital was a big job. As a business owner she understood that sometimes sacrifices had to be made to get a job done, but, damn, she really needed him here today.

She smiled at Richard's receptionist. "Looks like I'm going to have to reschedule."

Ava smiled and nodded politely. "It's no problem. You can go on in and tell Mr. Barrington. He's in there with his brother right now and said to send you in when you arrived." Ava stood and grabbed a folder from the chair. "I need to run these downstairs. It'll only take a second. When I come back, I'll look at his schedule for a new time later this week."

Yvonne thanked her and went to the door. It wasn't closed all the way. She assumed because they were expecting her and Nathan to show up at any moment. Richard and Michael's voices carried through the partially opened door.

"You can't go through with their show," Michael was saying. A warning in his voice.

Yvonne hesitated with her hand on the knob. Eavesdropping was rude, and Yvonne typically didn't listen in on other people's conversations. But when the conversation was obviously about her, she couldn't help but stop. All she'd heard up until now was that Richard thought their show was perfect for the network.

"Yes, I can, and I will," Richard replied in his self-assured professional voice.

"Richard, this is crazy. I get it, you want her back, but to go this far is ridiculous."

"It's not just to get her back."

Not just? Had getting her back even played a role in his offer? He'd said he'd been interested in the show even before he'd known she was involved.

"Then what is it about? You and Natalie made a choice to move the network to more original programming," Michael countered.

"This is original programming."

"Scripted shows. Not home improvement. Now you find out your old side piece is doing a show and you suddenly want to include them."

"She was never a side piece. The show is good. I know

what I'm doing by making the offer." The slightest bit of hesitancy in his voice.

Yvonne's hand tightened on the knob. Obviously, he wasn't so sure? Was he feeding her a bunch of lies about how viable the show could be?

"Natalie won't go through with it, you know," Michael's voice was resigned. "She's already angry you're coming to Atlanta every weekend. Once she finds out you're buying this show she's going to go ballistic."

"Natalie will be okay," Richard said dismissively. "Once the money comes in she'll get over herself."

"I don't think so. I saw her the other day at Mom's. She's threatened to sell her stake of the company. She said, and I quote, I'll run that business into the ground before I let him put that woman on the air."

There was a moment of silence. Yvonne imagined Richard thinking over what Natalie said. This is when he'd stand up for the show. When he'd say he had faith in her ability to bring a successful program to his network. When he'd say to hell with Natalie's threats and support Yvonne.

"Look," Richard said. "We'll film the pilot and test the show with some audiences. That'll give Natalie enough time to cool off and enough time for me to try and work things out with Yvonne."

Yvonne's stomach lurched. He'd played her. He'd been playing her all along. This had never been about wanting her show. It had been about getting back with her. Nathan had been right all along. She never should have trusted Richard. Never should have believed he would change. Risking his business wasn't worth taking a risk on her, and it never would be.

She pushed open the door. It hit the wall with a thud. Richard and Michael jumped and spun to face her.

"Was this your plan all along?" She threw the accusation

at Richard along with a glare. Pain she'd been sure she would avoid feeling again with his return exploded in her chest like bundles of emotional C4.

"Yvonne, this isn't what you think," Richard said calmly. He had the gall to look nonchalant and unfazed by being overheard.

"It's exactly what I think. I never should have believed what you said. All those words about wanting our show and believing it will be good on your network were just that, words. Just like before, you talk a pretty game to get me, then prove you're full of it with your actions."

She turned and rushed to the elevator. Richard's hurried steps followed. "Yvonne, listen to me. I do believe in your show. I wasn't lying about that."

She pressed the buttons on the elevator. "Sure, Richard."

He moved between her and the elevator. "It's the truth."

"And if it comes to picking up our show or losing your company because Natalie won't like it what will you do? Huh, Richard, what will you choose? Oh wait, you'll prolong filming so you can finish wooing me and getting me back in your bed."

"It's not about getting you in my bed. What I said the other night was true. I love you."

She crossed her arms and scoffed. Unwilling to be fazed by the apparent sincerity or pain in his eyes.

"But you let me know loud and clear I have no chance," he continued. "I was out of line on the Fourth. You were right, I didn't respect what you have with Nathan, and I did think our past was stronger than your present. I never should have kissed you, and when you left to go out of town with Nathan the next day, I knew I'd lost you."

"And whose fault is that?"

The elevator door swooshed open. They stared at each other. Her heart cracking. Her pride shattered. She'd been about to make a terrible mistake.

"I'll have our lawyer call to handle the contracts...and work out visitation between you and Jacob. Until then, please don't come by my house. Goodbye, Richard."

Yvonne went straight to Nathan's home after the meeting with Richard. She was going to tell him everything. The kiss, how her feelings for Richard weren't as nonexistent as she wanted them to be, why she thought their engagement was premature even though she did care about him, how she still wanted to do the home renovation show with him on another network, just not as his fiancé.

All of that was a lot to process, and she didn't expect responses to every revelation today. If anything, she expected Nathan to tell her he never wanted to see her again and kick her out of his house. That's about what she would have done if he'd come to her with similar confessions.

When she pulled up at his home and saw his car in the driveway, relief swept through her. She hadn't been sure if he'd already left for Savannah. She got out of the car and skipped up the steps to his front door. Thankfully, the media attention from the day before had died down. Only two photographers still hung out in front of Nathan's house. A big-name comedian in town for a show was arrested the night before for shoplifting. Which meant a bigger and more lucrative story. She ignored their calls as she pulled out her key to let herself into Nathan's place. She wasn't about to worry about letting herself in when waiting on him to answer would mean getting her picture taken a hundred times.

There were shouts from the kitchen. What was Cassidy doing there? Why were they fighting again? She slowly made her way to the kitchen. She was not in the mood to defuse another Nathan/Cassidy showdown.

"For the love of God, Nathan, go for what you want," Cassidy yelled. "We've tried to ignore this for too long."

"What about Mom and Dad?" Nathan fired back. "They would be devastated."

Yvonne frowned and stopped at the kitchen door. What could Nathan want that would possibly devastate their parents? A chill went down her spine. Was it her? She'd met his parents when they'd come to town a few months back. They'd seemed cool about her and Nathan, but that didn't mean anything. They could have been nice to her and gone back to tell Nathan and Cassidy they hated her.

Cassidy stepped closer to Nathan and pressed her hand to his chest. Her green eyes pleaded with his. "They love us." She ran her hand up Nathan's chest to the back of his head. "They'll understand."

Hold up! Was she talking about...them? *"Stepsister. It's not the same."* Her mother's constant comeback flashed in Yvonne's mind. She closed her eyes and shook her head. She had to be misreading things. There was no way Cassidy and Nathan were...Just no way.

Her eyes opened. They hadn't seen her. Cassidy wrapped her arms around Nathan's neck and jammed her mouth against his. Yvonne sucked in a breath. Waited. Nathan would push her away. Any second now, he'd shove her back. Tell her to stop. Wipe his mouth and say she was being foolish.

Any second.

The seconds ticked by. Yvonne's jaw dropping farther with each disbelieving heartbeat. Nathan's body shuddered. His arms slipped around Cassidy's waist and he kissed her back.

"Nathan!" The shout was out of her mouth before she could stop herself.

Nathan and Cassidy scrambled apart. Yvonne couldn't get her mouth to close. Nathan's shirt was pulled from the waistband. His face fire-engine red. Eyes wide.

What the hell was going on? How long had this been going on? Why had he even asked her to marry him?

She spun on her heel and ran toward the door. Nathan called her name and ran after her. His hand wrapped around her upper arm as she bent over to pick up her bag.

"Yvonne, wait, let's talk about this."

The plea in his voice made her want to kick him in the nuts. She jerked out of his grasp. When he came forward, she held up a hand. "No. We are not talking about this. You're kissing your sister?"

"Stepsister." He ran a hand through his hair then over his face. "It's complicated and screwed up."

"No kidding! And you expect me to sit here and listen while you try and explain. There's nothing to explain. We're through."

"Yvonne, please listen to me. I love you, but..."

"But I shouldn't have felt bad when Richard kissed me. That's what I came over here to tell you. Guess you wouldn't have cared much anyway, huh."

The words were angry and intentionally hurtful. She was hurting. The pain in her heart compounded with the pain from her fight with Richard. She felt like her heart had been ripped from her chest, dragged by a bus, and shoved back in. Battered, ragged and bruised.

Nathan blinked and shook his head. Confusion blended to realization and transformed to anger. "He what?"

"Don't you dare look at me as if I've done something wrong." She pointed toward the kitchen. "Not after what I've just seen."

"That never should have happened." He was instantly contrite.

Yvonne jerked the ring off her finger and threw it at his face. "And this shouldn't have happened either."

Chapter 24

When summer camp called Yvonne at the end of the week to verify if her mother was supposed to pick up Jacob, Yvonne gave them the okay instead of cursing a blue streak. Why had she expected Rochelle to not eventually butt in and force a confrontation? Not like she'd believe in giving her daughter space and time before digging into what was going on.

Yvonne left work and went to her mom's. Might as well get things over with sooner rather than later. Time didn't always make difficult discussions easier.

Her mom and Jacob were in the backyard when Yvonne arrived. Rochelle had gotten Jacob a bow that slung water balloons instead of arrows. Jacob was having a ball slinging balloons across the yard while Rochelle watched from her back porch.

Yvonne waved at Jacob and promised to watch as she walked over and sat down next to her mom. "You didn't have to pick him up today."

"I wanted to see my grandson. You were keeping him hidden."

"I was not keeping him hidden. We've been busy."

"Too busy to call Nathan back?" Rochelle smirked at Yvonne. "He called me last night. Asking if I'd talked to you and begging me to get you to call him back."

Yvonne couldn't believe he would pull her mom into this. "I can't believe he did that."

"You should be happy he called. Not many men would try to get back the woman they loved after she walked out on him. He thinks you're with Richard."

"What?"

"You heard what I said. He thinks you've gone back to Richard." Rochelle shook her head. Disappointment oozed from her body in rivulets. "I don't blame him either. The way you and Richard were practically drooling over each other at your cookout. I didn't say anything then because I didn't want to embarrass you in front of Richard's family. And when you went out of town with Nathan, I'd hoped you'd gotten your mind together. Then he calls yesterday and tells me you gave back the ring and are back with Richard. Yvonne, I don't understand you. I guess I should have known you would repeat my mistakes. I tried to tell you but—"

"Mom, stop!" Yvonne slashed her hand through the air. "Just...stop."

Rochelle gasped and jerked back. "Oh no, you are not going to tell me to stop. Not when I told you to keep those parts of your life separate. Now you're about to lose a good man—"

"Did Nathan tell you the part about him kissing Cassidy?" She lowered her voice, so the words wouldn't travel to Jacob, who'd started flinging balloons in the air and running to see if they could land on his head.

Rochelle whipped around so fast Yvonne was surprised her neck didn't snap. "He what?"

"Yes, Mom, Nathan, the so-called perfect guy, was shoving his tongue down his stepsister's throat the other day. I walked in and caught them right in the middle."

Rochelle gaped for several seconds. She looked around the backyard as if expecting a different explanation to sprout up from the grass. "Well...I..." She looked back at Yvonne. "Cassidy?"

Yvonne nodded. "I knew they were close but didn't expect that."

"Neither did I. I mean...I thought their relationship was odd. The way he was always so into her dating life, but you know brothers can be overprotective like that."

"Especially when they're trying to protect what they want."

Rochelle shook her head and leaned back in her chair. "Nathan? Are you sure?"

"Mom, the image is burned into my brain. I'm very sure."

"What happens now? And why did he sound angry about you with Richard after he did that?"

"Because I told him the truth. I told him that there was something there between Richard and me, but I let go of that fantasy. I was going to tell Nathan everything and see if he still wanted to do the show. Instead I find out he's possibly been cheating on me all along with Cassidy."

"Are you going to still do the show?"

"I don't know. We signed the contract, but they signed on for a happily engaged couple. Not one who can barely be in the same room with each other."

Rochelle reached over and placed a hand on Yvonne's. "Are you okay?"

The concerned question surprised Yvonne. She'd expected her mom to make excuses for Nathan, or try to justify what he'd done. Maybe even say Yvonne had pushed him toward messing up. Rochelle had never steered clear of finding the fault Yvonne played in her previous relationships. She hadn't expected this to be much different.

"I'm going to be okay. I was going to break off the engagement anyway. He made it easier to do."

"I thought you were in love with him."

"I did love him, but I wasn't ready to marry him."

"I wasn't going to say it, but I didn't like the way he proposed. In front of all those people so you had to say yes."

"I thought you were ecstatic. You loved Nathan and kept telling me how lucky I was."

Rochelle squeezed her hand then pulled back. "I meant what I said. I was happy for you. I wanted you to have what I couldn't have. I thought Richard was going to mess things up."

"Why were you so sure of that?"

"Because Richard is the one that got away, and your child's father. He'll always hold a spot in your heart. Why do you think I cheated on my husband and lost my family?"

Yvonne frowned. "You never said you'd had a relationship before with my father."

"Because no one knew about it. When I met him, he was a hustler who made his money scamming people, but I didn't care. The man was charismatic, and he had me so wrapped up in him I couldn't think of anything else. Then he went to jail and I met Valerie's father. The opposite of what I was used to. He treated me like a queen and was so sweet. I fell for it and told myself I didn't need the excitement. Then, your dad gets out of jail, he's found Jesus and started preaching. At *my* church, no less." Rochelle's eyes got a dreamy, faraway look, as if she were looking back and remembering the irresistible charm that came from being reunited with the one she'd lost. "I tried to ignore things. He'd gotten married, they were having a baby, I was supposed to be happy. But then one thing led to another and we were meeting up in the church basement almost every night. Charisma works on the street corner and in the church."

Jacob laughed as a water balloon landed on his head. "Did you see that?"

"I did, baby." Yvonne called back. She and Rochelle both clapped at his achievement.

"I'm going to do it again." His hand plunged back into the large tub of water balloons in the yard.

"Do you think I'd be making a mistake if I were to go back to Richard?" Yvonne asked the question hesitantly. Almost afraid to put the idea back into reality.

"I don't know. Richard isn't a bad man after all. He loves Jacob. He's rich." Rochelle shrugged. "And he's not sleeping with his stepsister."

Yvonne laughed. "True, but he did lie to me. He wasn't as interested in the show as he was in getting me back. I don't know if I can trust him not to hurt me again." If she were giving up one fantasy for another.

"Then take your time and figure it out. My biggest mistake was rushing back into things. I saw that in you. The way you jumped into things with your whole heart open. I worried it would mess you up the same way I messed up. Trust your heart, but don't let Richard or Nathan put you in a position to make a hasty decision. Men are good at that. At the end of the day remember you're the prize." Her mom shook her head. Her lips rose in a small smile. "We women would avoid so much trouble if we understood that from the start."

Chapter 25

The press release announcing her and Nathan's split went out the following week. She hadn't talked to Nathan. They'd handled the breakup like civilized people through their publicist. Richard texted the next day.

Are you okay?

She didn't answer. Partly because she didn't want to give him the impression he had a right to know. She'd trusted him again. Believed he was different, that he was serious about supporting her show on his network. Instead he'd used the show to get back on her good side. She knew he cared about Jacob. The emotion when they were together couldn't be feigned, and for that she couldn't completely cut Richard out of her life, but she was no longer going to give a hint of a chance for them to get back together.

The other reason she hadn't answered was because she'd avoided thinking about whether she was okay or not. Now she had to think about it. She was angry about the way she'd found out about Nathan and Cassidy. In hindsight, maybe she should have noticed that their relationship was a little too close. But she was even more disappointed about not being able to sell the show. Though her original goal when she started her interior design business hadn't been to eventually land on television, she'd gotten excited about the prospect of showing what she could do to a larger audience. Now that opportunity was gone.

I'm sorry. Please let me know you're okay.

As much as she wanted to ignore the message, she also accepted Richard would continue to check on her. **I'm fine.**

If you need anything let me know.

I'm fine.

If she needed anything she wouldn't go to him. No more looking for a perfect Prince Charming. She wasn't going to settle for anyone who wasn't sure they were ready to give as much in the relationship as she was. No more settling for the image of happiness instead of true happiness.

The next several days went by in a blur. She ignored phone calls and texts from Nathan, and the ones from Richard that weren't about Jacob. She finished work on several designs and started new projects. She accepted that her schedule was getting out of control and told Lashon she wouldn't be doing any more articles. Ignored that Lashon didn't seem to mind as much now that Nathan was out of the picture. She blatantly ignored Bree's attempts to get her to go and "get back out there." She wasn't closing herself off to love one day, but she also wasn't ready to jump back into the dating pool after nearly drowning in disappointment.

"Mommy, when is Daddy coming back to visit?" Jacob asked from the back seat of the car.

They were on the way to his summer camp. Yvonne gripped the steering wheel as she eased into the parking lot of his school where the summer camp was being held. Richard had taken Jacob out the previous weekend, but since then they were working out the visiting schedule.

"We're working out the next visit." She'd called her

lawyer to help finalize the details of visitation. Richard wanted Jacob to visit him this summer. Yvonne knew Jacob would be okay to spend time with Richard, but she was still worried. If Jacob went to D.C. it would be their first real separation. She had to get her mind right for that.

"He can't just come to the house anymore?" Jacob reached over and unbuckled the seatbelt going over his booster seat.

"Your dad has his own house and he wants you to visit him there sometimes." She got out of the car and went around to help Jacob.

Once he was out of the car and they were holding hands to walk in Jacob stopped and looked up at Yvonne. "Can't he come live with us?"

What about Nathan, was the first thing to pop into her mind. She didn't voice that question. When she'd explained to Jacob she wasn't marrying Nathan he'd immediately asked if it was because she was marrying his dad. The joy in his voice had been like a sizzling knife across her heart.

"Your dad lives somewhere else and he likes it there. He doesn't have to come stay with us."

"Don't you want him to live with us? Then we can be a real family." Jacob smiled at her as if he'd just made the offer of the year.

Her heart twisted. Partly because a piece of her did want them to be a real family. "It's not that easy, baby. Remember what I told you, it's going to be just us again."

She was saved from more questions by another parent walking out of the school speaking to them. Then one of Jacob's friends ran over, and they moved on to getting him signed in for the day.

Back in her car, Yvonne headed to Sandra's. The last of the furniture for Sandra's home had arrived, and the project was complete. The magazine that interviewed her and Nathan was interested in getting pictures of the interior and Sandra agreed.

The article was supposed to be in the issue two months

from now. The press release announcing their split was released too late to pull the article. Which meant the article about the loving couple would have to come with a footnote. *Yvonne and Nathan unfortunately split shortly after this interview. Nathan is no longer waiting for the right woman and is happily having sex with his stepsister on kitchen counters across America.*

The thought made her lips twitch, and before she knew it, she was chuckling at the absurdity of it all. Her life had become a soap opera plot line. There was no way she could handle any more surprises. Not unless some long-lost aunt on her absent father's side left her a castle in England and a title. She could deal with being a duchess.

Sandra greeted her with a big smile and hug. "The house looks perfect!"

Yvonne followed her inside and had to agree. She'd focused on complementing the architectural features of the home. Natural colors along with the excellent lighting, and bolder colors in areas that needed to be brightened. Heirloom antique furnishings and fresh transitional pieces coalesced to create a stylish and welcoming feel to the home.

"I'm glad you like it." She was proud of her work. This was why she loved interior design. She got to make people's homes speak for themselves. She made sanctuaries, work spaces, and havens for her clients.

"With the house being photographed today I thought it would be a good idea to have you on my show in the same month your article with Nathan comes out. It'll be good publicity."

Yvonne stopped walking. "About that."

Sandra turned around. She wore a long, red and purple silk tunic dress that brushed her feet and swirled when she moved. "The rumors about you and Richard Barrington. I wondered if you were going to bring them up or if I should."

Not surprising Sandra was well caught up on the gossip. For some reason, the woman was tuned in to what happened in Yvonne's life. "There's nothing to the rumors." Not really, now that she'd told Richard she wouldn't be with him. "But Richard wasn't the reason Nathan and I broke our engagement."

"What were the reasons?"

"We want different things." Different people.

Sandra crossed her arms over her chest and she lifted a brow. "I wondered when you would realize that."

Not the answer she'd expected. So, Sandra had assumed she and Nathan wouldn't make it. The thought irritated her. "I don't understand where you're coming from."

"I saw the look on your face when he asked you. I watched the video over and over, and each time nothing changed. You looked panicked and surprised for a split second. Then you were all smiles, hugs and kisses. He did that and you two hadn't ever talked seriously about marriage before, had you?"

"You got all of that from watching the video of the proposal?" Yvonne raised a brow.

"It's my job to read people when I'm interviewing them. Split second facial expressions always give people away."

"Why were you watching the video over and over? Was it to make sure you were hiring someone who was legit?"

"No, it's because I'm nosey and I wanted to know more about you two. My parents were terrible at marriage and, let's be real, dating can suck. You and Nathan seemed too good to be true," Sandra said as if daring Yvonne to question her reasons. "Even though I thought that, I'm kinda bummed you two aren't going to work out."

Yvonne rolled her eyes. "Tell me about it. Guess I won't be gracing television screens with my designs."

Sandra cocked her head to the side. "Why not?"

"Nathan and I are split. We were doing the show together."

"You don't need Nathan to do a show."

Obviously, but doing a show had been Nathan's idea. He'd originally agreed when Judy approached them about doing that. He'd pushed to make sure their image was impeccable, so they could represent the "Southern Sophistication" the show they pitched was supposed to represent.

"It was Nathan's thing," Yvonne said.

"But that doesn't mean *you* shouldn't do a show. I mean, contractors are a dime a dozen. The spark in your relationship with Nathan was you. You're the one the people loved when you both were noticed on *Celebrity Housewives*. You're the one people want to know about."

"You think?" She considered Sandra's take. Sure, she was the one the producers on *Celebrity Housewives* noticed first. Her interactions with the housewife had become a focal point of one episode. When Nathan asked her out, that's when the producers began to pay attention to them both.

"I know. I watch that show and so do my listeners. And, to be honest, most of the online chatter is in your favor."

Yvonne shook her head. "One, what online chatter? And, two, I'd expect more people to be sympathetic to Nathan. I'm the one with the kid whose father showed up."

"First of all." Sandra held up a finger. "I need you to stop pretending as if there isn't online chatter about you. Second." Another finger popped up. "You and Richard aren't together. The question was asked if Nathan couldn't deal because Jacob's father came back. Which doesn't endear a lot of people to him for bailing after his promises of always and forever, let's wait until marriage, Yvonne is my best friend. He's not contradicting the rumors, and he was seen in Savannah with a redhead yesterday. Everyone is Team Yvonne on this split."

"Wow." She couldn't believe it. Maybe she did need to check out the online chatter. After the split, she hadn't wanted to see what people were saying. So, she'd focused on making the transition easier for Jacob. Even so, if people were sympathetic to her, and if the interest was in her personality, could she still have a show?

"Exactly. If I were you, I'd find a new publicist and start telling networks you're ready to still do the show without Nathan."

Yvonne nodded and smiled what felt like the first real smile she'd been able to muster since the disastrous day she'd had her relationships with Richard and Nathan implode. "Maybe I will. Hey, Sandra, I appreciate this. I know when we first met I was..."

"Standoffish?"

Understatement of the year. "A little. Through all of that you've always been extremely nice to me, and willing to go above and beyond. I appreciate that."

Sandra sighed then bit her lower lip. "Well, I have my reasons."

"Whatever they are, I'm happy you have them."

Sandra wrung her hands together. For the first time since Yvonne had known her, she appeared nervous. "You may not say so once you hear. There is really only one reason I want to not only know more about you, but also help you out."

"Mind telling me what that reason is?"

Sandra swallowed hard then grinned. A big, broad, nervous grin. "We're half-sisters."

Yvonne's jaw dropped. She had to be joking. She'd wanted a lost aunt who left her a castle and title. Not...this. "What the hell?"

Sandra held out her arms. "Surprise."

Chapter 26

Yvonne stared down at the piece of paper with the proof that Sandra was indeed her half-sister. She placed a hand over her mouth and took a long, considering breath. What in the world? She had another sister.

She looked up from the paper across the table to the only sister she'd known all her life. They sat in Valerie's office. That was the first place Yvonne had considered going after getting the results of the DNA test Sandra had agreed to. The DNA test wasn't really necessary. Sandra had nothing to gain by claiming to be Yvonne's sister. It wasn't as if Yvonne was about to inherit that castle she'd fantasized about, and Sandra ran a successful business and had a massive following through her radio show. If anyone would benefit from their relation, it was Yvonne, because she'd now have a sister who was tapped into such a broad reach.

"It's true then." Valerie said. Sunlight streamed in through the floor-to-ceiling windows in Valerie's office and the golden color on the walls gave the room a warm glow.

"What are you going to do?"

"What can I do?" Yvonne pointed at the paper. "She's my sister. I can't change that."

Valerie rolled her eyes then looked at Yvonne as if her brain wasn't functioning. "I mean, what are you going to do now that you know? Are you okay with it? Angry she kept it from you for so long?"

"I'm...happy."

"About what?"

"I finally have some link to my dad's family. It's not just this dark void of family history that I'll never get to explore."

"Are you going to spend time with him?" Valerie asked.

Yvonne shook her head. "No. Before we decided to take the DNA test, Sandra told me she'd spoken to her dad...our dad. He said she was making a mistake stirring up old dirt like this. He told her not to do it, and that if she insisted on going through with it, he didn't want anything to do with me."

"Really? After all these years, he still wants to be a jerk about this?" Valerie sounded like she wished Yvonne's dad was in the room so she could knock some sense into him.

"The thing is, I don't care about him being a jerk." Valerie raised a brow and Yvonne shrugged. "Okay, knowing he still wants nothing to do with me does sting." A lot. "But not as much as it did before when I knew nothing about him. I've had a long time to come to terms with my father not wanting me. This newest revelation isn't anything less than what I would have expected of him."

She hadn't even been able to muster up a lot of outrage when Sandra apologetically told her about her father's stance. She was angry her father hadn't felt the need to take care of his responsibilities. That he'd been willing to walk away from a child he helped create and never look back. But that was his problem. Letting that anger control her life would only cause her grief. Her dad was still out there living his life.

Not thinking about her. There was no reason to hinder her mental state carrying around the stress and anger of a situation she couldn't control.

Instead, learning she had another sibling. Not one who resented her or blamed her for the problems in her parents' marriage, but one who cared enough to find her, get to know her, and ultimately help her. Well, that didn't make up for her father being an asshole, but it damn sure made the sting of his rejection less potent. And knowing he was against Sandra getting to know her but Sandra insisted, made the petty side of her brain very happy. Everyone should indulge in the petty in certain situations.

"I guess you're right," Valerie said grudgingly. "I just don't know if I could be that...open to someone new in my life."

"The way my life has changed so much over the past few weeks, I can't help but be open to new experiences and sudden changes. I can't control what's happening around me, but I can control how I respond to what's happening."

"You sound like a training video on handling stress." Valerie looked skyward with the flatly delivered words, but her lips quirked up at the ends.

"I think I did hear that in a training somewhere." Yvonne grinned at her sister's I-knew-it smirk. "There's actually good information in most training videos. The problem is that people don't follow the advice."

"And you're following the advice and going to embrace having a new sister in your life. It's all slumber parties and let's braid each other's hair."

"I'm not saying all of that, but she has been there for me so far. She introduced me to one of the executives of Tribute Network. The talks are super preliminary, but he was really excited about the idea of doing a show with me."

"Seriously?"

Yvonne nodded. "Seriously. This may work out. Can you believe it?"

"I can. I know it was originally Nathan's idea for you two to try and do a home renovation show, but I know you can pull it off. You don't need him to carry you. You can carry yourself."

"I can carry myself." Yvonne nodded and let the words sink in and support her confidence. "I like the sound of that. It's true. I got so wrapped up in having a partner in Nathan, I forgot about how much I'd been able to accomplish on my own. I'm ready to tackle what's ahead."

Valerie tapped on the paper. "Including having a new sister."

Yvonne picked up the paper and studied the results. She thought about Jacob and Nadia, how she wanted them to know each other and have some type of relationship even if she and Richard hadn't worked out. If anything, she'd learned family was important. Her mom and sister had been her support system for years. Maybe not always providing support in the way she'd wanted, or even needed, but she'd known they'd been there. She wanted that for Jacob. For him to know where he came from and who he was connected to. The best way to do that was by also embracing her connections.

"No hair braiding and slumber parties, but, yes, I am ready to include having a new sister in my life."

Two days before Yvonne's radio interview on Sandra's show, Nathan came by her office. Bree was out of the office so there was no one there to pretend as if Yvonne was out for the day. Yvonne wanted to be annoyed by the interruption, but the time had come for them to talk. Her anger had died down, and now she only wanted to understand what had happened.

Nathan stopped at her door. He watched her warily with a hesitant smile. He looked good. More tan from working outside. His sandy brown hair lighter. The white button up shirt and jeans flattering against his lean, muscular form. She still cared about him, but she didn't feel the rush of love she'd once felt. Love that had been wrapped up in a sense of comfort like a baby in a blanket. Warm and protected with no worries, while someone else handled responsibilities.

That's how she'd viewed Nathan. As her protection from the storm of life, and the never-ending gale of worry and doubt. She'd thought she was struggling to make things work on her own and that Nathan would make things easier. When, in reality, she had been making it on her own. Nathan had been a bonus, but it took their relationship imploding for her to realize that.

Yvonne stood from behind her desk. "Come in."

Nathan closed the door, and she walked over to the round meeting table she kept in her office. Nathan crossed to her, his arms spread as if he were going to hug her.

Yvonne looked away and pulled out a chair before he could follow through. "How's it going?"

Nathan's hands lowered slowly. After a heartbeat, he pulled out the other chair and slid into it. He ran his hands over his pants legs. "I've been busy. We've got the hospital in Savannah under control. I'm starting on a few other projects. You?"

"Going well. I have the interview on Sandra's show in a couple of days. We're going to talk about my plans for the future."

"I heard about you getting your own show."

He smiled, and she searched to see if it was sincere. There was no hate in his voice or his eyes. She shouldn't have expected there to be any. Nathan had always been supportive. "Yeah, it's kind of amazing and scary, but I'm ready for the challenge."

"You deserve it. You were always the more interesting personality in our idea. I can't wait to watch."

"I appreciate that, Nathan. Thanks."

"Sounds like things have worked out." His pitch raised at the end of the sentence, turning it into a question.

She picked at the edge of her blouse. "Not all things."

Nathan grimaced and ran a hand through his hair. "Guess not."

"So...do you want to tell me about that?"

Nathan leaned back. He blew air out in a long steady breath. "The thing with Cassidy started a while ago."

"How long is a while?" She was ready to talk, and had let go of the anger, but if he told her he'd been messing around with Cassidy the entire time they were together she couldn't guarantee angry Yvonne wouldn't resurface.

His eyes widened as her meaning settled into his brain. Nathan held up a hand and shook his head. "Not like that. Not while we were together. Our parents got married when we were twelve. It was weird because we'd known each other from school. She was the cute girl my friends and I had just started to notice, and suddenly she became my sister. Mom and Dad really wanted us to get along, so that's what we did. We became best friends. That worked through middle and high school. Cassidy went to college, and I took over for my dad's contracting company. Whenever she came home, we went right back to being friends, but things shifted. Felt... different. We slept together after she graduated."

"That was years ago. Are you telling me you've been having this secret thing for years?"

Nathan shook his head. "That's not what happened. The next day we tried to tell Mom and Dad, but they were planning a family reunion and were looking through old pictures. They kept going on and on about how proud they were of us, and how lucky they were that we'd gotten along and become true brother and sister. I didn't have the heart to tell them. I felt terrible, guilty, dirty. Cassidy thought I was being stupid. I moved to Atlanta and made a pact to get over wanting

Cassidy. I thought lust was the reason for what happened. So, I decided to abstain. I wouldn't let lust and desire push me into making another bad decision. I swore off meaningless or spontaneous sex and focused on finding a wife."

Yvonne could understand the confusion that must have come after he and Cassidy slept together. She couldn't imagine being in his position and couldn't say what she would have done if put in a similar situation. Though she didn't agree with his plan of living like a monk as punishment for a perceived sin. That only suppressed feelings and lead to emotional explosions like the ones he and Cassidy frequently had. "You pushed yourself to try and be with someone you don't really want."

Nathan leaned forward and rested his arms on the table. "I'd say you were doing the same."

Truth tended to sting when people threw it back at you. When she saw Richard again, she'd known deep down he still had access to her heart. A part of her still wanted him. Couldn't shake that silly voice that said he was *the one*. The elusive person you were destined to be with. But if that were the case, and she really was supposed to be with Richard, why did he keep messing things up?

Maybe because you aren't his one.

That hurt to think about, so she addressed Nathan's accusation first. "First, Richard was out of my life for years. When we went out, I wasn't trying to be with someone I didn't want."

"I saw it in your face the moment he returned. You realized you were making a mistake."

That wasn't entirely true. When Richard returned, she had thought Nathan was the best choice. The safer choice.

"Richard isn't the reason our engagement was a mistake. When you asked me, I hadn't really considered marriage. We were good together. You were safe."

Nathan winced. "Ouch. Safe."

"You were. That, and you were great with Jacob. I thought

you wanted me for me despite all that I came with. It's been a long time since I've felt that way."

"I did want you for you. What I felt for you wasn't a lie. Neither is what I feel for Cassidy."

She believed him. Maybe they both had believed they'd found what they'd been searching for. He found the perfect woman who didn't have the potential to tear apart his family. She'd found the perfect man who was ready to embrace her and her son.

"What are you two going to do?" she asked.

"We're going to tell our family." His voice was confident. His eyes were nervous. She doubted this decision was easy for him. "Now that everyone knows you and I aren't together, my parents want to know why. I don't want to continue to hide my feelings." He smiled and looked like a guy about to take on an unexpected and scary adventure. "I don't know how things will turn out, but I need to find out. Saying this may be wrong of me, but, seeing you and Richard is part of the reason."

"How? You didn't trust Richard."

"That's because I know a threat when I see one. I thought he was only out to get you back."

Yvonne cringed. Again, stung by the truth. Except this sting was like being wrapped in the tendrils of a jellyfish. "You weren't wrong about that. I found out he was hoping to get me back. His ex-wife threatened to tear apart the company if he went along with the show. He was willing to let the show drop, but wanted to wait until he could work things out with me first. I think that's the only reason they made the offer in the first place."

Nathan frowned. "I don't think so. I didn't believe it when he said he wanted the show before knowing who we were, but Judy backed up his words. She told me the network liked the idea of a couple's home renovation show. Part of the push for original programming."

"Okay, but that doesn't take away from the fact that Richard tried to use the show to get close to me."

Nathan ran a hand through his hair then eyed her warily. "About that. I did talk to him man-to-man about that."

"You what?" When had Nathan even had the chance to be alone with Richard?

"I wanted to know what his end game was. He admitted he cared about you, but also that he only wanted you to be happy and to get his family together. If I had to be a part of the deal, then he'd be okay with that."

Yvonne's jaw dropped. A second later she snapped it shut. The stinging pain of Richard's words lost their potency. "He said that?"

Nathan exhaled slowly. "He did. That's when I knew I had serious competition. He still loves you, but he wasn't going to love you at the expense of forcing me out of your life. I didn't like it, but I had to respect it."

She looked away. Thoughts went through a spinner in her mind. Had she misjudged what he said? Did it matter if she had? What did this mean?

Nathan's hand closed over hers, jerking her back to their conversation. "I don't know what to tell you about Richard. What I can tell you is that I forced myself to conceal my feelings for Cassidy for years because of pride and worry about what other people would think. Lies kept you from the father of your child. The man you were in love with, and I don't think you ever got over that. How about we both stop letting unrealistic expectations and fears keep us from being happy."

That's why she'd fallen for Nathan. He was always so steady, so sensible, so supportive. No matter what happened, she knew she'd always want him as a friend in her life. She flipped her hand over and squeezed his. "I like that idea."

Chapter 27

"Are you ready?"

Yvonne looked up from the magazine she'd been reading while waiting for her segment on Sandra's show. Her nerves had finally died down from *I'm-going-to-throw-up* to *I'm-only-moderately-nauseous* levels. She wasn't sure why. She'd done interviews before, was filming the pilot for her television show, and had sat in confessionals during her short stint on *Celebrity Housewives*. But this felt different. Before she'd only seen the interviewer, or a cameraman, and she hadn't been live. Live for thousands of listeners.

Sandra hurried across the green room and sat next to Yvonne. "Don't panic. You will do great."

"It's that obvious?"

Sandra scrunched her nose then nodded. "Do I need to get you a bag?"

Yvonne laughed and took a deep breath. "No. I'm not going to be sick. Just a little nervous."

"Don't even think about the people listening. Just act like you're talking to me. That should make it easier."

That would make it easier. In the few weeks since learning Sandra was her sister, they had spent more time together, talking and getting to know more about each other and their childhoods. Yvonne had always assumed her father's kids with his wife lived some perfect ideal life. The perfect mom and dad with their happy little family. She'd envisioned Christmases with lots of presents, birthdays full of love and laughter, and proud faces beaming, giving standing ovations after every school event.

The reality of Sandra's childhood was much different. She'd grown up watching her parents fight constantly about her father's infidelity, until finally her mother had gotten a boyfriend. Her parents' secret, but not so secret, other lives caused an oppressive sadness in the home. Yvonne's childhood had been full of her mother's warnings not to make the same mistakes she had, but there hadn't been sadness or an absence of love. Her mom had been there for her and Valerie at every school event, and always struggled to make holidays and birthdays special, if meager.

"I think I can handle that," she said.

"And remember, I'm not going to go into our connection as sisters. That can be handled later if we want to." Sandra said quietly so they wouldn't be overheard by anyone walking by the green room.

They'd both agreed Yvonne's life was hectic enough with the announcement of her broken engagement and connection to Richard. They didn't need to add finding a long-lost sister to the mix. Besides, they wanted to spend more time getting to know each other before letting others in. Valerie was an exception of course. Her sister had insisted on getting to know Sandra. Yvonne hadn't argued. She loved Valerie and how she always had her back.

"Sounds good."

"We'll focus on your new show, your design background,

and maybe a little of the dirt from *Celebrity Housewives*." Sandra stood.

Yvonne laughed and got up as well. "Only a little. I'd like to keep the confidentially of my clients. It's good for business."

Sandra waved a hand, but grinned. "Fine, if you have to be honorable."

They walked out of the green room to the sound room where Sandra's show was recorded.

"You know, you really dodged a bullet by not doing the show with W.E.W.," Sandra said.

"Why do you say that? I mean, I'm ecstatic about the new deal, but W.E.W. is one of the top networks."

"Was one of the top networks." She glanced at Yvonne. She must have seen the confusion in Yvonne's expression because she stopped to place a hand on Yvonne's arm. "You don't know?"

"Know what?"

"Richard Barrington sold his shares in the company."

"What?" The question rang out between them.

"Yes," Sandra said, shaking her head. "He said he's ready for a clean start and is focusing on new opportunities. He's no longer tied to the network or any of his family's previous holdings."

"None of them?" She sounded like a parrot, but she didn't care. She could barely form another thought as she wrapped her mind around what Sandra was saying.

Richard had sold his shares in the company? "That makes no sense. His company is the most important thing to him."

Sandra raised a brow. "Is it?" She gave Yvonne a knowing look before walking into the sound room.

Yes, it was. He'd once been willing to sacrifice his own happiness for the company. Would do anything to grow and increase its reach and influence including marrying a woman he didn't love. What would make him give all of that up?

"You coming?" Sandra asked before Yvonne could complete her train of thought.

She pushed the shock of Richard's decision out of her mind. Right now, she was about to start the first round of promotion for her new television show. Her show! This deserved all her attention. Figuring out what was going on with Richard could wait.

"I'm ready."

Excellent interview.

The text message from Richard came thirty minutes after she finished her interview with Sandra. An interview she'd gotten through without throwing up. Her nerves had settled and once she and Sandra started talking, she'd gotten into the groove of the conversation. The time had flown by and she'd ended up having fun. Now she was on her way out of the radio station and on her way to pick up Jacob.

She'd effectively put the situation with Richard and his company out of her mind. With two words, he was right back in the forefront of her thoughts. Her heart did a small lurch. Her palms became sweaty around her phone.

Thank you.

That could be the end of their text conversation. She'd made sure to keep their conversations short, sweet, and to the point since walking out of his offices. Focused solely on his next visit with Jacob, how they would handle the transfer, and communications through their lawyers on the points of the long-term visitation schedule. It was all very civilized and responsible. She hated it.

Jacob was introduced to his dad casually. Which meant he didn't understand why the easy way his dad used to show up and hang out with them no longer happened. The disappointment on his face broke her heart every time.

I heard about you selling your shares? Why?

He didn't owe her an answer. If he chose to ignore her then she'd suck up her curiosity and move on.

She didn't want to move on. She wanted an answer.

I needed a clean break.

A clean break? Could Richard be any vaguer? Break from what and why? Okay, she was overthinking things. Over hoping things. Like hoping he realized he'd sacrificed enough already to save the company his father started.

She didn't like admitting how much time Richard had occupied in her brain since she'd talked to Nathan. Knowing he'd said the same thing to Nathan she'd overheard in his office made her reevaluate that entire conversation. Yes, he had been willing to drag things out to placate Natalie while he figured out how to make things work with her, but that didn't mean he'd lied to her about the show or his belief in the show's merits. Another revelation emerged from what Nathan pointed out—technically, he hadn't lied to her.

Jacob misses you.

She opted to text something safe instead of asking more about his need for a clean break. If he wanted to tell her, then he would.

I'm in town. I know it's not my day. I'd like to come by.

Here is where she could say no. She felt the slippery slope she was on. The unsteadiness of knowing that if she fell, things would hurt. Did she want to fall? Did she want to believe in Richard one more time? She took herself out of the equation and thought of Jacob. He'd be happy to see his dad. If she got a weird vibe off Richard, then she would send him home without giving anything more of herself.

Jacob would like that. We'll be home after six.

Thank you. I'll see you later.

Chapter 28

For the rest of the afternoon she barely focused on anything. A few clients called to ask for updates on their projects and to tell her she was great on the radio; she tried to give them her full attention. Eventually she gave up for the day. School was back in, so she picked up Jacob from afterschool care and dinner from a Tex-Mex place. With extra queso and chips for Jacob.

Once home, she connected her phone to a pair of Bluetooth speakers in the kitchen. Old school R&B filled the kitchen as she put away the cups, bowls and other things left out in their mad dash to leave the house on time that morning.

"Mommy, can I switch the music?" Jacob already had her phone in his hand. "I don't want to hear this lovey stuff." He frowned as if lovey stuff was terrible.

"Go ahead," she said, laughing.

Soon after the upbeat tones of Kidz Bop replaced her lovey music. Yvonne sang along to the pop song. Jacob's enthusiastic voice accompanied. Soon they were in the middle of a two-person dance party.

Yvonne turned up the music and held a wooden spoon like a microphone in front of her face. She jumped up and down and raised her other arm as she belted out the words off key. Jacob danced around her.

When the song ended, Yvonne and Jacob both laughed. Jacob wrapped his arms around her legs, his grinning face beaming up at her. She hugged him tight and kissed his head. She couldn't remember the last time she'd had a dance party with Jacob. This was what brought sunshine to her life. These perfect moments with her son. Finding time to live life to the fullest. She wouldn't neglect that part of herself again.

Someone knocked on the back door right before the next song started. Yvonne swerved to the door. Richard stood on the other side of the screen smiling at them. She'd left the back door open when she'd taken the trash out earlier. Her stomach tightened. He had shared this moment with them.

Three things registered in her brain. Yearning to wrap her arms around him and soak in the love she saw on his face. A trace of affection fluttering around her middle. Unexpected desire. What was noticeably missing was the wary protectiveness that once kept her on edge whenever he came near.

She wanted him. In her arms. In her life. Smiling at her like that.

Jacob tore away from her and ran to the door. "Dad! You missed the dance party."

Jacob pushed open the screen door. Richard focused on Jacob while Yvonne's world spun. Nathan had been right: she'd never gotten over Richard.

Realizing she still wanted Richard was like a punch from Mohammad Ali. Her ears rang, and buzzing filled her head. She wasn't sure if she should be exhilarated or scared. Going with this, accepting this, would put her back in the same space she'd been in years ago.

"I saw some of it," Richard said to Jacob. "Looks like you two were having a good time."

"We were. Mommy sings real good," Jacob said.

Richard looked up at Yvonne. A sparkle in his eye and a hint of a smile hovered over his lips. "She does. I'd forgotten how well you sing."

She lifted a shoulder and hurried to her phone to turn off the music. "I wouldn't expect you to remember everything."

"There isn't much about you I forgot," he said. "You were always so full of life. So ready to make people smile. It's good to see that part of you again."

Yvonne stared at him for a long second as her world pivoted. She quickly turned away. She pulled a strip of paper towel off the roll and wiped at her sweaty brow. Sweat from dancing, and a little from the I-still-love-him panic attack she was trying to avoid. "We were just about to eat."

"Guess I got here in time."

"I hope you like tacos," she said.

She faced him again. Richard walked over to her and pulled a small piece of paper towel that was stuck to her temple right near her hair line. Yvonne went completely still. The brush of his fingers on her face ignited a spark in her chest. She should have stepped back or walked away while his fingers lingered on her temple.

"I gratefully accept whatever you offer." His voice dropped. Grew husky. Questioning.

Warning bells rang in her head. She needed to step away. Her breathing hadn't slowed down, and she swallowed hard. His gaze traced over her face. Stopped on her lips. She remembered his kiss. He still tasted the same. Sweetness and temptation wrapped in warmth that penetrated every corner of her soul. Richard must have felt something too, because his fingers ran from her temple, down her cheek to the racing pulse at her throat.

"Thank you for allowing me to come over." He inched closer until the enticing smell of his cologne mingled with the heat of her body and made her light up.

She slipped to the side. Out of his reach, before Jacob got a firsthand demonstration of the lovey stuff he hated. "Who's ready to eat?"

Jacob jumped up and down. "I am!"

She clapped her hands. Forced down her raging hormones. "Let's do this."

They sat around the table for dinner. Jacob's enthusiasm to have them both there didn't disappear as they ate. He beamed at her and Richard the entire time. She didn't need to give a penny for Jacob's thoughts because they were written all over his face. He had his family and he was happy.

After they put Jacob to bed, Richard followed her back into the living room. The atmosphere between them tonight was different. The anticipation of words begging to be spoken vibrated around them like hummingbird wings. Words she'd suppressed from the moment he walked back into her life. Yvonne couldn't sit down, so she straightened the pillows on the couch and tried not to obsess about the last time they were alone in this room.

"You can relax, you know. I'm not going to push." Richard eased down onto the edge of the couch. She got the feeling he didn't want to make her even more jumpy with sudden movement.

"Push what?"

"You. Me. How we move forward."

"Do we move forward?" The question burst from her lips. Irritation suddenly itched across her skin. Why was he so calm and collected when her world still reeled? He said he still loved her, but he was acting as if they were a business deal he had to work out.

"I'd like to." He watched her closely. His body still. Waiting. "I'm sorry about you and Nathan. I know you loved him."

She walked around the couch and sat on the opposite edge from him. "Breaking up with Nathan was the right thing to do."

"I hope I didn't—"

"And it had nothing to do with you." She wasn't ready to tell Richard about what happened with Nathan. She still cared about Nathan, and until she knew what was happening with her and Richard she wouldn't put Nathan's personal life in Richard's hands.

Richard pressed his lips together. He ran a hand over his top lip. Guess she'd sparked his own frustration. "Yvonne—"

"I'd gotten over you. I'd finally gotten past the pain in my heart and believed I could move on. Finally decided to trust again and you come back. All my plans to give Jacob a stable life, ruined."

Richard slid closer to her on the couch. "You don't need him or me to give Jacob stability. You've already done that."

"I know I can provide for him. I wanted him to have what I didn't have. I wanted him to have a father."

Richard jumped up from the couch and paced toward the wall before swinging back to face her. He placed the palm of his right hand against his chest. "He has a father. I will never walk out on him."

"I want to believe that."

"You want to believe it because you know I'm being honest. You want to believe it because you know what's between us didn't go away after six years. We both know we would be together if we'd done things differently."

She stood and pointed at him. "Not us. You. You walked away. You killed us."

"And you buried our relationship under fifty thousand dollars." The words were stated simply with no accusation. She still felt the sting.

She tried to turn away, but Richard closed the distance and took her wrist in his hand. "To hell with the past. None of that matters right now. Let's stop rehashing it. When I said I needed a clean break, I meant it, but that's not the only reason I sold my company shares. I don't want to have to consult with Natalie before I do something with the business. The only thing Natalie and I should consult each other on is how we take care of Nadia. I gave up everything I ever wanted to carry on the legacy of a man who lied to me in the end. I don't want anything to do with my father's company, or his plans for me. I want you to know that nothing will pull me away from being the man who should have been there for you and Jacob from the start." He tugged on her hand and pulled her closer. "Build a future with me. Let's fix what others tore to pieces. I won't hurt you like that ever again."

"You said that before."

"Before there was Natalie. My dad, the business. Not anymore, Yvonne. Today, there's me and you and our son." His eyes were serious as he met her gaze. His hands clung to hers. "I won't let my father's corrupt idea of a legacy have control over the parts of my life I want to embrace."

"I didn't ask you to do this. I didn't want you to give up everything to prove something."

"I didn't give up the business to prove anything to anyone. I did this to prove something to myself. When I walked away from you before, it was because I tried to do the right thing. Not only for Natalie, but for my family's corporation. I lost so much more instead. Natalie and I both knew we weren't in love, but convenience and money made everything else seem okay. I couldn't imagine a world where I wasn't there for my child. Instead I turned my back on you and lost so much time with Jacob." His voice broke. He cleared his throat and took a deep breath. "Family is the most important thing to me. You, Jacob, Nadia, and, yes, Natalie because she is the mother of my child. But you're the woman I want to be in my life. You've always been the woman I want in my life. I don't want to push; I know your engagement just ended, and that you're afraid to trust me. But I'd like to know if there is even the hope of a future for us. I'll give you all the time and space you need, but please let me know if we have a chance."

Yvonne closed her eyes. She knew exactly what she wanted to do. Not because she needed him in her life. Not because she wanted a father for her son. Not because she couldn't be happy if she didn't have the perfect family. She wanted him because the ache in her heart she'd hidden from the world, from herself, had only intensified each day since he'd walked back into her life. Years ago, she'd given him her heart without a second thought and he'd crushed it to mush. Despite all of that, she'd forgiven him. Accepted that their time hadn't been right six years ago, but maybe they were right for each other now.

The relief of letting go of her pain manifested itself in silent tears. Warm, strong fingers brushed away her tears with a gentle caress. His forehead pressed to hers. His hand cupped her cheek. Richard wrapped his arm around her waist and pulled her body closer against his. He held her close, cradling her as if she were precious.

"Why can't I get over you?" she whispered. Pain, longing, and fear squeezed her lungs. This man had the power to give her joyous expectation and panic.

She opened her eyes. Hope and a small hint of relief filled his dark gaze. "If you hurt me again, I'll survive, but if you hurt Jacob, I'll hurt you."

"I know you will," he said seriously. He brushed his thumb over her lower lip. "Can I kiss you now?" His voice was a low, rumbling caress.

Yvonne tilted her head up and brushed her lips over his. "No, I can kiss you."

He trembled just a little. His arms pulled her in closer. Six years of craving made their kiss wild and desperate. The walls were down. There were no bonds or commitments to stir up guilt as she led him to her bedroom.

"Look at me," he said later when she lay breathless in his arms. A thin layer of sweat coated their bodies. Her memories of how good things were between her and Richard had not been inflated.

Yvonne slowly lifted her lashes. The emotion in his eyes took her breath away. "I love you. Always you. Only you."

His words sent a thousand flutters over her skin, into her heart, down to her soul. Had she ever stopped loving Richard? She'd cursed him, wished she'd never met him, but she hadn't been able to kill the love she'd had for him. She knew that.

She placed her hand on his cheek. Leaned in and kissed him slowly. "I love you, too, Richard."

Chapter 29

"I still can't believe it's been a year for you."

Richard's groan vibrated in his chest beneath Yvonne. The revelation of his celibacy came during their second round of post-sex discussion when she'd told him she was on birth control. After the greatest "uh oh" of her life, Jacob, Yvonne hadn't trusted taking a pill a day and opted for an IUD after having Jacob.

"Why do you keep bringing that up?"

Yvonne grinned at him. "You don't seem out of practice."

Richard laughed and ran his big hand down her back to caress her backside. "I don't ride a bike every day, but that doesn't mean I forgot how to ride one."

"True." She ran her fingers through the hair on his chest. A year was a long time. She knew his divorce was right before he'd come back into her life. "And you never once..."

"No. I never stepped out on Natalie," he said forcefully.

She believed him. Richard didn't like complications and having a mistress would have caused too many. That, and he really wanted to be an honorable guy. "Why did you two get divorced?"

His heavy sigh seemed to rise from deep in his soul. His fingers ran through her hair and he frowned at the ceiling. "We couldn't pretend to make it work anymore."

"Pretend?"

"Natalie didn't trust me after we got back together," he said. "I don't think she would have gone through with the wedding if it wasn't for Nadia and the merger."

"Would the companies have still merged if she hadn't gotten pregnant?"

Richard shrugged. "Our dads really pushed the merger. Two family companies that wanted to grow but keep it all in the family. That was their mantra. I'll admit, during the time Natalie and I were split, the talks began to break down. Natalie's father wasn't happy about trusting the man who'd just left his daughter. Money can go a long way to healing wounded pride, he was just beginning to come around when Natalie told me about the pregnancy."

"Even though she didn't trust you, she stayed with you?"

"The first year was okay. The second I actually thought we could build a happy life." He said the last part as if he were surprised he once believed that. She wasn't surprised. Richard didn't do anything halfway.

"What happened?"

His brows drew together. "I dreamed of you one night. Woke up thinking of you and called her your name. Our marriage steadily declined after."

Yvonne cringed and lifted her head. "How are you still alive? I would have killed you."

"I'm not proud of that moment." He ran a hand over his face. "But that moment forced me to admit I'd made a mistake marrying Natalie. That was right before congestive heart failure finally took my dad's life. Our last disagreement was when I told him I shouldn't have married her. That I was going to consider a divorce."

"I would think that would've been the time he told you I'd taken fifty grand and ran."

"I've thought back on that day and wonder the same thing. Instead, he reminded me of my responsibility. Natalie and I had a place in society. We were a business power couple. Partners in business and life, and if I couldn't make it with her then I couldn't make it with anyone. Then he hit my conscience hard. Don't ever say taking care of your child and marrying your child's mother is a mistake. That's what he said to me."

"He made you feel guilty." She couldn't imagine one day using guilt to make Jacob stay in an unhappy situation. Above anything she wanted Jacob's life to be filled with love, laughter, and success, but not at the expense of him being unhappy.

"His words made me try harder to make my marriage work."

"Realizing you shouldn't have married Natalie even though she was pregnant with your child shouldn't make you feel bad." Yvonne shifted until she was on her back next to him.

Richard rolled onto his side. Gentle hands traced up her stomach to the valley between her breasts. "I know that now. It won't be easy, but we can make this work. All of us, for the kids."

"I want to believe you."

He turned her, so they faced each other, and their eyes met. "We'll do this together and we'll be the bigger people. For Jacob and Nadia's sake."

The way ahead was sure to be as hard as a concrete slab, but she remembered the way Jacob and Nadia laughed and played together. She wanted her son to know his sister and have a real relationship with her. Natalie may not want to play nice, but if they sat down like adults who wanted the best for their children then maybe they could make this work.

She pushed away her doubts. Pushed away the pain of their past. Right now, she was happy. In his arms, someplace she never thought she'd be again, she was happier than she'd ever admit to him. She ran her hands up the muscles of his chest and rested them on his broad shoulders. She rolled him onto his back and straddled his waist. "Let's give it a try."

Chapter 30

Yvonne had to travel to New York to film a special for her show. *Her show!* She still couldn't believe viewers were excited to watch her do her thing, but she sure enjoyed every minute.

She'd hoped Richard would have had the chance to come up from D.C. and see her while she'd been in the Northeast, but he'd gotten caught up in business meetings. Apparently selling his shares hadn't been as easy a process as he'd told her it would be. Natalie fought him, and even though his brother wanted to purchase Richard's share, Natalie fought that idea even more.

Yvonne wasn't an I-told-you-so kind of person, but finding out that Natalie wasn't going to make their future easy wasn't something she wanted to be right about. Her plane home was delayed, which meant she didn't get back in Atlanta until after eleven. She called her mom to ask if she'd keep Jacob over one more night and take him to school the next morning, instead of her coming to pick him up late. Rochelle agreed, and Yvonne headed straight for home.

While she'd enjoyed New York, she preferred the warm, fall nights of Atlanta. She was tired and wanted nothing more than to be in her bed.

She pulled up to her home eager to get out of her clothes and into pajamas while putting off thoughts about the next project until tomorrow.

"What the hell?" she murmured to herself. A car with a rental tag was in her yard. Luxury sedan.

The light in her living room was also on. Whomever had come by was in her house. She pulled out her cell phone to call the police when her front door opened. Richard. She'd given him a key the week prior when he'd needed to get in with Jacob when she'd worked late.

She cut the engine and got out of the car. Her heart still pounding. "You scared me half to death. I was just about to call the police. What are you doing here?" she said as she rushed to the front door.

The closer she got, the better she got a look at him. His t-shirt and jeans weren't wrinkled but there was stubble on his jaw, lines around his red rimmed eyes, and pain in his expression. Forgetting about the scare, Yvonne hurried forward to him. "Richard, what happened?" She placed her hands on his jaw and looked into his eyes.

Richard wrapped his arms around her waist and crushed her against his chest. His body shook as he held her. Yvonne wrapped her arms around his neck and held him. She ushered him inside and used her foot to kick the door closed.

"Richard, you're scaring me. What's wrong, baby?"

"She's not mine." He straightened. His eyes strained. "Nadia. She's not my daughter."

Yvonne's world spun. No, that would be too wrong. He loved Nadia so much. She gripped his shoulders. "No, you must be mistaken."

He shook his head. "No mistake. I had Nadia earlier this week. When I took her home, I hoped I could talk to Natalie about fighting the sale. That she'd be less defensive if it were just the two of us. She knows it's inevitable. Then she...she said Nadia wasn't mine. I don't think she meant to tell me at first. Then she gloated about it. Said I deserved to have my world broken after all she gave up for me."

Yvonne wished Natalie were in front of her right now. She'd snatch out every strand of hair on her head for putting that haunted look in Richard's eyes. She took him into the living room. Kicking off her shoes and dropping her purse on the floor, Yvonne settled into one corner of the couch and pulled Richard down until his head rested in her lap. All her earlier fatigue was forgotten as she took care of him.

"Tell me everything."

"She admitted she hadn't been faithful long before I broke things off with her, but she'd preferred being the fiancé of a millionaire than the girlfriend of a blue-collar worker. Until I broke things off, and so she tried to make things work with the guy she really loved. I should have noticed, but honestly, I didn't pay much attention to what Natalie did when we weren't together. When I ended the engagement, she was free. Except he didn't want to be a father and rejected her when she told him about the pregnancy. That's when she chose option two. Tell me she was pregnant, and it was mine."

The more he talked the more Yvonne wished she could get her hands on Natalie. She'd caused so much pain with her lies.

"Richard, I could kill her—"

"Don't. She said I should have asked." He shook his head and stared off as if he were watching his past on a projector. The protagonist about to run down a deserted alley to escape the serial killer instead of to the crowded street. "I didn't ask. I didn't even think to ask. I just believed her and did what I thought was right."

The raw pain and loathing in his voice seared her heart. "I wish I knew what to say." She ran her hand over his hair.

He stared up at the ceiling. "There's nothing anyone can say. The entire situation is bad."

"Are you going to tell Nadia?"

He closed his eyes. Yvonne wiped the tear that trailed down his cheek with one hand. Wiped her own wet eyes with her other. "One day," he said. "Not now. She's still upset about the divorce and me moving out. Maybe if her..." he swallowed. "If her father were in the picture it might be easier, but I can't turn my back on her. I can't forget I raised her for nearly seven years." His dark eyes popped open and met hers. "She's my daughter, Yvonne."

"I know." The love in his eyes when he looked at Jacob was the same love when he looked at Nadia. Love that didn't disappear just because of a revelation.

"Afterwards...I think Natalie realized she'd messed up. She begged me to forgive her. To still be a part of Nadia's life." He sat up and faced her. "Can you live with that?"

Yvonne frowned. "Why are you asking me? I wouldn't dream of telling you to walk away from her." Her father had walked away from her. She wouldn't wish that pain on Nadia. Biology aside, Richard was Nadia's father.

"Because it involves you, too."

"How?"

"I know we're just finding our way back to each other, but one thing is true. I've got you back in my life and I don't want to lose you again. I love you. I love Jacob, and the idea of losing you both scares me. Just when I thought we could work things out, this happens. If you don't want to deal with Nadia knowing she isn't my daughter..." He swallowed hard. "I'll have to respect that."

She thought about what he asked. The difficult road they faced if she agreed to be with him. She thought of Nadia.

How the sweet girl didn't deserve any of this. The vicious games Natalie had played with their lives. Watching Jacob try to understand why the sister he liked was suddenly not his sister. Telling Richard he could love her only under the condition he ignored the love he felt for a child he'd raised for six years.

She placed her hand on his damp cheek. Rubbed the growing stubble on his jaw. "We'll get through this together."

His shoulders shook, and he crushed her against him. "I love you so much."

Yvonne squeezed him tight. Seeing the relief in his eyes, after he'd arrived so broken, turned on a light inside of her. The pain of Natalie's lies wasn't gone, and she'd have to call on every saint in heaven to not strangle Natalie the first time she saw her, but she would no longer let the lies of the past overshadow the light of their future. She would spend the rest of her life making sure no one ever got the opportunity to manipulate and hurt her family ever again.

Chapter 31

Yvonne, Valerie and her mom visited Richard in D.C. later that year for Christmas. Michael had a new drone and was showing Richard and Jacob his new toy in the backyard. Sandra and Rochelle were debating if Denzel Washington or Idris Elba was sexier. Yvonne looked up from the glass of wine she was pouring at Valerie, next to her in the kitchen.

Yvonne shook her head. "Can you believe them?"

Valerie chuckled and shrugged. "I don't know. Mom is making a good point. Denzel is more likely to make you hot just from a conversation. Idris only has swag."

Yvonne bumped her sister with her shoulder and grinned. "You're stupid and wrong." She handed a glass of wine to Valerie.

Valerie took the wine. "Hey, I'm just contributing to the conversation." She looked around. Some of Richard's things were packed in boxes stored in the corners. "When is he moving?"

"After the New Year," Yvonne said with a nervous grin. "He wants to spend the holidays with Nadia. Give her an entire year to get used to him living in Atlanta before the next holiday."

"When is he going to tell her?"

Yvonne held up a hand. "When the time is right. Not before." Just the idea of telling the little girl broke Yvonne's heart. She and Jacob loved each other. They were so proud to have a sibling. Damn Natalie's lies for taking that away.

Thankfully, her sister changed the subject. "Is he seriously thinking of investing in a coffee house?"

Yvonne's shoulders relaxed with the new, more promising topic. "He is. That and a few other things. For the first time, he's been able to invest in things he really has an interest in, and he's enjoying it."

Richard had always been a lover of spoken word poetry. She'd met him at a poetry night all those years ago. When he learned about a coffee house that catered to poets and other artists that were struggling, she hadn't been surprised when he'd decided to take an interest in the property.

"Well, if he needs a broker, I'm his girl. Plus, I like that space. It's a great venue for events. Hopefully, he'll make it work."

Yvonne crossed her fingers. "I hope so."

"Then you can give your favorite sister a discount for events?" Valerie leaned her head on Yvonne's shoulder.

Yvonne wrapped an arm around Valerie's shoulder and hugged. "Haven't even made an offer and you're already asking for a discount."

"You know it!"

The doorbell rang. Yvonne shook her head and headed toward the door. Valerie had been throwing out the "favorite sister" comments a lot more lately. At first Yvonne had thought her sister was being funny. Now, she was pretty sure Valerie was being deliberate.

Yvonne and Sandra had grown closer. They talked a lot

more than she talked with Valerie, mostly because Valerie was always busy brokering deals and selling properties. She and Yvonne had never been the talk-on-the-phone-every-day type of sisters, but they loved each other. Once Valerie found out that Yvonne spoke with Sandra almost daily, mostly because Sandra called her more often and asked Yvonne to do stuff with her, Yvonne had gotten the impression Valerie was feeling like her territory was being infringed upon.

For a second, she wondered about getting Richard to answer the door, but reminded herself he'd said his house was her house. Besides, Richard was having too much fun playing with the drone out back.

She opened the door and her gaze met Natalie's. Yvonne's smile slowly melted away. Natalie's eyes widened, and her lips pressed into a thin line. Yvonne squeezed the doorknob. This was the first time they'd come face-to-face since she and Richard reunited. Yvonne still wanted to snatch her hair out for the pain she'd inflicted on her life, but she didn't.

Yvonne lowered her gaze to Nadia. "Hey, Nadia," she said with a grin. "Jacob is out back with your dad. They're playing with a drone."

Nadia's bright eyes sparkled, and she jumped up and down. "Ohh, can I go out back, too?"

"Sure thing, sweetie. My family is in the kitchen."

Nadia turned to Natalie and gave her a hug. "Bye, Mom."

Natalie hugged Nadia back. "I'll be back in a few hours."

Richard mentioned Nadia coming by today. She was supposed to come with his mom. Not Natalie. Yvonne watched Nadia run in, and a few seconds later heard her voice speaking to her family.

She turned back to Natalie. "Natalie, we don't have to like each other."

Natalie flipped her hair over her shoulders. "Thank God for that."

"But, we have to be civil for the sake of the kids. I personally will never forgive you for the lies you told. The part you played in keeping Jacob from his father. How you lied about Nadia."

"I would do it again," Natalie said with a lift of her chin. No sign of remorse in her features. For the first time, Yvonne noticed how beautiful Natalie was. Flawless skin the color of desert sand, wide soulful eyes, the perfect cupid's bow mouth. Combined with a tall, curvy frame that would be hard pressed to look bad in any outfit. So much beauty hid such an ugly heart.

"I did what needed to be done," Natalie said.

"By lying to Richard about me."

"Yes. Richard would have run back to you in a second. I sacrificed too much to let that happen."

Her sacrifice? She'd lied and manipulated everyone, and she had the nerve to talk about her sacrifice? Forget ugly heart, the woman had no heart. "You hurt him in a way I don't think you'll ever understand, and because of that, I will never trust you."

Natalie crossed her arms over her chest. "He should have asked."

"Don't give me that. He shouldn't have had to ask."

"What do you want with me?" Natalie's voice became defensive. "You got the ultimate prize. Not only did you get fifty thousand dollars, but you're back with your boy toy. You should be happy."

Yvonne stepped out of the door and onto the front step. She took a measure of pleasure that Natalie stepped down one. "You don't get it. That money will never replace the years Jacob lost with his father. The pain Nadia will feel when she's old enough to learn her mother lied to her. Being with Richard isn't a jackpot. He's a good man. He loves his kids and he tries to do what's right. I love him, and I will protect him from letting you ever hurt him, my son, or your daughter like that again." She took a step forward. "Let this be a warning. If you use Nadia to hurt him you won't have to worry about Richard, because I will come for you. Richard fights fair. I won't. Don't make me come for you. It won't be pretty."

Natalie raised her chin. She glared at Yvonne with anger, contempt, and a trace of fear. Good, because Yvonne meant every damn word.

The door opened behind her. Natalie's gaze went behind Yvonne. She quickly turned her features impassive. "My daughter wants to be here, otherwise, I'd tell you two to go to hell." She turned and scuttled off the porch.

Yvonne knew Richard must be behind her. He didn't say anything until Natalie got in her car and drove away. His strong arm wrapped around Yvonne's waist and pulled her against his front. He kissed her temple. "Thank you."

"For what?"

"That." He pointed toward Natalie's retreating car. "I appreciate it. Even if I don't need protection. I can handle Natalie."

"I know you can, but I want her to know that I'm not letting you face her bitterness alone." She turned in his arms and met his eyes.

"She isn't going to make this easy." He shifted from one foot to the other. Regret in his gaze.

"Maybe, maybe not. But we'll get through it because our kids are depending on us."

"You sure you're okay with that?"

"If anything, the past few months have taught me that I can handle having a blended family. We may not be conventional, but I wouldn't change a thing."

He relaxed and rested his forehead on hers. "I love you. I can't believe we made it back to each other."

Neither could she. Even when she'd stepped into his

office and he'd said he wanted his son in his life she hadn't thought they'd be back together. Now, she couldn't imagine not having him in her life.

"I'm glad we did."

He lifted his head. A wicked sparkle in his eye. "I also have a surprise for you later."

"What?"

"Our mothers have agreed to watch the kids. I'm taking you to open mic night tonight."

She grinned and squeezed him. "Does that mean you're going to get on stage and try to blow me away?"

Richard tossed his head back and laughed. His eyes were bright with happiness when they met hers again. "We're just going to listen . . . but I may be working on a poem to read to you."

Yvonne drew back. "Seriously? You're writing a poem for me?"

"I'd do anything for you and our kids. Including write bad poetry."

Yvonne wrapped her arm around his neck and kissed him. "I don't care if it's bad, but I reserve the right to duck under the table if it's too cheesy or about to make me cry."

His laugh filled the air and he hugged her. "Then be prepared to duck under a table."

The sun sparkled off the engagement ring on her finger. Yvonne's heart nearly burst. This was how joy was supposed to feel. Not how she expected. Not how she'd pictured, but that wasn't the point of happiness. Happiness may not always be perfect, but who needed perfection anyway?

REDESIGNING HAPPINESS

ABOUT THIS GUIDE

The suggested questions are included to enhance your group's
reading of Nita Brook's *Redesigning Happiness!*

Discussion Questions

1. What were your first thoughts of Yvonne when you met her?

2. Did you agree with Yvonne and Nathan's reasons for waiting? Why or why not?

3. Did you agree with Yvonne's decision to take the money and accept Richard's father's terms?

4. Should Yvonne have waited longer before introducing Jacob to Richard? Why or why not?

5. How does Yvonne's sense of abandonment play into the decisions she makes?

6. What do you think of Yvonne's relationship with her mom? How does that relationship affect her choices?

7. Did you think there were warning signs about Cassidy early in the story?

8. Should Sandra have revealed her connection to Yvonne earlier?

9. Were you #TeamRichard or #TeamNathan and why?

10. Should Richard have asked Natalie about Nadia when she told him she was pregnant?

11. What did you think of Richard's decision to keep Nadia in his life? Were you surprised that Yvonne was okay with his choice?

Connect with U s

Visit us online at
KensingtonBooks.com
to read more from your favorite authors, see books
by series, view reading group guides, and more.

for sneak peeks, chances to win books and prize packs,
and to share your thoughts with other readers.

facebook.com/kensingtonpublishing
twitter.com/kensingtonbooks

Tell us what you think!

To share your thoughts, submit a review,
or sign up for our eNewsletters, please visit:
KensingtonBooks.com/TellUs.